Also By Jass Richards

This Will Not Look Good on My Resume

The Road Trip Dialogues

The Blasphemy Tour

Dogs Just Wanna Have Fun

License to Do That

License to Do That

Jass Richards

Magenta

Library and Archives Canada Cataloguing in Publication

Richards, Jass, author
  License to do that / Jass Richards.

Issued in print and electronic formats.
ISBN 978-1-926891-61-3 (pbk.).--ISBN 978-1-926891-62-0 (ebk.).--ISBN 978-1-926891-64-4 (pdf)

  I. Title.

PS8635.I268L52 2014   C813'.6   C2013-908066-X
                        C2013-908067-8

uess what happened while we were away," Dylan said to Rev. They were in her screened porch, Rev sunk lengthwise into her couch staring out at the sparkling lake, Dylan stretched out on a lounge chair staring at his open laptop.

They'd just come back from their infamous 'blasphemy tour', ostensibly a series of speaking engagements at American Bible Colleges, sponsored by the Atheist Alliance Consortium, to talk about their recent adventure in court. They'd been charged with blasphemy when they'd added "'Blessed are they that taketh and dasheth thy little ones against the stone.' — Psalms 137:9" to a billboard just outside Algonquin Park. A Right-to-Life billboard.

A great number of things, Rev thought, would have happened while they were away. An infinite number of things, if Dylan was including events that had occurred in alternate universes. If she took into account his interests, that would narrow it down. But not by much. Ah. The laptop. If he was reading the news, then, given the news producers' interests, that would narrow it down to just half a dozen things. Politics, business, sports, cars, houses, and travel. Well, one thing, really. Money.

"Are you rea—"

"You're just supposed to say 'What?'" Dylan said.

She thought about that for a moment. "Why?"

He groaned, grinned, then sighed. Bloody hell, but he was going to miss her. He was a professional housesitter, and so didn't really have a home of his own, but since their serendipitous meeting about a year ago, some twenty years after they'd gone through teachers' college together—at the end of which they had both been voted most likely to be brilliant teachers and, simultaneously, least likely to be hired—he'd been spending half his time at her cabin on a lake in a forest, near Sudbury. He had a housesit scheduled in Argentina for two weeks hence, but, he thought now, maybe he'd cancel it and just stay here. Stay home, he happily amended.

"Okay, where?" Rev had decided to narrow it down.

"What?"

They stared at each other.

"Have some Froot Loops," he said and held the box out to her.

"There's no pizza left?"

"Someone ate it all."

"Hm."

He returned to his laptop, and she returned to the sun-glittering lake. She had missed it dearly while they were away and now couldn't get enough of it.

"So," Dylan tried again, "have you read the news recently?"

"No," she replied. Then added, "Not since the early 90s."

He looked up from his laptop in disbelief, stared at her expectantly, and was not disappointed.

"It's always the same old shit," she explained. "About which I can do nothing, since I am the epitome of powerlessness. So what's the point? Stupidity doesn't entertain me."

Dylan snorted.

"Which means, by the way," she continued, ignoring the snort, "that I depend on you to tell me when some Nero's gone nuclear. Or some yahoo gets the blueprints for the reactors mixed up and installs the earthquake supports backwards. Again. So I can go up to the loft."

"That's not going to stop you from getting irradiated."

"No, but it's where I keep my suicide kit."

He considered that information for a moment.

"Why the loft?" he finally asked.

"I figure, generally speaking, if I'm that depressed, I'm too depressed to climb the stairs. So it's a—"

"Got it. Good idea."

And then another moment.

"And what's in your suicide kit?"

"A bottle of Jack Daniels, a razor blade, and lots and lots of Nyquil. And a pen and some paper."

He nodded. "To write what, exactly?"

"Oh, you know, last words about the meaning of life, the universe, and everything. Or maybe just our epitaph."

"Which would be?"

She thought about that for a bit. "'I told you we were sick.'"

He laughed. "Indeed."

"And yet," he said then, pointing at his laptop, "guess what happened—"

She glared at him. Sort of.

"Canada passed the Parent Licence Act," he said quickly.

She slowly turned her gaze from the lake to him. "You're kidding."

"Nope. The NDP voted for it because it would piss off the Go-forth-and-multiply Conservatives, and the Conservatives voted for it because it would piss off the You-can't-touch-our-civil-liberties NDP."

He passed his laptop to her so she could skim the article.

"Wow," she said when she was done.

"And," he continued, happily, "*That Magazine* wants me to do an article about it."

"What magazine?"

"*That Magazine*. Remember? There's this magazine called—we've been over this before. Haven't we?"

"Oh yeah. Cool!"

She turned her gaze back to the lake.

"You should call up Hugh LaFollette," she said after a few moments, "if he's still alive. He published a paper on the idea back in the 80s. And Jack Westman wrote a book about it. You could cover the legal implications, the moral implications, you could interview parents, Family Services, the Church ... " She was off and running. As he knew she would be.

Dylan was typing away. A moment later, he hit 'Send' and a note arrived in Argentina.

T hey worked for a bit. Rev was a test development freelancer, writing logical reasoning questions that went on
the LSAT. What else does one do with degrees in Philosophy, Literature, and Education? And Dylan started gather-
ing background for his new assignment. He was a freelancer as well
and typically wrote travel articles, which fit well with his housesitting and his degrees in History and Education, but occasionally, more
often since reconnecting with Rev, he wrote pieces with a little more
substance. Such as this one.

After a while, they decided to go into town to rectify the pizza deficiency.

On the way, Dylan summarized his findings for Rev.

"So, you have to be eighteen."

"That makes sense," Rev said as she drove her pine-tar-spattered
car along the dirt road that lead from their driveway to the main
road. "You've got to be eighteen to drive. Surely parenting requires
the same level of maturity."

"More, I'd say," Dylan replied. "Maybe driving has greater potential for physical injury, but—"

"But getting in a car accident doesn't mean you'll end up with
maggots in your diaper."

Dylan looked over at her. "Not usually, no."

"But," she backed up a bit, "we're assuming a correlation between age and maturity."

"Good point," he pulled out a little pad of paper and a pen and made a note to himself.

"According to Covell and Howe," he recalled, "professors of psychology and political science, respectively, and both directors of a children's rights center in Cape Breton, people should demonstrate the ability to be responsible for their own lives before being allowed to assume responsibility for a child's life."

"But, again, that's assuming a correlation," she turned from the dirt road onto the main road. "If that was the rationale for the age thing. Being a certain age doesn't mean you've taken responsibility for your own life."

"True." Dylan thought for a moment. "What would?"

"Having moved out of your parents' house? And lived on your own for a year? I heard a guy in the hardware store once whining about how now that his wife had left, he'd had to figure out how to cook his own dinner once he got home. Poor baby."

"No surprise as to why his wife left."

"And yet the woman at the register was so sympathetic. She actually cooed."

"Whereas you ... "

"Oh I was sympathetic too."

Dylan thought this highly unlikely.

"I agreed that figuring out how to turn on an oven could be tricky for a man of forty."

They passed the graveyard of a gravel pit. It had been in full operation twenty-four hours a day, six days a week, for eight months while the highway had been four-laned. Rev couldn't stand the noise, which, due to the acoustic corridor formed by the long lake, reached her cabin despite being miles away, and she'd had to move for the duration. At her own expense, of course. Neither the township nor any Ministry she called was willing to intervene. The pit owner had a right to run his business as he saw fit.

"Okay, what else?" she asked.

"No drug addictions."

"And what are they counting as drugs?"

"Gotta get that list," he made another note to himself.

"No mental illness," he continued. "Gotta get that list."

"I wonder if they'll consider religious belief a mental illness."

"They could consider atheism a mental illness."

"Who's 'they', that's the question. Get *that* list."

"No mental retardation," Dylan resumed.

"That's going to upset the disability lobby."

"Yeah, I should interview someone about that." Another note to self.

"Ask them if they'd hire the special person down the street to build their house. Unsupervised."

"Hm."

"What else?" she asked.

"You have to have a minimum income, 20% above the poverty level."

"Well, it does take money to raise a kid. Food, clothing, music lessons. Or something. But we don't want it so only the rich can have kids." She noticed in passing that the only remaining independent gas station in the area had finally, inevitably, gone out of business.

"Well, 20% above poverty level doesn't exactly make you rich," Dylan replied.

"True. Though if you're living at poverty level, an extra 20% can make you feel rich," she remembered back a couple decades. There was a time she was scrubbing toilets at the hockey camp for minimum wage, despite the three degrees in her back pocket.

"Would we rather have kids fully funded by the state?" he wondered aloud. "They could have made it like in China. People who agree to have only one child get priority access to housing, health subsidies, and pensions, and the kid gets priority access to nurseries, schools, and employment. People who have more than one child have to pay an 'excess child' levy, which is, I believe, quite steep. I think it's a ten percent deduction from their total income, until the child reaches sixteen. In addition to having to pay for all the medical and educational expenses for the additional kid. Benefits like that would be a real incentive to get licensed. I wonder why—"

"Because it would've been an incentive to have a kid just for the money?"

"But if the money wasn't paid directly to the parents—and it wouldn't be, in the case of access to housing and schools—"

"I think I prefer the minimum income thing. Why should I pay for someone else's kids?" Rev asked. "They had 'em, *they* should pay for 'em. Do they pay for my choices? When I decide to take a trip—"

"Well, they pay for some of your choices. If you'd broken your leg when you fell off what's-her-name's Harley—"

"Yeah, but—"

"And we already do. Pay for other people's kids. We pay for their education, to a point. And their broken legs. And—"

"Yeah, and I've never really been happy about that," she said. "It's like the biochem cube thought experiment."

Dylan glanced over with raised eyebrows.

"Suppose John Smith makes biochem cubes," Rev recalled the experiment. "Biological-chemical cubes of something or other about one metre by one metre. With an input for the resources required for sustenance, and an output for the unusable processed resources.

"Why does John Smith make biochem cubes? Good question. Truth be told, they're unlikely to make the world a better place. And he doesn't sell them.

"So. Should we make allowances for John Smith? Should we give him a bigger salary? A break on his income tax? After all, he has, let's say, ten biochem cubes to support. If they are to stay alive, he has to provide. He needs a bigger house. More electricity. More food.

"Should we encourage his 'hobby'? Or should we censure it? Because once his biochem cubes become ambulatory, the rest of us have to go around them in one way or another. And when we're both dead, his ecological footprint will have been ten times mine. Or yours. More, if the biochem cubes he made are self-replicating."

"Well, when you put it that way," Dylan said after a moment.

"Though you know," Rev thought aloud, "if only qualified people will be able to have kids, there may be fewer broken legs. Or what have you. And I don't mind paying for the pure accidents. It's paying for the consequences of other people's stupidity, or thoughtlessness, that I mind. And I guess I can generalize that to the kids themselves. I mind less paying for a cherished, wanted child than for the result of some drunken or otherwise mindless fuck."

"To put it delicately."

She grinned.

"What else?"

"You have to take a course on child development," he said.

"Good. Is it a long course?"

"Don't know the details. Yet."

He made a note.

"No prior convictions for child abuse. Which will upset the child abuse lobby."

She glanced over quickly to see if he was serious. "There's a child abuse lobby?"

"People have rights!" he parodied.

"There has to be a minimum of two partner-parents," he continued, "and since this is Canada, there are no specifications as to sex, sexual preference, or skin color of said partner-parents."

"Cool."

"But," he summarized, "all that applies only to those who want to raise the child."

"What do you—ah. Right. Of course." Then, several moments later, when she'd fully caught up, "Wow."

"Wow, indeed," Dylan agreed.

"Mandatory testing?"

He nodded.

"Mandatory engineering?"

He nodded again.

"Wow. That used to be illegal in Canada. Now it's mandatory?" Then a few seconds later, "*That's* opening a can of worms."

"And yet—"

"And yet, like the other, it doesn't have to. Are they insisting on genetic enhancement or just ... whatever it's called when you correct genes. Like for, what, Parkinson's, Alzheimer's, Lou Gehrig's—" She paused for a moment, thinking. "What disease would you want to be named after you?"

W hen they walked into the pizza place, they saw a new guy back in the kitchen area. He lumbered out to the counter, a perfect picture of boredom and fatigue, then reached for a pen and the pad of pre-printed order forms. He waited.

"One with green olives and pineapple, one with black olives and mushrooms ... "

"One with onions and peppers," Dylan said, then turned to Rev, "and one Veggie Special?"

"Sounds good."

The man ticked off various boxes.

"All large," Rev anticipated his question, "and all undercooked a bit."

Driving into town for just one pizza would be environmentally irresponsible, so she ordered several each trip, then froze them, heating up one slice at a time in her toaster oven. Four large would be a month's supply. In theory.

The man re-entered the order into the computer system.

"And a bottle of Pepsi," Dylan added.

"Yeah, make that two," Rev said.

They waited a few moments.

"That'll be $103.76," the man said. Rev handed over her credit card.

"So," she said to the guy as he processed the payment, "what do you think about the new parent licence thing?"

"What?"

"The new law that says you have to get a licence before you become a parent. He's writing an article on it," she nodded to Dylan.

"I think it's stupid," the man said.

Dylan nodded. "I'll be sure to put that in my article."

THEY STEPPED OUTSIDE with half an hour to kill.

"While we wait, shall we check out the word on the street? What I have so far is—"

"An unrepresentative sample?"

"Maybe. Hopefully. Probably not."

"Okay, sure," Rev said. They looked to the right. They looked to the left.

"Okay, maybe the word in the mall?" Dylan suggested.

Rev hated malls. They were everything she—hated. "Another day. The park?"

"Yeah, but the ice cream place first."

So they walked down the empty street to the ice cream place. It was a seasonal establishment and had just recently re-opened. Soon the summer people would stream in every weekend with their loud and large self-importance, but today they had the place to themselves. Dylan considered the possibilities, walking along the freezer with its selection of ice cream in brown cardboard barrels, then looking up to study the sign that listed extras. He asked for Strawberry Cupcake with green sprinkles. Rev asked for Triple Chocolate, then wandered to the adjoining fudge counter.

"Pity it's not cheesecake," Dylan said what was clearly on her mind.

"Yeah. Even so ... a piece of the Egg Nog fudge too, please," she said to the youngish woman behind the counter who was busy scooping their choices.

"So what do you think about the new parent licence thing?" Rev asked her she handed their cones to them. "He's doing an article about it."

"I think it's about time," she replied, slicing off a piece of Egg Nog fudge, then wrapping it. "I've got a little girl, just turned eight, and I swear I spend half my time undoing the influence of other people's kids. Do you know how difficult it is to refuse your own kid when everyone else's kid has it or is doing it?"

"I never thought of it that way," Dylan said, taking a lick of his Strawberry Cupcake. "Thanks for your comment."

She scowled as she rang up their order. "I just know she's going to want to give blow-jobs when she's ten."

THEY PAID FOR THEIR cones and the fudge, then crossed the street and entered a small park. Once they had walked around the perimeter, they sat on a bench, idly watching some kids on the brightly-coloured playground equipment.

Suddenly Dylan got up, tossing his cone, and rushed to the monkey bars to rescue a purple-faced upside-down toddler.

"Hey, get away from my kid!" A large woman, followed by an even larger man, stomped toward Dylan from one of the other benches.

"I was just helping—"

"He didn't need any help!" the woman shouted.

"Actually, he did," Dylan said. "At that age, there's no way he'd've been able to pull himself back up. In a moment, he would've fallen off."

"Then he would've learned an important lesson!" the man grunted. "Not to climb up there in the first place."

"A moot lesson for a paraplegic and/or vegetable," Rev commented, having joined the circus.

"Are you calling my kid a vegetable?"

"If he'd fallen, on his head, which he would've have, given—" Dylan decided to withhold the physics lesson, "that's exactly what he would've become."

"But you probably wouldn't've noticed much difference," Rev assured the couple.

There was a moment of dead air.

"Are you saying I'm a bad mother?" the woman challenged Rev.

"Duh." She licked her Triple Chocolate.

"But I *love* my kids!"

"Oh please," Rev responded, "the word means so many things, it's useless. Whatever, your love is obviously insufficient."

"But I'd do anything for them!" she insisted.

"Except take Child Care 101," Dylan said dryly as they returned to their table.

"You know," Rev commented, as she offered Dylan a lick from her cone, "one article isn't going to be enough."

"Not even close," he agreed.

ylan looked at his watch after they'd picked up their pizza. "It's only 4:30, are you up for a quick detour to the parent licensing office? I can get whatever materials they don't have at their website and make an appointment for an interview."

"Sure, let's do that," Rev said, taking another bite of her slice of warm, gooey pizza.

They headed to the government office building. It housed the unemployment office and the health card office, as well as the offices for getting a driver's licence, a marriage licence, a liquor licence, a fishing licence, a hunting licence, and a lottery licence.

"So what's it called," Rev asked, as they got out of the car and started walking up the steps, "the Ministry of Parenting? That sounds a bit—Orwellian. And yet, it's about time, isn't it. We have Ministries for Natural Resources, Energy, the Environment, Health, Labour—"

"Silly Walks."

"No, wait," she stopped at the top, "aren't ministries provincial? This whole Parent Licence Act, it's federal, right?"

"Yes. So it's called the Department of Parent Licensing," he nodded to the list at the entrance, which indicated that the Department of Parent Licensing was on the third floor.

They headed to the elevator, pushed the up button, then stood back to wait.

A few seconds later, a man bursting with intelligence, compe-tence, and everything that's Male, strode to where they were waiting. He pressed the up button.

"Oh, is *that* what that's for?" Rev asked him.

He glanced at her with incomprehension, ineptness, and every-thing—

"HELLO," DYLAN SAID TO the receptionist conveniently stationed immediately outside the elevator. "I'm doing an article on parent li-censing, for *That Magazine*, and I wonder if you have any literature I can take away with me that you don't already have on your website. And I'd like to make an appointment to interview—someone."

A woman had walked out of an inner office at just that moment and had overheard Dylan's request.

"I can give you half an hour now, if you'd like," she said. "I'm the Regional Director."

"Oh, fantastic, that'd be great!"

"Cheryl, bundle up one of everything for him—the pamphlets, the interim reports, the backgrounder ... " She led the way to her office, and Dylan and Rev followed. Dylan was almost skipping.

"So," she sat behind her desk, and gestured to the two chairs op-posite, "what would you like to know?" She was an incredibly no-nonsense person. What you saw was what you got. Rev liked her immediately.

When she saw Dylan pull a teeny tiny notepad from the third pocket he checked, she opened one of her desk drawers, took out a legal-sized pad of paper from it, and pushed it toward him.

"Thanks," he said, a little shamefaced. Then held up his pen. He had a pen. He quickly wrote her name, Aletha Jackson—it was on the nameplate on her desk—and her title on his big pad of paper.

"We were away for most of the past year, and didn't keep up," he started, "and I imagine I can get a lot of the information I need from the material Cheryl's putting together, thank you for that, but one thing I'm curious about, and it's actually not the most im-portant thing, but—why is parent licensing under federal, rather than provincial, jurisdiction?"

"Actually, that has been an issue of contention. Not only whether we should be a Department, or an Agency, or a Board, but whether parent licensing should be a federal or provincial matter. Traditionally, if it's private in nature, it comes under the auspices of the provincial governments. Health, welfare, education, property, civil rights—all of these are provincial."

"So why did it end up being federal?" Dylan asked. "Wouldn't parenting be considered—"

"I'm not really sure," she interjected. "And frankly, I suspect that might change in the near future. The important thing, though, is that we're independent. We are politically independent. Completely."

"That's a relief," Rev said. "We wouldn't want this to pave the way for *The Handmaid's Tale*."

"Indeed, we would not."

"Okay, good, thanks," Dylan said, making a few notes. "Another question—and this *is* important—what happens when an unlicensed woman gets pregnant? Is she forced to get an abortion? Or put the child up for adoption?"

"Does it matter whether the father is also unlicensed?" Rev added, glaring just a little at Dylan.

"Yeah, that's the biggie," Ms. Jackson replied. "For now, we're assuming that people are reasonable and law-abiding."

"How Canadian," Rev said.

"And actually, that scenario might not happen as often as you think, once we get the vaccine out there. It was supposed to pre-date the legislation, but somebody somewhere messed up and ... "

"Wait a minute," Rev interrupted, leaning forward slightly, "a *contraception* vaccine?"

"Yes. You get it at puberty and you're good to go until, if and when, you get the antidote."

"Wow." Rev sat back. This was revolutionary. Truly revolutionary. "That'll change—that'll *reverse*—the default mode. Instead of people having to do something to *not* get pregnant, they'll have to do something *to* get pregnant."

Ms. Jackson nodded. "Having a child will *require* a deliberate choice."

"And—"

"No side-effects that we're aware of at the moment," she anticipated Rev's question.

"Wow," Rev said again. "What—"

"What took so long?" she smiled and raised her eyebrow.

"Yeah."

"I suppose somebody somewhere thought that now with the legislation, there would be a demand, so suddenly there's profit in it. We'd actually considered making the vaccine mandatory—"

"Whoever manufactures it was in favour of that, I'll bet," Dylan interjected, scribbling away.

"They were indeed. But the civil rights people were concerned that the antidote might someday become inaccessible."

"Yeah, that'd suck," Rev said. Which was, she was fully aware, an understatement. "How expensive is it?"

"Expensive," she said, "but the government will be paying for it."

"Really?"

"Of course," she said. "It'll be paying for the antidote as well."

"But then—"

"It'll be hard to get," she said, cryptically.

"You're not saying you have to be licensed in order to get it, are you?" Dylan asked. That way surely led to *The Handmaid's Tale*.

"No. I'm saying it will be as complicated a process to get the antidote as it is now to—"

"Get an abortion?" Rev suggested. Ms. Jackson smiled. Cryptically.

"What about those who were pregnant when the bill passed?" Rev asked.

"They were 'grandfathered,'" she said, glowering. "Can you believe they said that? In *this* of all situations?"

"Why didn't those women abort?"

"Many did. Some didn't find out in time, or didn't decide in time. Or abortion wasn't an option. Many clinics—and, as you know," she nodded to Rev, "there aren't that many—or weren't, before this legislation—many clinics were booked solid for months. And women couldn't afford to drive halfway across the country to one that had an opening."

"Back up a bit," Rev said. "This legislation has *increased* the number of abortion clinics?"

"And the availability of contraception, both Plan A and Plan B types. It would have to."

"Yes, I suppose it would," Rev thought it through. "If people are expected to comply, to not reproduce if they don't have a licence, they have to have the means to do so."

"Hence, the contraception vaccine."

"Okay, another question we had," Dylan said, "was who exactly determines whether someone gets licensed? That's a lot of power."

"It is, and we're well aware of that. So we built a lot checks and balances into the system. And we diffused the power as much as possible. So, in a very real sense, no one makes that determination. If someone meets the criteria, they get a licence, no one really makes a final decision.

"And," she anticipated him, "we consulted a great number, and a great variety, of people as to the criteria. Psychologists, teachers, lawyers, philosophers, geneticists, economists, sociologists, social services people, parents, grandparents, and on and on. It was a zoo," she grimaced. "But we are now multicultural, multidisciplinary, multiracial, multigendered, and multigenerational. And," she concluded, "we ended up with, I think, a really solid program.

"Then again," she added, "we had so many models to draw from. Adoption, custody, in vitro fertilization, even cloning. They've all worked through all this already."

"You're right!" Dylan hadn't thought of that before. He wrote another note to himself on his big pad of paper.

"What we kept in mind was that we weren't trying to figure out who makes the best parents, we were just trying to identify the worst. The very worst."

"But the worst parents won't bother to get licensed," Rev said.

Ms. Jackson sighed. "Which is why the vaccine should be mandatory, and the antidote available only upon obtaining a licence. We went around and around on that very point."

"Which is better," Rev summarized, "a democracy of idiots or the risk of a malevolent dictatorship."

"Exactly."

"Well, we've truly failed at turning our democracy of idiots into one of the well-informed. Dylan and I were on the front lines there, for years."

"Days," Dylan corrected, for himself. "Day, actually. I quit teaching after one day," he said sheepishly to Ms. Jackson.

"Maybe we'll be more successful at preventing the dictatorship from turning malevolent," Rev said hopefully.

"Hm. I should say that identifying the very worst," Ms. Jackson came back to that point, "was easier than you might think. Whether the child is likely to have insufficient clothing, or get sick due to in-adequate hygiene and/or inadequate nutrition, or have accidents due to inadequate supervision, these things are pretty easy to pre-dict. Usually a single home visit will do."

"And a home visit is part of the process?" Dylan asked.

She nodded. "And a background check. Similar to that done by many employers before they hire you to work with kids."

Dylan nodded. That made perfect sense.

"You know," she continued, "people imagine all sorts of unrea-sonable and intrusive 'shoulds' and 'should nots', but the require-ments for a licence are pretty basic. You've got the list?"

"I do, yes. I downloaded it from your website. And, one of the things I noticed, if you'd care to comment, is that there's no maximum to the number of children people can have."

"Very astute," she smiled. "We're hoping that once people get through the course, they'll realize on their own that one or two is enough."

He had a follow-up question. Sort of. "Has there been any back-lash to the mental competence requirement?"

"You bet. We're ignoring it."

"Because you're Canadian?" Rev smiled.

"Because mentally-challenged and mentally-delayed applicants won't pass the course. So it'll become a moot point."

"Clever."

"Not as clever as leaving out that requirement altogether would have been," she replied.

"There's a minimum age requirement," Dylan said, "but no maximum."

"We considered a maximum, but then thought we'd wait and see. Youth has energy, but age has wisdom. Sometimes. So, again, we're hoping that people who are 'too old' to parent, whatever that might mean, will realize that once they go through the course."

"But isn't it a lifetime licence?"

"Yes and no. Like the driver's licence, we made it so people over seventy have to renew every three years. But we don't anticipate that happening. We think most older people are actually rather content to be grandparents, rather than parents."

"The course," Dylan changed direction, "it's free?"

"Absolutely."

"And who determines the content, the evaluation ... "

"That was part of the forementioned multi-everything process. And rather than get into that now," she glanced at her watch, "I invite you to simply sit in on a few classes, speak to our teachers, and so on."

"Good idea, yes, thank you. Just one more thing, if I may—"

She nodded.

"—I wonder if the program will act as a self-selection thing. People who will make the very worst parents might not even bother going through the application process. Because, truthfully, they probably don't really want to be parents. Any comment on that?"

"I think you might be right. Anyone who can't commit to attending a class two nights a week and doing a shitload of homework isn't going to be able to commit to raising an infant. Too soon to tell though."

Dylan got it all down. On his big pad of paper. "Thank you," he said, tearing off the top several sheets, and handing the remainder of the pad back to her.

"Keep it," Ms. Jackson said to him. "I think you'll need it."

"Thanks," he replied. She was right, of course. They stood up to leave.

"I will say this though," Ms. Jackson stood as well. "Despite all the criticism of the parent licensing legislation, which you may or may not be aware of yet, my opinion is it can't hurt. It's not like the existing system is working. One third of all girls in Canada, that's one in three, experience some form of sexual abuse—and eighty percent of the abusers are family, variously defined. And that's just one aspect of abuse. So why not try this?"

"So, what," Rev said, "Canada's an experiment? We're guinea pigs?"

"Well, why not?" Ms. Jackson opened the door. "We have to do something to make up for the fact that we're the third biggest energy guzzlers, per person, in the world, we're the third biggest producers of greenhouse gases, per person, in the world, and we're number one when it comes to garbage. Per person. In the world."

"So we're already—pigs," Rev summarized.

"IMAGINE IF WE CHANGED the default mode for being alive," Rev mused, once they were back in the car and on their way home. "If you had to do something to stay alive, instead of, as now, doing something to kill yourself."

"But we do," he said. "Here, have another slice."

"AND YOU KNOW," SHE said several miles later, "I'm not sure I would have gotten the vaccine."

"Really?" He thought, hoped, actually, that she would've been first in line.

"I mean if you know for sure, why risk long-term hormonal interference when you can get a simple cut and cauterize?"

"Ah. So when did you know for sure? And when did you get—neutered?"

"Oh I knew for sure at fifteen. And I got neutered a five years later. On Mother's Day."

"Yeah? I did it on Father's Day!"

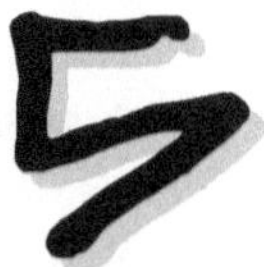

couple days later, they were again in the screened porch, Rev gazing at the lake, working on some LSAT items, Dylan making his way through the literature he'd received from the Department of Parent Licensing and planning future interviews.

The phone rang. Rev ignored it. Dylan wasn't surprised. He cocked his ear and heard the blast of a cruise ship, followed by the Captain inviting them to hurry and claim their free boarding pass.

A few minutes later, a bank called asking if Rev was happy with their service and whether there was anything they could do for her. She flew off the couch, relatively speaking, to take that call.

"No, I'm not happy with your service," Dylan heard her say, loudly, angrily, "and yes, there is something you can do for me! You can stop interrupting me when I'm working. You can stop interrupting me when I'm not working. You can stop invading my home with your calls. There is nothing wrong with my account. This is not an important call. This is a lame attempt to get more business. I don't know which marketing genius told you that a way to get more business was to badger existing customers with unwanted phone calls. You know what happens instead? When you badger existing customers with unwanted phone calls? They close their accounts!"

No sooner had she hung up and taken three steps back toward the porch than the phone rang yet again.

"What?!" Rev all but screamed into the receiver.

Dylan cringed. And hoped it wasn't someone returning one of his calls. One of his polite requests for an interview. The call lasted several minutes, and since Rev wasn't shouting, he couldn't hear her end of the conversation.

When she returned to the porch, she asked in a perplexed tone, "What's the opposite of a murder mystery?"

Dylan thought about that and had no answer.

"That was Anita," she settled back into her couch. "From the shelter. Apparently one of their current residents has been charged with unlawful parentage—or something—they don't have a name for it yet—"

"She was raped? Without a licence?" He winced when he realized what he'd just said.

"No, not exactly. One of her eggs—she sold what she had left when she got a tubal ligation, or maybe it was a hysterectomy—one of her eggs has been fertilized."

It took Dylan a moment. "What?"

"Someone committed—illegal fertilization? Illegal insemination? You know, that's interesting."

"What. Exactly." He actually found several aspects of the matter interesting.

"We have several words for the unlawful ending of a life. First degree murder, second degree murder, manslaughter, euthanasia, suicide. But nothing for the unlawful creation of a life."

"Yet."

"Hm. I wonder what exactly 'wrongful death' is," she mused. "Maybe we could call it 'wrongful birth'."

"No, that sounds like the person who's born is at fault. 'Wrongful life' maybe."

"Put that on your list of questions to ask a lawyer. A lawyer's on your list, isn't it?"

"Yes. Now."

"There's such a thing as reckless driving, right? How about reckless insemination?" she snorted. "Negligent fertilization?"

"Yeah, but that's all male agency. We have to have something that encompasses what the woman could do too."

That stumped them both.

"Wrongful pregnancy?" Dylan suggested a few moments later.

"Yeah, but wouldn't it be better to have a single crime that could apply to either the man or the woman? Reckless engendering?" Rev tried again. "Negligent conception?"

"Illegal conception. Illegal replication."

"Those are good. Nicer if it had its own single word. Like murder and suicide ... " They thought about it for a few more moments, but came up dry.

"So why did Anita call you?"

Rev glared at him.

"No, I meant—do you two know each other?"

"I used to work there."

"Ah." He realized the operative phrase was 'used to'.

"And I got fired," she anticipated his question, "for asking too many questions. Apparently why a woman decides to go back to a man who beats her up is none of my business."

"Which is why they called you now, for this. They need someone who will ask too many questions."

"Ironic, isn't it."

"It would be if they were going to pay you."

She gave him an odd look. That quickly blackened. "See? I didn't even think of asking to be paid. That's why you're all so rich and we're not."

She went back to the kitchen, Dylan trailing after her, and picked up the receiver. Oddly enough, or not, she'd never had occasion, or desire, to call someone back, so she didn't know what numbers to press.

"Asterisk, 6, 9," Dylan said. "And it's a sharp, not a pound," he muttered to himself. "Let alone a hashtag."

"Yeah," Rev ignored the muttered bits, "but that'll probably cost me $8.95 plus PST plus GST. Or HST." She put the receiver down and pulled the phone book out of the drawer.

"Probably," he agreed.

She thumbed through the book. Couldn't remember the shelter's formal name. Didn't know whether it would be in the residential section or the business section. Checked 'Shelter' in the yellow pages and found the Humane Society. And the Animal Rescue Association, the Society for the Prevention of Cruelty to Animals, and DogHaven.

"Oh for—"

Dylan reached over, picked up the receiver, pressed asterisk, 6, 9, then handed it to her.

"Hey, Anita, I'll be getting paid for my investigation, right?"

Dylan whispered, "Three hundred a day plus expenses!"

"Fifty an hour plus expenses," she said to Anita.

"Okay, that's fine," she said a long moment later.

"Well?" Dylan asked when she'd hung up.

"Twenty an hour. No expenses."

"Rev!"

"Dylan! They've got a waiting list of over a hundred women, each one living with an asshole who's beaten them up at least once. And one or two kids he may or may not have already started on. They can't afford to establish another shelter, they certainly can't afford to pay me—"

"Well, all that might change, mightn't it?"

"What do you mean?"

"Well, surely the main reason women who are being beaten up don't just leave is because they have no income of their own, they have no job. And the reason for that is they've got kids. If they'd had to get a licence—"

"They might still have those kids. And no job."

"Or might not. If the licence requirements include, even implicitly, a stable relationship and a stable, sufficient income—maybe part of why those assholes are beating up their wives is because they also don't have a job—"

"Stable jobs with sufficient income are lost every day though. Which of course means they weren't stable, but … "

"Yeah." He thought about that. "But maybe a man who so easily resorts to assault doesn't really want kids in the first place? Wouldn't have gone through the hassle of applying for a licence?"

"Maybe. Or maybe not. I think a lot of the time, people who want kids want the *idea* of having kids. They're just thinking about it in the abstract. For men, having kids is a measure of their manhood. It's only once they're actually there that they understand they're a lot of work. And a lot of responsibility."

"And having kids must triple the stress load of a relationship," Dylan agreed. "I wouldn't be surprised if the abuse doesn't start until the first kid arrives."

"Actually, that's often exactly when it starts," Rev confirmed. "With impressively incorrect logic, he blames her for the kid. For the extra stress, psychological and financial. Plus, because of the kid, she's suddenly less available to him, emotionally and sexually."

"But if the course they have to take makes them understand exactly what they're getting into—I wonder how many people drop out?" Dylan went back to the porch to make another note to himself.

o," Dylan said later, "are you up for the mall today? We can poll the opinion of the masses."

"Okay," Rev said, after looking out the window and seeing that it was too windy to go out on the lake in her bright red kayak, something she did pretty much every afternoon for several hours. It was a solitude of bliss and beauty, being out on the lake, paddling along the undeveloped shoreline of the several coves and up the little river that fed the lake, seeing the loons, and beavers, and otters. Every now and then she saw a moose or a deer. Once she saw a little mink.

"And while we're in town," she added, "I'd like to go to the shelter and ask a few questions."

"Okay, and I'd like to buy a bike."

"A bike?" She hated the noise of the dirt bikes and ATVs that used the trails. Most were driven by young men, in turn driven by testosterone, who had yet to consider other people. They even modified the mufflers so they could be heard by everyone within a hundred square miles. 'Don't mess with me,' they roared, 'I'm on a motorized bike with a two-stroke engine!'

"Yeah. I miss it." He had been an avid cyclist way back when tenspeeds first became popular, but ever since he took up the housesitting life, it was hit and miss as to whether he had access to a bike. And of course, they had spent the entire blasphemy tour in their van.

"There's miles and miles of trails here, right? Crown land? Accessible from your place? You used to run them, didn't you?"

"Yeah … " She did indeed. Back when she ran. Five, ten, fifteen miles. She loved the distance, the silence. Now, well, knees don't last forever, apparently. And at some point, she figured she could either keep running, then have to use a walker when she hit sixty, or stop running, and quite possibly walk to eighty.

"I'd like to bike them," Dylan continued. "Therefore, I'd like to buy a bike. Am I ready for the LSAT or what?" He grinned, but then noted her lack of enthusiasm.

"A trail bike," he clarified, then thought that's not actually what they were called. "A mountain bike." Though he wouldn't be biking any mountains any time soon. "Not a dirt bike." He would, however, be biking on dirt. Marketing people clearly didn't pay much attention to words, he realized. No, that's wrong, they paid a lot of attention to words. It's just that they chose the most manipulative for their purposes, not the most accurate. So was 'dirt bike' supposed to attract boys who like getting dirty? Presumably, a large market? "A bike with pedals," Dylan tried again. "That go round and round."

"IF YOU'RE GOING TO go into the forest," Rev said, once they were on the highway, "and, actually, even if you're not, you'll need a bug jacket. Add it to your list."

"They make jackets for bugs now?" Dylan asked.

Rev laughed. "No, it's sort of like a beekeeper outfit. Keeps out the blackflies, and the mosquitoes. The only other thing that works is DEET. But long-term studies about the interactive effect of DEET and benzophenones are still in-progress and—"

"—and I don't want my skin to start coming off in strips a few years hence," he finished her thought. "Can't you just—" he waved his hand, "wave them away?"

"No," she replied decisively. "The little buggers crawl all over you, most annoyingly along your hair line—high on your forehead, your neck, and around your ears. And they bite. You can, actually, just pick them off. But for a few weeks they swarm. You'd need ten arms. Each with a hand."

"And silly me, I left my other arms, each with a hand, on the mothership."

"And now with the Arctic ice melting, our mosquitoes are getting more dangerous. West Nile's been here for a few years now. Dengue fever and malaria are now in Toronto. Without a bug jacket, you'd be quarantined inside the cabin. Except on windy days."

"I'll need a bug jacket then," he agreed. And added it to his list.

THERE USED TO BE A bike shop in town, owned by a guy who also did repairs, but it had gone out of business when kids started riding dirt biks. So they pulled into the parking lot of the Canadian Tire store. It was as big as the store itself. That was the way in Canada. Given the distances, and the lack of an efficient public transportation system between towns—actually, the lack of *any* public transportation system between towns—people needed cars. Men, however, needed pick-ups. In case they ever picked something up. Which would be unlikely, Rev thought, given how much garbage she herself picked up from the forementioned trails.

"I'm surprised this isn't a—what's the American equivalent of Canadian Tire?" she asked as they walked across the parking lot. The Bay had been replaced by Walmart, Zellers by Target, Home Hardware was being pushed out by Home Depot.

"American Tire!" he grinned.

"No, I mean—"

"Lowes?"

"No, aren't they more a Home Hardware/Home Depot store?"

"I think you're right, yes. In any case, it doesn't have colourful monopoly money," Dylan said.

"So?"

"So there you go. Canadian Tire's future in Canada is safe."

They entered the store and walked toward the bike section.

"I'd like a purple one with a basket in front and streamers on the handlebars," Dylan told Rev. "Turquoise streamers."

She thought about that for a moment.

"And a bell. You'll need a bell to scare the bears away," she said.

"Oh. You've just got black bears here though, right? No grizzlies?"

"Do you know how to tell the difference? I mean, if you come across some bear scat?"

"No," he replied, thinking that would be useful indeed.

"Black bear scat has berries in it, leaves, and maybe little bits of fur. Grizzly scat has little bits of bells in it."

"I'll get a big bell. Just in case."

They arrived at the bike section without seeing a customer service rep on the way. Fortunately, the bikes weren't chained together. Dylan selected one that looked the right size. Unfortunately it was black. Rev pointed out a purple one further down, but it looked a little smaller.

"Aren't these adjustable to some degree?" she asked.

Dylan took a look. The wheel size of the purple one was the same as the black one, and yes, the seat and handle bars looked like they could be extended. He got on. Yes, he definitely needed a longer reach to the pedals.

"I'm going to find someone," he said and pedalled off. Almost as soon as he turned out of sight, she heard a crash. Then an "Oops."

"Hey Rev," he called out a few moments later. "Will *this* scare the bears away?" He honked a horn. It sounded like one of those clown horns.

Rev grinned, pulled a candy red bike from the row, and pedalled off to join him.

The next aisle was, she saw, the bike accessories aisle. Dylan had a shiny silver horn in his hand and as she approached, squeezed its black rubber bulb again. It honked loudly.

"Well, it'll certainly let them know you're there. What they do with that information is up to them. If it were me ... "

Dylan grinned and honked yet again.

And still no customer service rep appeared.

"Look, streamers!" He reached out for turquoise ones, but then had nowhere to put them. "No baskets," he said, sadly.

"Well, we can check Walmart," Rev said. Sadly. It had put a lot of local, small businesses out of business. Not that she cared much about local, small businesses. It was the diversity that was important. Now, if Walmart didn't have it, you couldn't buy it. Unless, of course, you could get it on Ebay. Ebay was God. For people, like her, who hated to shop. But pretty much knew exactly what she wanted.

"I can get the fenders here though," Dylan pointed down the aisle. "I don't know why they're not standard—"

"I think the idea is that these bikes are stripped down for speed."

"Yeah, but the idea is also that they're ridden through mud. Without fenders, you get that lovely skunk stripe up the back of all your best tshirts."

"No kickstand either," he realized when he got off the bike to better look at the fender selection. "Do I need a lock?"

"Not at my place. Will you be riding it in the city?"

"Probably not. But—hey, remember the combination locks that fit around the back wheel? Before those big clunky U-things?"

"Yeah! I wonder why—oh yeah. People started stealing bikes by just lifting them into a van or something. So you had to start locking your bike *to* something. Hey, do you want a rat trap?" Rev was walking her bike up the aisle. "You could put a milk crate on the back like you used to have."

"You remember?"

"Of course! It was blue." He'd often stop by her place on the way to classes.

Still no customer service person had appeared.

"And you'll need a helmet." Even if it hadn't been a legal requirement these days. The trails were rough. And rocky.

They moved down the aisle a bit to look at the helmet display. "I was really hoping for a purple and turquoise one," Dylan said.

"Maybe they have more in the back," she said. Then looked around for the still non-existent customer service person.

"I'm *really* surprised this isn't a Lowes yet," Dylan added, in response to the non-existent customer service. They'd just spent almost a year touring the States, occasionally shopping, and much as it challenged the stereotypes of friendly Canadians and obnoxious Americans, they had to admit that by comparison Canada knew *nothing* about customer service.

"This is ridiculous," she said. "Give me that," she grabbed his horn and pedalled off. Honking.

Dylan grabbed another horn from the rack and pedalled after her. Also honking.

At the end of the aisle, they split, going into different directions. They proceeded to pedal down aisles 1, 2, 3, playing 'Marco Polo' with their horns. They saw a great many customers, most of them wandering, apparently lost and in despair, since many tried to flag them down, but they saw no customer service rep. They covered aisles 4 through 26. Still no customer service rep.

"Security to the exit, Security to the exit."

Rev and Dylan reached the Check-out at the same time. "Actually, it's Customer Service we're after needing," Dylan said. Rev honked her horn.

"Customer Service to the exit, Customer Service—"

"To the sports section," Rev corrected. In angry disbelief. And honked her horn again.

"We'll meet him or her there," Dylan said, as they pedalled away.

"Sorry," a young man said as he rounded the corner at a trot shortly a second after they got back to the bike aisle. "I'm the only one on today."

"But it's Saturday!" Rev protested.

"I'm aware of that," he said, tightly. Clearly he had an application in at Walmart. And Target. And Home Depot.

"Okay, so, I like this one," Dylan said, "but I want to be sure the handlebars and the seat have another six inches."

The young man looked at Dylan's bike, then walked along the row of bikes, stopping halfway to the end. "Excuse me, sir?" he called back to Dylan, pulling out an almost identical one from the row. "That's a ladies'. You'll want this one."

Dylan looked at the bike he'd pulled out. "No, I'll want this one," he said, pointing to his choice. The one with the crossbar angling down from the handlebars toward the seat. Not the one with the ball-busting horizontal crossbar. "They got the designs mixed up way back in the 40s. Think about it."

The young man did so. "Good point," he said, putting the 'men's' version back into the row.

"So, adjustment potential?"

The young man took a look at the model number, entered it into the nearby computer terminal, then confirmed that both handlebars and seat had sufficient extension capacity.

"Good, okay, thanks. Now, helmets. Do you have any more in the back? I was looking for a purple and turquoise one," he gestured vaguely at all the manly black and silver ones.

7

s soon as they pulled into the driveway of the shelter, which was a nondescript two-storey house, three very pregnant women who had been sitting on the porch rushed inside.

"Looks like a home for unwedded mothers, which I didn't think they had anymore," Dylan said. "Except for the running inside part."

"Yeah, it's—why didn't they have any homes for unwedded fathers?"

They pondered gender, sex, and disgrace for a while.

"They won't let you in," Rev said eventually.

"What? Why? That's—"

"An unfair generalization. I know. But making generalizations—That stove burned us when we put our hand on it, so we assume all stoves are hot. And good thing we did."

"I'm not a stove. I went through a teapot phase, I'll admit, but I've never been a stove."

"I know that. You know that. But they don't know that. And they have good reason to assume the opposite."

He thought about that for a moment. "You're right," he sighed. "Whenever I'm housesitting in a city, and I happen to be walking at night, if there's a woman ahead of me, I cross the street. Or stop and window shop until she's far ahead of me."

"You do?"

"Of course I do. I hate it, it's awful going through life knowing that half the species is afraid of you, but—shit, we're fucked up." He gazed out the car window.

"How close is Walmart? I can go get a basket for my bike while you do your thing here. And spray paint for my helmet."

"That's a good idea," she said, as they both got out of the car. "And Home Hardware is right beside it. They've got good bug jackets. Okay, right at the corner," she told him. "Or maybe left. Then another right. Or a left. You have to get onto Lansing, I think, then just follow it to Lasalle. Maybe a mile? Two?"

He stared at her.

"I could take my new bike!" he said after a moment.

"You didn't get a lock for it."

"Right. Pity. Okay, then, I'll see you outside Walmart in, what, an hour? Maybe two?"

REV WALKED UP TO the gate set in the chain link fence that surrounded the property. She rang the buzzer, then waited until whoever was on the desk checked the monitor to see who it was, did a camera sweep of the sidewalk to the left and right of her, then activated the unlock mechanism.

Anita met her at the door. "Rev," she said, smiling broadly as if she was greeting a long lost friend, instead of someone she had fired. "So good to see you! Come on in!"

Rev stepped into the small entrance area, and saw the three women from the porch sitting in the living room. They seemed to be chatting about baby names.

"How about Dennis?" the one in the striped tent said. "Dennis Garrett."

"'Lover of fine wines'," the one with the book said, and they oohed with approval at that, imagining the child growing up to be some sort of connoisseur, "'armed with a spear'."

They tried to giggle. Didn't quite make it.

"Oh, oh," the woman had been flipping through the pages, "if it's a girl, you can call her Olivia. 'Elf army'."

"Hey all," Anita said, leading Rev into the room. "This is Rev, the woman I told you about. Okay if she talks with you a few minutes?"

They all agreed, mostly because they had nothing else to do, and Rev sat down.

"That's Susie," Anita said, pointing to the woman in the tent. "And Raquelle," the one with the book. "And Brittany." The one whose face was still bruised and swollen. The problem with the term 'domestic violence', Rev thought, not for the first time, is that it makes it sound all nice and cozy. Instead of brutal.

"Okay, so," Rev said, "one of you has been charged with—"

"It's probably Bobby who did it," Susie spoke up. "He started hitting me after Billy was born, and then when I got pregnant with—Olivia," she grinned at the others, "I got my tubes tied. And since I needed the money, if I was going to leave Bobby, I had my eggs out at the same time. Sold 'em to the egg bank."

"It's legal to sell your eggs now?" Rev asked, turning to Anita. "When did that happen?"

"Last year some time. Sperm too. It's become quite common. What with more and more people going to fertility clinics ... Each city has an egg bank now. And a sperm bank. They've already got a blood bank."

"Yeah, but don't we just donate our blood?"

"Not anymore. You can sell it now. And why not?" Anita asked. "We sell our physical resources all the time, our muscle power, our brain power—"

"And surrogacy?" Rev was curious. "Can you rent a uterus now too?"

Anita nodded. "But you have to be licensed, of course. That's right," she said then, "you've been away."

"Yeah, I'm just getting up to speed about the parent licensing thing."

"Then you may know there are two parts to it. If you want to be a surrogate, you just have to get the bioparenting part. Whoever wants to raise the child has to get the other part."

"Yeah, what are they calling that other part?"

Anita thought for a moment. "I can't recall. Psychosocial parenting? Nurture parenting? I know both terms have been in the news."

"Okay, so," Rev brought the conversation back on topic, "you think Bobby broke into the egg bank, found the right test tube, and jizzed on your eggs?"

"Eew," Raquelle said.

"Well, it's no different from—right. Eew," Brittany said.

"Maybe they keep them in petri dishes," Raquelle said. "You know, if they're already developing. One of those super duper petri dishes, what do you call it?"

"A uterus," Rev said. Which is why surrogates *should* get paid, she thought. "Okay, how would Bobby have gotten in?" she turned back to Susie.

"He's got skills," she replied, and Brittany snickered. Susie ignored her. "He did a lot of B&Es when he was younger."

"And why would he have done it?" Rev asked.

"Because he can," Raquelle said.

Ah. Right. Rev had presumed a rational motive. Perhaps she'd given him way too much credit. She turned to Susie for her answer.

"Why does he do anything?" she shrugged.

Rev thought for a scarey moment that she wasn't saying she didn't understand his reasons, but that he genuinely didn't have any.

"Maybe he's punishing her," Brittany said. Anita looked at her sadly.

"For what?" Rev asked.

"Being alive," Anita answered.

"So what will they do with it?" Rev asked after a moment. "The fertilized egg."

It seemed no one had thought that far. Rev shot a glance at Susie, who didn't seem too upset as she considered, presumably, the various possibilities.

Anita stood up then. "Rev and I are going to talk a bit, you three have to get ready for class, yeah?" She turned to Rev with an explanation. "They all want to keep their babies, so they've all applied for a licence."

"So what do you think?" Anita asked anxiously when she and Rev were in her office.

"I think you're an idiot," Rev said. Then explained. "You don't need me, you need a lawyer. Doesn't the shelter still have Agnes Fenelon on retainer?"

Anita nodded.

"Well, you should've called her, not me! What were you thinking? The surgeon who extracted Susie's eggs can establish that they were unfertilized at the time, and surely the egg bank or whatever it's called will verify that. A biologist with a super duper pee stick can determine time of fertilization, probably to the hour. The residents here still have to sign in and out?"

Anita nodded.

"Then my guess is Susie has a solid alibi. Have Fenelon insist they do a DNA test. Since Bobby has a record, his DNA will be on file, right? Why the police even pressed charges against Susie, I have no idea. Why did you let them get away with that?"

Anita had visibly crumpled. "You're right. You're absolutely right. It's just—" she waved her hand, and her eyes started to tear, "it's just that I'm so fricking used to it. A woman gets beaten up by her husband, it's her fault. A woman gets raped, her fault. So this, when they implied it was her fault ... "

"You've been here too long then," Rev said. Thinking of burn-out, frogs, and pots of boiling water.

When Dylan walked into the big, bright, and busy Walmart, the seventy-year-old greeter smiled at him. "Good afternoon!"

"Good afternoon," he smiled back, "where will I find bicycle baskets?"

"Aisle 12, half way up, on the left."

"Thank you!" He was impressed. And wondered whether she gave that answer to every query.

But when he found Aisle 12, right there between Aisle 11 and Aisle 13, he saw half a dozen bicycle baskets halfway up, on the left. All for $9.99. All made in Taiwan. All in pink and white.

He took one then went to the checkouts. Each had a line. Long enough to reach Taiwan. He chose the speedy one, the one that had three cashiers, for people with under six items. Of whom there were about twenty.

"Please proceed to Checkout One," an fake-nice robotic voice said cheerfully from the speaker placed at the front of the line. The line moved forward one person.

Twenty seconds passed. "Please proceed to Checkout Two," the fake-nice robotic voice said cheerfully. The line moved forward one person.

Half a minute passed. "Please proceed to Checkout One," the fake-nice robotic voice said cheerfully. The line moved forward one person.

Fifteen seconds passed. "Please proceed to Checkout Three," the fake-nice robotic voice said cheerfully. The line moved forward one person.

When Dylan got close enough, he picked up a 9V lantern battery from the impulse shopping display and smashed it against the speaker.

"Pleeeeeeeeeeeeeeeeee phgflt."

Everyone cheered. The cashiers the loudest.

Then a pompous little Manager swooped into the checkout area and made a beeline for Dylan.

"Sir, I have to ask you to come with me."

"Why?" Dylan said, the battery still in his hand.

The Manager nodded to the ex-speaker, then to camera mounted across from the checkout area. "You have destroyed property that belongs to Walmart. I am willing to hold off on pressing charges," he said in a fake-nice voice, "if you are prepared to pay for the damage immediately." Everyone booed.

Dylan shrugged and followed the man to his office. It was filled with monitors. Apparently Walmart had cameras everywhere.

"Just out of curiosity," Dylan said, as the man went about filling out some forms, "why don't you have just a discreet pixel counter that indicates which checkout is free? Or, here's an idea: assume that people can tell the difference between a checkout that has a customer and one that doesn't, and that the person at the front of the line will be paying sufficient attention to make that determination."

"Because the person at the front of the line *isn't* always paying sufficient attention."

"So the person behind him or her gives him a nudge."

"We have found that that sort of thing costs 6.4 seconds. On average."

"Oh. Well. God forbid your cashiers get a 6.4 second break every now and then."

A FEW MINUTES LATER, he returned to the checkout, since he had yet to pay for his little basket. The receipt now sitting inside it was for the single amount of $249.53.

As soon as he approached the speedy checkout area, the people there began to cheer again. He smiled, and as he made his way through the path that cleared for him, they started tossing money into his little basket, loonies, toonies, bills even. He felt like a little flower girl. So when he got to the front of the line, he turned and curtsied.

9

ev pulled into the Walmart parking lot and saw Dylan standing at the entrance, a cute little pink and white bicycle basket in his hand.

"Apparently they don't make manly baskets," he said happily as he got into the car.

"And do they all come with money in them?" she asked, nodding to the assortment of coins and bills inside.

Dylan told her what had happened.

"How—me of you!" she said. "Smashing the speaker. Not buying a little pink and white basket."

"Got that. It is, isn't it." He smiled. "So how did it go with you?"

"Anita's resigning."

"And you say you have no effect whatsoever on people. Did you make her cry first?"

He got into the car, setting his pretty basket into the back carefully beside the bike.

"Still up for this?" Dylan asked. "The mall? On a Saturday?"

"But of course!" Rev said, driving the kilometre to get to the far end of the lot where there was a vacant space.

"That was sarcasm, right?"

They got out, locked the doors, walked back past Walmart around the corner to the mall entrance.

"What the—"

Just outside the entrance, there was a new awning structure under which sat rows and rows of what looked to be motorized ATV/wheelchair hybrids, each with a shopping cart trailer attached to it.

"Did we also miss the passage of some new disability act?"

They watched, stunned, as an overweight couple disengaged one and then another of the vehicles, got onto them with a heave and a sigh, then started driving through the extra-wide door and into the mall.

"Un-fucking-believable."

They watched as another person wrestled a vehicle from the row and got onto it. Her kid climbed happily into the cart trailer, needing only two tries to get in.

Once inside, Rev and Dylan were stunned yet again. The McDonalds had moved to the entrance end of the mall—it used to be at the food court in the middle—and there was a line–up at the drive-through window. They paused at the front of the line as the person placed an order for a dozen mini-burgers, fries, and a shake.

"And he's wearing an Oilers hockey shirt," Rev observed.

"And Nikes," Dylan added.

They negotiated a path away from the line-up, but soon found themselves having to constantly walk around one of the slow-moving vehicles.

"Shit!" Rev said as she all but fell over one that had suddenly stopped in front of her.

"Excuse me!" the woman was indignant. "Watch where you're going!"

"Excuse me!" Rev retorted, "don't fucking stop in the middle of the—this isn't a even a road, for gawd's sake, get out and walk, you fat ass!"

"Who are you calling a fat ass?" she demanded, trying to get out of the vehicle. Unsuccessfully, because her fat ass was stuck.

Rev started laughing. She couldn't help it. Dylan pulled her along.

"You know," she said, "I bet people like that *really* piss off the *really* disabled. I mean they're born with this perfectly good body, and then through their own negligence and lack of self-discipline, they turn it into something—like that," she pointed to a similarly overweight person struggling to extricate himself from his vehicle.

"Sometimes it's genetic," Dylan said. Weakly.

"One in four Canadians is clinically obese," Rev replied. "Twenty-five percent of the population can't help it? At all?"

It looked like most stores didn't allow the vehicles inside, for obvious reasons, so people had to park in front of the stores they wanted to enter. And leave their parcels in the cart? Not likely.

"What do they do if their cart isn't there when they come out of the store?" Dylan wondered aloud, as they watched someone wrestle several bags out of her cart before entering Dollarama.

"Want to find out?" Rev asked.

"I do, yes," Dylan said after a moment. "But we're here to find out what people think of the Parent Licence Act, remember? We're here to get 'the word in the mall'!"

"Oh yeah," Rev sighed.

"So," she said to next person to walk by, "what do you think of the Parent Licence Act?"

"What?"

She turned to Dylan as if he had a camera, mimed having a microphone in her hand, and said, "And there you have it. The word in the mall is 'What?'"

Dylan grinned and pulled out his mini recorder. Rev raised her eyebrows. He had a mini voice recorder? And he had the foresight to bring it with him?. He set it to record, hoping the high level of background mall noise would not be a problem, then approached a woman with a couple kids clinging to her.

"Excuse me," he said, "I'm writing an article about the new parent licence law, and I'm trying to get a sense of public opinion on the matter. May I ask your opinion?"

"Sure!"

There was a bit of dead air.

"What is your opinion of the new parent licence law?" Dylan said.

"Oh, I don't know," she said amiably. "I suppose it's a good thing."

"And why is that?"

"Oh, I don't know," she smiled. "I suppose because it's a good idea."

Dylan was undeterred. He stopped a pair of young women. "Hi there, I'm writing an article—what do you think about the new parent licence law?"

"I think it's a great idea," the first one said. "You need a licence to own a gun."

"A kid's not a gun," her companion said.

"Could be."

Dylan stepped back out of the way of a few motorized vehicles, and the women walked on.

"Excuse me," Rev said to the next man to pass by, on his own two feet, "What do you think of the new parent licence law?"

"I think the government has no business telling me whether I can or cannot engage in sexual relations."

Rev let a moment pass.

"Yeah, but what do you think of the new parent licence law?"

"I just told you."

"There's a difference between having sex and reproducing."

He snorted.

"I think that right there is the problem," she said to Dylan as the man walked away. "Apparently some men haven't heard about condoms yet."

Oddly enough, the next man said something similar. "I have a right to have sex whenever and with whoever I want."

"Okay, let's do the math," Rev said. "Say you have sex twice a week. 50 weeks, that's 100 kids per year. But since the odds of fertilization are only 20%, that's 20 kids per year. Assuming, of course, you have sex with at least 20 different women over the course of that year.

"Okay, so 20 kids a year, over 20 years, you'd've made 400 kids. How are you going to feed them? Where are they going to sleep?

"And if each of them thinks the way you do, or doesn't think, the way you don't, then 200 of them, assuming 50% are male, will each make their own 400 kids, which means you alone—"

"—and the women," Dylan inserted.

"—will have added over 80,000 people to the world. And if each of your grandsons—"

"Stop," Dylan said, noting the glazed look in the man's eyes. "You lost him. Probably at 'have sex twice a week'."

They walked on, zigzagging with increasing irritation around the many stopped vehicles, and slowing to a crawl behind people, most of them, who were walking at zombie speed.

"Excuse me, what do you think of the new parent licence law?" Rev tried again, approaching an older man in one of the ATV things.

"What's next, needing a licence to breathe?"

She looked at him, at the aggressive look on his stupid face, and thought that that actually might not be a bad idea.

"Excuse me, what do you think of the new parent licence law?" she turned to a family of four coming their way, and Dylan held out his recorder.

"I say welcome to Nazi Germany," the man said. "Eugenics. The whole nine yards."

"And do you also say it's okay to create a little human being that will be in pain from the moment it's born?"

"What do you mean?" His wife gently tugged at him to move on, while the three kids tugged at her to move on, but he ignored them all.

"What do you mean, what do I mean?" Rev replied. "There are many genetic conditions that cause excruciating pain. We should knowingly let fertilized eggs with those conditions develop? Why, in god's name?"

"I think that there's your answer," Dylan said.

"Hm."

They scanned the people nearest them and approached a young couple with their arms around each other. "Excuse me, what do you think of the new parent licence law?"

"I have to say I'm a little bit nervous about it," the woman said. "Giving the state power and influence over the reproductive decisions of its citizens ... If they restrict the right *to* reproduce, won't they go on to restrict the right *not* to reproduce? I don't want the right to contraception and abortion taken away."

"I share your concern," Rev replied, delighted to engage someone so thoughtful and articulate, in a shopping mall, on a Saturday, "but prohibiting incompetent people *from* driving doesn't entail forcing competent people *to* drive."

"That's true," the woman replied.

"The guiding principle isn't control over reproduction, per se,"

Rev continued, "it's reduction of harm. Limiting access to contracep-tion would be causing harm, because it's forcing pregnancy. So to be consistent, the state wouldn't *restrict* the right not to reproduce, it would *ensure* the right not to reproduce."

"If the state were interested in being consistent."

"Point taken," Rev said.

"But," Dylan said, "in order for the new law to work, it *has* to keep contraception and abortion accessible. Or prohibit sexual inter-course."

"Which," Rev said, "Bubba's been saying, 'ain't gonna happen'."

"Still, the law's open to all sorts of abuses," the young man of-fered.

"Of course it is," Dylan agreed. "As are all licensing programs."

"True, but when this goes wrong, it'll go very wrong. Good people will be denied the right to have children." The couple moved closer together.

"But as LaFollette points out," Dylan said, "the harm done by not licensing at all is surely greater than the harm done by mistakenly denying licences to some."

"Greatest good for the greatest number," the young man recog-nized the principle. "I dunno ... "

"Innocent people get life in prison," Rev noted. "Doesn't mean we should retract the laws that put them there, does it?"

"No, but ... "

"Thank you for your opinion," Dylan said, seeing that the two of them were eager to move on. They nodded and did just that.

Rev and Dylan had reached the other end of the mall. Where there was a Tim Hortons. And another line-up.

"Gimme a dozen donuts," they overheard the man in front of them say to the counterperson. "What do you want?" he turned to his wife in the vehicle beside him.

"You know," Rev said, staring at the two of them, "this is why I don't support blanket national healthcare. Why the fuck should I pay for their triple bypass surgeries?"

The man turned to her, having heard her, and opened his mouth to respond, but was then distracted by the dozen donuts the counterperson held out to him. He paid and moved on.

"One Pepsi, please, and one honey cruller," Rev said. Tim Hortons' honey crullers were to die for. Literally, if you ate a dozen at a time.

"Same for me, please," Dylan said, slipping his recorder into his pocket, "but I'll have an apple fritter."

They wandered out into the mall again, since all of the chairs were taken. Or blocked by vehicles. Once they'd finished their do-nuts, and Dylan made a quick trip into a craft store, having forgotten to buy spray paint for his helmet in Walmart, they resumed their in-terviewing.

"Excuse me, what do you think of the new parent licence law?" Dylan decided it was his turn, and had his Pepsi in one hand, his re-corder back in the other.

"You can't legislate a thing like that. It just happens."

"It just happens?" Rev asked.

"Yeah, my own kids were accidents, if you know what I mean," the man snickered.

"Actually, no, I don't," Rev replied. "How did you accidentally ejaculate into a vagina? Did you mistake it for something else?"

Dylan sprayed Pepsi out his nose.

"Or did the woman in question catch some ejaculate with her vagina—by accident? 'Cuz if that's the case, I'd really like to know what it was she was actually trying to do."

They walked away, and Rev muttered angrily to a still-recovering Dylan, "'I created someone by accident'! That should be just as horrif-ic, and just as morally reprehensible, as 'I killed someone by acci-dent.'"

Dylan just nodded his agreement, then sputtered "Reckless re-production!"

They started to walk up the other side of the mall, tossing their empty bottles into a recycling bin as they passed by.

"You've read Joseph Fletcher?" Dylan asked. "He said it's depress-ing to realize that most of us are accidents."

"Yeah," Rev replied, looking around, "especially since some of us are considerably more of a train wreck than others."

"Excuse me," Dylan approached some people in a cluster, "what do you think about the new parent licence law?" He held out his re-corder.

"I'm not in favour of it," one of the women said. "The idea of re-quiring a licence in order to bear children—it violates what it means to be human."

"Yeah," Rev agreed, "I guess. If being human is all about being led by the nose by your driven-to-replicate-DNA."

They moved on.

"Excuse me, what do you think of the new parent licence law?" Rev tried again, with the next person, a woman who was idly watch-ing a boy and a girl chase each other around one of the many benches conveniently placed along the length of the mall, stepping on the feet of the people who were sitting on the bench, eliciting various 'Heys!' and "Watch its!'

"Coercion never works," the woman said. "You can't force people to do things."

"But the law isn't forcing you to become a parent. It's just saying that if you want to become a parent, you have to know what you're doing."

"And," Dylan offered, pleased with the chance to show off the results of his research again, "As Chasteen points out, it's unrealistic to expect individual parents to act in the best interest of society—they must be legislated to do so."

"And it's not just parents," Rev added. "Most people have trouble acting for the common good, on their own volition. Look at energy use, fossil fuel emissions, recycling for gawd's sake. Even that didn't happen until it was *required*."

"Well," the woman said, still staring dispassionately at the kids still running amuck, "but I think we should have tried parent educa-tion first. They should have a course in school, maybe even in the community centers."

"Would you have taken such a course?" Rev asked, raising her el-bow just a bit too late to clip one of the kids on the chin as they ran past them and then back to circle the bench.

"Well, no," the woman admitted.

"And are you a parent?"

"Well, yes."

They walked on.

"Matthew! Penny! Get over here!"

"Excuse me, what do you think of the new parent licence law?" Dylan approached one of the people, an elderly man, sitting on the bench.

"We already have a licence to have kids. It's called marriage."

They thought about that for a minute.

"He's got a point," Rev said to Dylan. "At least to the extent of financial provision."

"But anyone can get married. So it doesn't really—"

"Well, no, don't you have to be a certain age?" Rev asked.

"Yeah, but isn't that about it?"

"This one's a much better licence," she said to the old guy.

"And what do you think?" Dylan asked the elderly woman beside him, whose cane was tucked beside her.

"I say bring it on! Bring. It. On."

Rev grinned at her, then they moved on. A shriek split the air, and they turned to look. Matthew lay sprawled on the mall floor. Seemed he tripped over someone's extended cane.

"Excuse me, what do you think of the new parent licence law?" Dylan asked a young man whose pants were halfway down his butt, exposing several inches of worn, greying underpants. He had a baseball cap on backwards and the hood of his hoodie up. It looked like he was growing a little shelf out the back of his head.

"My parents didn't have no licence and I turned out okay," he said.

"Are ya sure?" That was Rev.

"Hey, I ain't never killed nobody!"

"Well, goody for you!"

He turned to her then, glowering. "I don't need this!" he practically spit in her face.

"And the underlying premise there is that I exist to provide only what you need?"

Dylan pulled her along. "That's the standard?" she said to him. "Two hundred thousand years, or six, and that's the best we can do? 'I ain't never killed nobody'?"

"It's a hundred and eighty degrees from where we started."

"Still."

"Still," Dylan agreed.

Three stores down, there was a traffic jam. Dylan and Rev watched for a while with amusement. The vehicles didn't have a reverse. And it took forever for it to occur to someone, anyone, that he could get off and pull his vehicle free of the mess.

They walked on.

"Excuse me, what do you think of the new parent licence law?" Rev asked the next person they passed.

"No one's going to tell me whether I can have sex!" the man fumed. "There's no place for the state in the bedrooms of the nation. President Clinton said that."

"No one's saying you can't have sex, you dumbfuck. You can jerk off all day long if you want. The new legislation isn't even saying you can't reproduce. All it's saying is you have to prove competence before you do so."

"And actually, it was Trudeau," Dylan said. "*Prime Minister* Trudeau."

They walked on.

"Excuse me, what do you think of the new parent licence legislation?" Dylan approached a man just about to enter a store, three bags already in his hands.

"Oh, I don't know," he said. "I haven't really thought about it."

"Are you a parent?" Rev asked.

"Yes, I am."

"And do you think about that? Really?"

"No."

"And that doesn't bother you?"

"Why should it?" He looked impatiently toward the store.

"YOU KNOW WHAT I think?" Rev said to Dylan as they walked out to the car, "the Department of Parent Licensing could save a lot of time by just asking applicants what they think of the program. Those in favour get a licence. Because they're the ones who get it. They get the importance of becoming qualified, developing competence. They're the ones who'd make responsible parents."

"I think you're right," he sighed.

10

O h, look, it's 50s and 60s night at The Dive," she said as they drove by. The neon sign hanging outside said as much.

"It's a bit early, and it's been a long day, but we could go get dinner somewhere and then come back?" Dylan sounded eager. And Rev desperately wanted to get the mall experience out of her mind.

SO AN HOUR LATER, they opened the door, and took in the dreary, dreary scene. Overly made-up and underly dressed young women were dancing in a cluster on the floor. Actually, they were not so much dancing as advertising. In a most dispirited fashion. And no wonder. There were half a dozen young men, overly drunk, standing at the bar. Watching the women with bored expressions, talking to each other about sports, no doubt. Rev knew the scene. It played out at every local bar she'd ever been to. When a slow dance came, about every five songs, the men would move en masse to ask one of the women to dance and if she said yes, they'd stand there in full body contact stepping from side to side while they made a full circle or two during the course of the song. Because of course real men don't dance.

So when Dylan moved onto the floor, by himself, the men stopped talking. Dylan didn't so much dance as personify the music with movement. He punctuated the lines with his body, he dipped when the music dipped, he literally changed direction when the music changed direction. No steps, no patterns, nothing at all conventional, he just let the music move through him. He danced like a child might before it got ruined by dance lessons. And before they even saw anyone else dance. She reminded him of one of the dancers on *So You Think You Can Dance*—Mark Kanemura, from Hawaii. The one who did that brilliant piece to Queen's "Bohemian Rhapsody".

She went to the bar, bought a couple drinks, put them on one of the empty small tables, then joined him on the floor.

"Chantilly Lace" had finished. The next song was "Shout". They started out doing some synchronized steps in the Platters style, Dylan leading, Rev following as best she could, then as the music raced faster and faster, they broke into a game of dance tag, chasing each other around the floor, but pausing to look up and throw their hands in the air each time 'Shout!' came. They ran on the spot at one point, then when the music suddenly slooped into the loose bit, they did the same. It was ridiculous. It was silly. It was great. And by the time it was over, they had to sit down.

"Oh God but that was fun," Dylan said, joy plastered across his face. He picked up the drink, raised it in thanks to Rev, and downed half of it. She pretty much did the same.

"In the Still of the Night" had come on, so all the men had moved to the floor and the dismal shuffle had started.

"'What the hell are they doing?" Dylan asked horrified. "Most of them aren't even in time!" A few seconds later, he said "I can't watch." He moved his chair around to the other side of the table so his back was to the floor. At that moment, the thick bouncer walked over to their table.

"I'm afraid I'm going to have to ask the two of you to leave."

"What? Why?" Dylan said. "We're over age. Here—" He reached into his pocket for his wallet. Rev grinned.

"You were running around the dance floor. Someone could've gotten hurt. It's a *dance* floor."

"Tell that to *them*!" Dylan nodded to the floor. "Duke of Earl" came on. "Oh, oh," Dylan got up. The bouncer stood in his way. "I won't run. Please. I *have* to dance to Duke."

The bouncer didn't move.

"You can too, you know. 'Duke, Duke, Duke,'" Dylan thrust his head out from his neck like a goose with each word, "'Duke, Duke, Duke of Earl,'" he looked at the no-neck bouncer. "Okay, maybe not," he stepped deftly around him to the floor. Rev joined him, thrusting her head out at him on her way, "'Duke, Duke, Duke … .'"

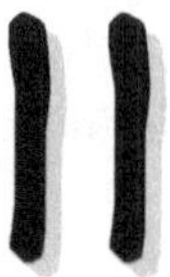

'm heading into the forest," Dylan announced the next day, with a honk of his horn. He was straddling his new bike just outside the back door of the cabin. Despite the warm June weather, he had long pants on. And his new bug jacket. Bug season had arrived.

Rev popped her head out the door.

"So if I'm not back in twenty-four hours, come look for me?"

"I thought you were going to paint your helmet purple and turquoise," she said, peering closely through the mesh that covered his head.

"I was. But then I decided it should match my little basket."

She nodded. "I like the glitter."

"So ... the bit about my not coming back ... "

"Yeah, yeah." Then added, as she turned to go back inside, "It's the middle of the afternoon. All the bears are at the dump."

ALL THE BEARS BUT one are at the dump, Dylan corrected as he stared at it, slumped on the ground against a tree in a bushy clearing of sorts. He was pleased with himself that he didn't mistake it for Bob. As had happened the year before when they were in Algonquin Park. Despite the fact that Bob had left him. For Fifi. Actually, mistaking it for Peanut would be even more understandable. Peanut was the infinitely lovable Newfoundland dog attached to Tucker, their border guard escort during the blasphemy tour. Peanut was no doubt over-the-top happy doing his rescue thing on the Jersey coast somewhere and hadn't given Dylan a second thought since they parted ways at the end of the tour. But Dylan was still in love with him. He should call Tucker and ask if he and Peanut want to come for a visit, Dylan thought. Peanut would love the lake. And he could show us all his new dances.

The bear's head moved.

Oh, right. Okay, Plan B. Plan A had been to just tiptoe past it. Plan B wasn't fully formed yet. It wasn't that big, Dylan thought. But then what the hell did he know. Even a small bear could probably overtake him on his bike. He didn't see any little cubs snuggled up beside it. So that was a good thing, right?

The bear stopped his head nodding and stared at Dylan. It looked—pleasantly satiated with a belly full of raspberries? Dylan looked around. He didn't see any raspberry bushes. He looked back at the bear again—wait a minute. Dylan recognized that look.

AN HOUR LATER, REV heard Dylan's honking horn. Normally, such a noise would irritate the hell out of her. But there was nothing normal about Dylan. She got up and went to the back door.

"Guess what I found in the forest?" Dylan reached into his little basket, pulled out a bunch of weeds, and showed them to Rev. "Look!"

"Pretty," she said. Understandably unimpressed.

"No, *look*!"

She stepped closer. "Oh," she said then. "Is that what I think it is? I thought they destroyed them all."

"You knew about this?" He got off his bike and leaned it against the cabin.

"Well, I knew the OPP found a huge grow-op out here somewhere, arrested the guy, and destroyed his crop. But that was a couple years ago."

"Well, they must have missed some. There's a healthy little patch out there." Dylan took the weed into the kitchen, set it onto the table, and started sorting through it.

"Paper bag?"

"Plastic box."

He groaned. "We need to put this in a paper bag," he'd separated out ripest-looking bits, "and then put it in the microwave. The rest I'll hang upside down somewhere."

"Like bats."

"Like bats," he agreed. "So. Paper bag?"

"I have lots of paper," Rev replied. "And I have lots of bags. But, oddly enough, it does not follow that I have paper bags."

"You're getting stoned just thinking about it!" he laughed.

"Maybe," she grinned. "It's been a while."

"It has indeed," he agreed. "Okay, where's your paper?"

Rev brought a thick stack of paper from her study and set it onto the table. Unlike Dylan, who used a laptop, she still wrote with pen and paper. So she kept all the articles she printed out but then didn't use, and just turned them upside down. Frontside back?

Dylan selected a sheet and began to fold it. A minute later he had a pretty origami buffalo.

"Where'd you learn to do that?"

"A Bunch of Drunken Indians taught me."

He was referring to the band he'd joined up north when he quit teaching.

He put the bits he'd selected into the buffalo's humpy back, placed it carefully into the microwave, and set it for defrost.

They stared at it as it went round and round.

"Kinda like a buffalo merry-go-round, isn't it."

"SO, SHALL WE GO GET the mail?" Rev asked, butting out the joint they'd shared.

"Sure," Dylan replied.

As soon as they headed to the closet for their bug jackets, Rev started giggling.

"What?"

"Remember when we did the laundry stoned? Putting the shirts onto hangers completely flummoxed me."

"Flummoxed." He giggled.

She stared at her bug jacket, hanging there on its hanger. "It doesn't have a neck hole."

"Sure it does. It's just full. Of the head hood."

"But if a hole is full, then it's not a hole."

"You're right."

They considered the situation again. "So if it's not a hole," Dylan said, "how is it the hanger neck goes through it?"

"The hanger has a neck? Does it have a neck hole too?"

"I don't think so. But I don't know why, exactly."

"So does that mean you can put a hanger onto another hanger?"

"It should, shouldn't it."

They considered the situation a bit longer.

"It's just a mile."

"And there's a bit of a breeze."

ABOUT FIFTY YARDS from the driveway, Rev said, "You know, I'm really tired."

"Me too. Really, really tired."

"Yeah. Maybe we should take a rest."

"Yeah. There's a good spot," Dylan pointed to the ditch at the side of the road.

"Yeah." Rev wobbled into the ditch and sat down. Then decided to fall over. Dylan joined her.

FIVE HOURS LATER, they woke up. In the dark.

"Are you awake?" Rev asked Dylan.

"Yeah, you?"

A moment passed. "No."

Another moment passed. "So are we old or what?"

"Pretty moon."

NEXT MORNING, LATE, they were in the porch, as usual. Except for the Absorbine Jr. smell. They'd discovered, no surprise really, that they were covered with bites. Blackfly bites. Mosquito bites. No-see-um bites. Deerfly bites. Horsefly bites. And, between the two of them, three unidentified bites. Or points of entry made by alien probes.

Once the itching started, they quickly exhausted her supply of calamine. The Absorbine Jr. was actually quite effective.

"So," Dylan said, idly scratching his arm, while he read the page he'd googled, "the problem was the trichomes were too ripe. When they're clear, you get a cerebral stone. When they're milky, you get a lethargic stone."

"So we're not old."

"We're not, no. Even so, we'll need a magnifying glass to check the trichomes. For future reference."

"Ebay."

12

ext day, since they were out of pizza, and Froot Loops, and
calamine, and Absorbine, Jr., they made another trip into town.

"Okay if we swing by the shelter?" Rev asked. "I'd like to touch base, see if they've found the guy."

"Sure. But it's too hot to sit in the car," Dylan said. "I'm going to go for a walk."

"Okay. Fifteen minutes tops."

They got out of the car, Dylan headed to the sidewalk, Rev to the gate. She rang the buzzer, waited for it to pop open, then walked up to the door.

"Hi," Rev said to a woman she didn't recognize. "Anita's day off?"

"Sort of," the woman replied. "She's on indefinite leave. I'm Pat. Who are you?"

"Chris Reveille," Rev said, extending her hand. "Used to work here. Anita called me about the problem with Susie, and I thought I'd just drop by and see if it's been resolved. Have the police dropped the charges against her? Have they picked up her ex?"

"Yes to the first, no to the second. Susie!" she called into the adjoining living room. "A Chris Reveille is here to see you!"

Susie waddled out of the room. "Oh Rev, hi!"

"Hi yourself. You're doing well?" Rev asked. She didn't really give a damn, but knew it was polite to inquire about the health of people you didn't care about it. And to make trite observations about the weather. But not to connect the weather to climate change and the people to blame for the coming devastation. Go figure.

"Yeah, thanks," she said, rubbing her hand over her belly.

"And Bobby? Have they found him? Is he the one who—" Okay, they really needed a bunch of new words. "—illegally fertilized your egg?"

Susie giggled. "No, if he doesn't want to be found—"

There was a sudden banging on the door.

"Susie, are you in there? Suze? Baby?"

All three of them stared at the door. Then the glass broke—which wasn't supposed to be possible—and a thick hand reached in and turned the knob. Pat ran into the office to call the police.

Bobby was a large man, Rev observed. A brute of a man, it was accurate to say. Especially judging by the expression on his face.

"Susie, come on, we're going home." He reached out to grab her.

Susie stepped back, bumping into the wall behind her. Fear paralyzed her face. And her vocal cords.

"Clearly you don't love her," Rev said, "and, in fact, you must hate her, given what you've done to her. So why do you want her to come home? I'd've thought you'd be glad the bitch left." She was stalling for time, and trying to take his attention off Susie, well aware that her being visibly pregnant wouldn't stop further assaults, but she was also genuinely puzzled by this sort of behaviour. She didn't get countries that refuse to let their citizens emigrate either.

"I *do* love her. Susie, baby, you *know* I love you!"

Susie didn't move.

"Well isn't hitting her a weird way of showing it?" Rev asked.

"You stay the fuck out of this!" Bobby roared and threw a punch at Rev. She ducked.

His movement had the effect of unfreezing Susie. She reached into a pocket and pulled out her stunner. Each woman who arrived at the shelter was given one of the new high-tech guns as part of the orientation package. In case of this very occurrence. There had been too many close calls, and the police never showed up in time. While Rev had worked there, though, these sorts of incidents had just resulted in property damage. No one had ever gotten in before. Where the hell was Pat?

"Go away, Bobby," Susie pointed the gun at him with a badly shaking hand. "I don't want to come home. I'm never coming home again."

Yes! Rev cheered silently to herself. All too often, they went. Meekly.

"Ah honey, you don't mean that."

"Yes, she does!" Rev said. "Why is it you guys never think a woman means what she says? 'No' means 'no' and 'I don't want to come home, I'm never coming home again' means 'I don't want to come home, I'm never coming home again'! And 'You're a fucking asshole' means—"

"I told you to stay the fuck out of this, are you deaf?" He roared menacingly at Rev. She involuntarily took a small step backwards, then hated herself for it. Then again, she didn't have a stunner in her hand. Note to self.

"Come on, baby," he turned his attention back to Susie, pleading sweetly, "you know you're not going to shoot that thing."

"Yes I am. If you come any closer." Susie had also taken a step backward. Well, sideways, since the wall was still behind her.

"No you won't, you're too afraid. You're afraid of everything," he taunted with disgust.

She fired. He was electrified. And went down.

Then staggered to his feet again.

"Go away or I'll fire again."

"No you won't, you can't do anything right. Look, that didn't even hurt me."

Come on, Susie, keep it together, Rev thought.

She fired again, with a still shaking hand. He went down again.

And got up again.

"Put it on a higher setting," Rev said to Susie, conversationally. As if she was simply suggesting an experiment.

But Susie *was* afraid. She was terrified.

"I'll get Billy and you'll never see him again," Bobby said, waiting, confidently and arrogantly, for Susie to give it up.

Susie paused. She lowered the gun. That can't happen, it just can't. Billy— Then just as Rev was about to open her mouth again, the stunner came up flashing. Bobby went down a third time. And thrashed around a bit. The stunner flashed again. Bobby thrashed again. Flash, thrash, flash, thrash. After the sixth time, Susie started smiling. Just a little. After the tenth time, Rev stopped her. In part because Bobby was no longer thrashing. At all.

And then the police politely pressed the buzzer at the gate.

DYLAN ROUNDED THE corner just as the police car drove away. He instantly broke into a sweat and sprinted to the driveway, arriving just as Rev came out of the house. Okay, relief poured through him, she's okay.

She wordlessly got into her car. He followed.

Once there, Rev turned the key in the ignition, then viciously turned off the radio in the middle of a sappy love song. "That and hip hop needs to be banned."

"Especially when played back to back." He immediately saw her point. And guessed correctly what had happened. "Susie's okay?"

"Yeah." She said nothing more while she got them out of the neighbourhood and onto the highway toward home.

"And you're okay?"

"I listened to the radio almost non-stop while I was growing up," she said. "As most people do. So I self-indoctrinated. Every frickin' song is about needing someone, wanting someone, finding someone, not finding someone, leaving someone, not leaving someone— Essentially, I inundated myself with messages about the importance of having a romantic/sexual relationship, the all-pervasive role in one's life of said romantic/sexual relationship."

"As most people do."

"Combine that with an inundation of the aggressive violence and misogyny of most hiphop, rap, urban music, or whatever the hell it's called—"

"Imagine," she said a mile later, and they both smiled at the Lennon reference, "if as many songs that are currently about romantic/sexual relationship were about, oh, changing the world. Imagine how we would be."

N ext morning, they carried their coffee and cold pizza into the porch—the perfect breakfast as far as Rev was concerned—set it on the table between her couch and his chair, then eased into its comfort, its gorgeous view of nothing but trees and lake and—

"That's new." Dylan said. They saw a motor boat parked across the little cove smack dab in the middle of—everything.

Rev sighed. "Actually, it's not. The property recently changed hands, and the new guy parks his boat there. When I saw that it wasn't there, when we got back, I thought maybe he'd moved it, but I guess it was just out for repair or something."

Dylan stared at it. He stood up and walked to both ends of the porch. There was no way they could not see it. He sat back down and stared out at it. "God, but it wrecks the ambiance."

"Tell me about it."

"Doesn't his property go all the way to the little creek? So he owns—must be three hundred feet of shoreline—couldn't he just park it a bit further up?"

"He could."

"Does he know that he's got it exactly where—did you ask if he'd move it?"

"Of course, I asked him," Rev said, now visibly upset. "I begged him. I explained that I spend all day, every day, staring out at the forest and the water—it's the same from my couch inside—"

"He leaves it there all winter? But—"

"—and that after all these years, the view still takes, took, my breath away—and now, for the rest of my life, or at least for as long as he owns the property— And he just got this stupid amused look on his face. As if I was being dramatic or over emotional.

"Then I asked if he could at least throw a tarp over it. Even bought him a dark green one."

"Well, yeah, it's sheet metal. That thing's going to glint like crazy when the sun's—"

She nodded.

"Even when it's cloudy—you can't not see it," Dylan insisted. "It stands out like a—"

"Middle finger."

"Why didn't you buy it? That stretch of cove, when it was for sale—could you have afforded to buy it?"

Rev nodded. "I tried. I offered a couple thousand more than the assessed price, then I doubled my offer, then I tripled it."

"And the guy refused?"

Rev nodded.

"Why in god's name?"

"He said he thought he could get more for the property with the cove attached."

They looked out through the screen for a while. At the brightly shining boat.

"God, but it wrecks—everything," Dylan said. "I'm going to go over and ask him."

"What, you think because you're a man, he'll listen to you?" Rev was angry.

"That's exactly what I think, yes. If he's the kind of asshole it seems he is, then to comply with a woman's request is to give in—to a woman. He'd never do that, no matter how reasonable the request. Or how politely made," he added. Just on the off-chance. "He'll be more apt to comply with the request if it comes from a man, because that wouldn't involve subordinating himself to a woman."

Rev went slack-jawed. As her whole life flashed before her eyes.

everal days later, Dylan took off on his bike, heading into the forest, a watering can and a few garden tools in his little basket up front, a bag of fertilizer in the milk crate he'd attached to the rat trap in back, and himself cocooned in his bug jacket.

Rev went out onto the lake in her beloved red kayak. The sun was sparkling on the water, the wind was just a breeze, and no one, not one person, was chainsawing or lawnmowing or dirtbiking. It was sublime. Absolutely sublime. Except for the blackflies, so she was similarly cocooned.

SHORTLY AFTER SHE returned, pleased to have once more gotten out of the kayak without going overboard—given her knees and the tendency of her body to stiffen after even short periods of inactivity, she figured it was just a matter of time—she had provided Dylan with unending entertainment during their recent tour through the States by repeatedly falling out of the van after long stretches on the road—Dylan returned as well.

"Rev!" he called, urgently but softly. She heard him from her couch on the porch and, intrigued, came around to the back door.

"Do you know whose dog this is?" He nodded to a pup standing warily about ten feet from him, panting and looking—expectant. "It showed up in the middle of the forest, when I was—gardening, and then wanted to come home with me. Followed me all the way. I tried to pick it up and put it in my basket, but it kept dancing away from me. So I just went slow. It's still a baby, I think. And it must be exhausted."

Rev looked at the scraggly, forlorn, little creature, wavering a little unsteadily on its feet. It was apparent that it wanted nothing more than to sit down, even lay down, but felt it had to remain ready for flight. Or something.

"It looks like it's been lost for a while," Dylan added. "Do you know where it belongs?"

She looked at the animal. "The forest."

"What?"

Rev waved at the cloud of blackflies hovering around her head, "I don't think that's a dog."

"Well, it isn't a bear." Dylan was sure on that point. And proud of it.

"No, it isn't a bear," Rev agreed. "It's a wolf."

Dylan looked at her. Then at the little— "Really? How can you tell?"

"Pointier ears, longer muzzle, longer legs," Rev summarized. "And she was all alone in the middle of the forest."

"But ... "

Rev went inside, and returned with a bowl of water. She knew better than to walk toward the little wolf, so she casually set the bowl down some distance away from it, and from the two of them. The little wolf went to it without hesitation and lapped greedily. Then looked at Rev for more. Rev approached slowly to pick up the bowl, letting the little wolf dance away from her. Dylan followed her back inside.

"It'll be hungry too," he said. He opened the fridge. There was no pizza left. And certainly no steaks in a vegetarian's fridge. He opened the cupboard. Ah. A moment later he set a bowl of Froot Loops beside the bowl of water. The little wolf started munching away like it was dog kibble. Wolf kibble. Finished the entire bowl. Then sat back on its haunches and looked up at Dylan. Who poured more into the bowl. It stepped back just a bit to allow him to do so, then emptied the second bowl as well. Dylan emptied the box. Eventually sated, the little wolf again sat back on its haunches and looked at them.

"Her mom probably got trapped," Rev said.

"There are traps in the forest?" Dylan was aghast. "I thought that was illegal!"

"Leg holds, yes. Not that that would stop anyone around here from setting them. But there's a guy up the river who sets snares. He sells the pelts. The wolves run through a wire noose to get at the food he places on the other side and then slowly strangle to death. Much more humane than leg holds."

"Poor thing."

"Yeah, but Dylan, we can't keep it."

The little animal dug a hole in the dirt beside the dishes, and then curled up in it.

"She thinks otherwise."

They looked at her, eyes already closed. So sweet.

"She won't be able to survive on her own," Dylan said. "And it's our fault—our species' fault—so it's our responsibility. Let's keep her, at least until she can make it on her own."

"Okay, but let's not let her into the house. We don't really know what we're doing."

"Agreed."

"Oh did you see that?" Dylan added. "She wagged her little tail!"

"SHE'S GOING TO BE hungry again when she wakes up," Rev said after they'd both gone inside. "Mom might've taken several days to die, and she was probably tucked close beside her the whole time."

Whimpering, Dylan thought, and crying her little eyes out.

"I'll go into town," Dylan said, "to get some dog kibble. Where's our list?"

Rev took their 'to get' list from the end of the kitchen counter. It was beside their 'to do' list.

He grabbed the car keys and went out the door. The little wolf was immediately at his side—well, a cautious five feet from his side—and followed him to the car in the driveway. Dylan walked back to the house. The little wolf followed him back to the house.

"Rev?"

It seemed the little wolf had imprinted on Dylan. He was her surrogate mom. Dylan was honored. And couldn't be more pleased. He had visions of her tucked beside him in bed.

"I'll go," Rev said. "She's had enough trauma for a while."

She took the keys from him, got into the car, and slowly backed out. Dylan quickly went back inside for his bug jacket, then sat down on the ground by the back door, leaning against the cabin. The little wolf sat down beside him, two feet away. Then it lay down beside him. Crawled a foot closer. Dylan tentatively, slowly, reached out his hand, let it linger in front of her nose for a bit, then gently, gingerly, stroked her. Once. Twice. She seemed okay with that. In fact, she wagged her tail again. Dylan beamed.

THEY BOTH SAT UP with attention as Rev's car pulled back into the driveway some time later.

"Pizza!" Dylan cried out as he watched Rev unload several large boxes from the passenger seat of the car.

"It's for the little wolf." Rev said. "The top one. Not all six." Oh, the horror.

Dylan took the top one and opened it. "A Meatlovers'!" he exclaimed. "Brilliant!" He set it onto the ground beside the two dishes.

"Don't you think we should cut it into—"

The little wolf tore off a large piece, trotted a few steps away from the box, then threw it into the air, clearly delighted. Or ensuring its death by plummet. making sure it was dead from the impact before she ate it. She rolled onto it. Yay! Pizza fur! Then she practically inhaled it. She returned to tear off another large piece. Trotted away. Threw it into the air. Rolled on it. Inhaled it. Returned a third time. Repeat. Until the large pizza was gone.

"That's probably enough. We don't want little wolf puke to deal with," Dylan said.

"Well, *she'd* probably deal with it, but—"

"Froot Loup. I named her Froot Loup. Not Froot Loop. Froot Loup."

"Got it. Clever."

Dylan grinned. Rev handed the rest of the pizza to Dylan to carry into the house, then returned to her car.

"Did you know," she called out, "there's a line of all-natural dog kibble that has, like, wild rabbit, or wild salmon, in it?" She hefted a bag of Alpha Dog with Rabbit out of the car and followed Dylan into the house.

"Can't get any more natural than that, I suppose," he commented.

"Unless it came with an assortment of viruses, bacteria, and parasites."

"Hey, do you think we should take her to a vet? For the standard pup vaccinations?"

Rev thought about that. "I don't know any vet that would take a wolf. And she might freak out in the car."

"Good point. But what if she gets injured? Would any of the local vets make a house call? For a wolf?"

"Might be worth calling around about. Just in case."

Dylan got the FoodStore bags from the car, containing Froot Loops—three boxes—and various other goodies.

"I think she's an eastern wolf, not a gray wolf," Dylan said, having brought his laptop outside at one point to do some research. "They tend to be grey-reddish. Like her." Dylan smiled at Froot Loup, following them back and forth. "And she's probably about 3 months old."

They returned to the car for another load.

"What's in the garbage bags?" he saw three hefty garbage bags squished into the back of the car. She'd put the seats down to make room for them.

"Straw," she said. "I stopped—you know where that woman has a horse? I figured she might sell us a couple bags. We can make a nest for Froot Loup in the shed. Since we're not letting her into the house." She grinned at Dylan.

So as soon as they unpacked the groceries, they went out to the shed. After some consideration, they decided Froot Loup might like one of the corners closest to the entrance. So she wouldn't feel cornered. So to speak. They moved stuff out of the corner on the left, then dumped the straw out.

"She needs a little—box," Dylan decided. "A mini-cave. A den. This is too open."

Rev looked around. "What about a kindling box?" She pointed to several wooden crates at the other end of the shed, obtained from the grocery store when produce was still shipped in wooden crates. Each one was full of kindling for starting woodstove fires in the winter, and she brought one at a time into the cabin once winter started.

"Bloody hell" Dylan said, going over to look. "I haven't seen these in a long time! You could probably sell them as antiques!"

"Yeah, well."

"I think—why don't we just move them here, to make a wall, sort of, on either side," Dylan started moving and stacking the crates, "and then if we had a tarp or an old blanket or something—"

Rev walked to another corner of the shed. "Here we go," she pulled a blanket out of a plastic garbage bag and shook it out. "Probably a bit mousey, but that might please Loup."

Dylan draped it across, making a low roof, then adjusted it so it hung down in front as well.

"What do you think?" he asked.

"Not as roomy as a refrigerator box, but if I were a homeless little wolf pup, I think I'd like it."

They moved Loup's food and water dishes, newly full of Froot Loops and water respectively, from the yard into the shed, tucking them just inside the enclosure. Froot Loup followed, but stopped at the shed doorway. She saw where they'd put them though. Dylan went back out, picked up the now-empty pizza box, then returned to the shed. The little wolf followed him, or the pizza box, this time getting up the nerve to enter the shed, but stopped just inside the door. She saw him put the pizza box just outside her new little den.

"I'm after a swim," Dylan said then. Rev decided the water was still too cold, but Froot Loup clearly didn't agree. Much to their surprise, she followed Dylan down the hill into the lake. They dog-paddled around for a bit, then Dylan called up to Rev, "Do you have any biodegradable shampoo or soap?"

Rev went back into the cabin and returned with her favourite shampoo, an Ebay find. She watched with disbelief as Dylan gave

Froot Loup a bath, standing in the shallow water just a few feet from shore.

"She's probably covered in dirt, and bugs," he said, as he gently ran his fingers through her fur, stroking her as he did so. "This probably feels great, doesn't it, Loup," he continued to croon to her, as she stood beside him, even leaning into his legs. "And once we get all your little furry bits clean, you can paddle around to rinse," he murmured, "and you'll be the cleanest little wolf in the forest. Your fur will be so soft and snuggly and—cherry cheesecakey," he looked up at Rev and grinned when he recognized the scent. Once he was done with the shampoo, he swam out, and sure enough, Froot Loup followed. They paddled around until the soap was out of her coat.

Once back on shore, Rev was ready with a towel. Two towels, in fact. It turned out that only one was necessary. Loup shook herself vigorously once she was back on shore, then took off.

Curious, they rushed up the hill back to the cabin, eager to see if she'd gone into her den, but they found her tearing around Rev's patch of lawn, such as it was. They watched, mesmerized, as she threw herself into a shoulder body surf, propelling herself with her back legs, essentially plowing through the grass. She got up and started running around again, then did the shoulder plow thing again. Repeat. Until dry. Then find a sunny patch, lay down, and fall asleep.

"She's still not coming inside," Rev anticipated Dylan's query.

"I know. She has to get used to—we have to get— We have to start from now preparing for her to leave us," he said sadly. Like Bob. Like Peanut.

REV DECIDED TO WORK for a bit on her in-progress LSAT reasoning questions, and Dylan had a lot of notes for his articles that he needed to organize, so they made coffee, grabbed a couple slices of pizza, and headed for the porch. Where they saw Froot Loup, curled up on Rev's couch, fast asleep, with the sweet contentment and over-the-top trust that only babies can have. Of any species.

Rev looked at the screen door. Now torn.

"I'll fix that," Dylan said quickly. "Put screen on the list," he added, mostly to himself.

"And new shoes," she said, nodding to one of Dylan's running shoes, tucked between Loup's paws, already significantly chewed up.

"Maybe she's teething. Where'd the comforter come from?" he said then. Rev didn't have a red comforter on her couch. Usually.

"It's my winter comforter. I keep it folded up, behind the couch."

"You sit out here in the winter?"

"Into the fall some. Until it starts to snow. And again in spring. But that's not the salient point. Is it."

"No," he grinned, "the salient point is that Froot Loup actually dragged the comforter out from behind your couch and then pulled it up onto your couch and made a little nest for herself. In dogs, manipulating their environment like that is a sign of intelligence. Bob used to get his squeaky frog and bring it to bed every night. No matter where he might have left it or," he added devilishly, "where I might have put it. He wouldn't come to bed until he'd found it." Froot Loup's eyes opened.

"Down!" Rev said sharply to her.

"She doesn't—"

The little wolf got down. Then turned around, put her little paws up onto the couch, and strained to reach Dylan's shoe. Dylan edged closer and pretending surreptitiousness, reached out and nudged his shoe toward her until it was close enough for her to grab. Rev not so surreptitiously pulled the blanket off the couch.

"Can't she—she's just a little baby—"

She bunched the blanket into a nest in the corner of the porch, beside Dylan's chair. He grinned. As did Froot Loup, who, after fixing the blanket a little more, just so, no just so, curled up in it. Dylan's shoe tucked beside her.

"ACTUALLY," REV REMEMBERED, half an hour later, butting out a half-finished joint—if they finished it, they'd probably fall asleep, she thought—then forgot what she was saying.

Dylan waited. Or pondered the word 'actually'.

"Oh yeah—I have a roll of leftover screen in the basement." She waved a mosquito away, then reached for the blackfly that was crawling along the back of her neck.

"No wonder she wants to be in here," Dylan nodded to Froot Loup and tried to slap at a mosquito at the same time. He ended up slapping his head.

"Yeah. It seems to be turning into a particularly bad, and particularly long, bug season."

"Are there other kinds?"

"No, not really," she confessed. "But that doesn't invalidate my comment."

After a very long time, Dylan agreed.

A little while later Rev remembered what she'd said about the screen and went into the basement to get it. Dylan rummaged in the kitchen for scissors and then went into Rev's study for her stapler.

Half an hour later, Dylan went to the top of the basement stairs. "Are you lost?"

"Possibly." A moment later, "I also forget what I came down here for."

"Can't help you there," he replied, then went back to the porch and saw the scissors and stapler on the little table between his chair and Rev's couch.

Froot Loup smiled at him.

"Screen!" Dylan shouted. He turned to repeat his message and bumped into Rev.

"Screen!" she'd shouted at the same time.

They proceeded to replace the torn bit with a measured and cut new bit. It took only an hour.

Rev returned the roll to the basement, Dylan returned the scissors to the kitchen and the stapler to Rev's study, and when they both returned to the porch, they saw that the screen was torn again. Froot Loup was on her blanket in the corner. So was her pizza box. She looked up at them with the paper from the bottom of the pizza box in her mouth. What?

"She was probably thirsty too," Dylan noted.

"Yeah, but do we really want to move her dishes in here?"

"Oh! Oh!" Dylan did his Horschach imitation. *Welcome Back Kotter* was responsible for his decision to become a teacher. "We could make it a swinging screen!"

"Yes! Brilliant!" And then, "Could we?"

Dylan went back to Rev's study for her letter opener. He carefully pried the staples off. There were a great many of them. And they were very small. And the same color as the screen.

"That's not right," Rev observed when he had finally completed the task. "I think you should have left one edge stapled."

A long while later, after Dylan painstakingly had restapled one edge to the door frame, she noted, "Yeah, I'd've gone with the top edge, myself."

o," Rev said, late the next morning as she came into the porch, "I just got off the phone and it turns out—hey, the boat's gone!"

Dylan looked up from his laptop and smiled. He'd noticed it right off too. "And now you don't know whether to be pissed or pleased."

"I'm both. Of course."

"Of course."

She sank into her couch and looked out at the gorgeous lake, nothing but trees and water, sun sparkling. God, but that fricking boat had ruined it, for so long, and for nothing. There was no reason whatsoever it couldn't have been parked twenty feet to the right all this time. Damn right she was pissed. And so very pleased.

"So what were you saying?"

She refused to tear her eyes from the view. "What?"

"You were saying it turns out ... "

"Oh yeah. It turns out that it wasn't Bobby. The egg bank thing." She turned to face Dylan and just then noticed that Froot Loup was in the corner with his shoe. Apparently now her shoe. Rev suspected she'd crept from her den into the porch shortly after Dylan had put her to bed—in the shed. "One, it's not his DNA. And, two, whoever it was jizzed on a whole shelf of petri dishes. Which is just eew."

"Maybe he just didn't know which one was—the one he was after."

"Or maybe he was just obeying that selfish gene in his primal brain, the one that instructs him to replicate itself as much as possible, as often as possible."

"Some people are such tools," Dylan said out loud what Rev was no doubt thinking. "Literally."

"Anyway, so now they're thinking it wasn't personal. That it's orchestrated by someone. Or some group. And since they've never been impressed with police intervention, they still want me to ask questions."

"Well, if I learned anything from my degree in journalism, it's 'Follow the money!'"

She thought about that. "You don't have a degree in journalism."

"Well, if I learned anything from my degree in history, it's 'Follow the money!'"

"Okay, let's do that," she said, lighting up the half joint from before. "Who stands to lose money from the new legislation?"

"If the new legislation leads to better kids—"

"Which, let's admit, isn't necessarily going to be the case. Even educated people do stupid shit."

She inhaled, then passed the joint over to him.

"Granted." He inhaled. "But let's say—what were we saying?"

"That if the new law leads to better kids, then the people who will lose money ... "

"Are the people whose job it is to fix kids," he said. Proudly.

"Psychologists? Counsellors?"

"Okay, that's good," he said. "We should write that down. Otherwise we'll forget."

"Forget what?"

"See?"

"See what?"

"See?!"

"See what?!"

"The legislation will also lead to fewer unwanted kids," she said a few seconds later, when she remembered what they were talking about. And then she realized that she'd remembered. And then she got sidetracked thinking about Libet's research, which showed that our awareness of an intent to do something actually occurs *after* we start doing it. Which totally fucks up free will. And moral responsibility.

"So, adoption agencies," Dylan said.

"What?"

"See?"

"See what?"

Dylan passed the joint back to her.

"Okay, so Child and Family Services," she was inexplicably back on track. "And social workers. For messed up families in general," she said. "When the parents aren't ready to put their kids up for adoption, or haven't yet had them taken away, but there's still need for intervention," she clarified. Or simply gushed on in the general area her brain found itself in.

"So the court system too?"

"Oh! Oh!" Rev was on a roll. "And the civil liberties lobby! And the disability lobby! They won't lose money, but they might be so ideologically against the legislation, they might stage something like this."

"Yes, good, we should write that down!"

"The Church!" Rev absolutely crowed. Froot Loup looked up from her shoe, then decided there was no cause for alarm. She happily resumed gnawing the toe.

"Yes, good!" Dylan said. "No wait, how would the Church lose money if people had to get licensed?"

"I don't know! But they've got a lot of it. And they're evil. So we can infer that they had something to do with this. Since this is evil and, and, may involve money!"

"We can?" He didn't think that was quite how inference worked.

"Yes! Probably!" She took a draw on the joint.

"Oh! Oh! I know! Licensed parents won't raise believers!" Dylan was pleased with himself. "They'll encourage their children to be critical thinkers, who will see through the lies the Church tells us, who will see the overwhelming lack of evidence for the existence of god!"

"Yes!" And a few moments later, "So?"

"So we should also investigate the television industry and the junk food manufacturers," Dylan said. "And the people who make Barbie dolls and toy guns."

"Because they go to Church?"

"No, silly, because— I forgot."

"Because parents who are licensed won't raise tv and junk food addicts!" Rev shouted.

They high fived each other in a celebration of their brilliance. And the movement made Rev fall off the couch.

Next morning, or thereabouts, when Rev and Dylan made their way into the porch with coffee and pizza to start their day's work, Loup was again already there. Along with a multitude of blackflies and mosquitoes. Dylan looked at the door and saw the problem: the screen was so stiff that when Loup walked through, it bunched up instead of falling back.

"We need to put a weight along the bottom," he said to Rev. "Then it'll hang straight without bunching."

Rev ignored the 'we' part of the sentence and settled into her couch with a sigh as she looked out at the gorgeous, absolutely gorgeous, view.

Dylan went out to the shed, and found a piece of strapping. He went back into the porch and measured the screen. Then went back to the shed, found Rev's saw, sawed a piece of strapping, found Rev's sandpaper, and sanded the ends. Then he went back to the porch. Then he went into Rev's study for her stapler. He returned to the porch and stapled the strapping to the bottom edge. The screen hung perfectly flat. No bunching at all.

"There you go!" Dylan said cheerfully to Loup, and when he left to put the saw, sandpaper, and strapping back where it had been, Loup followed. Tried to follow. Couldn't push through as easily as—there, that did it.

Dylan looked behind at the torn screen and dangling piece of strapping.

He sighed, then studied the problem and decided to put a piece of screen, unweighted, on each side of the door. Then when Loup went through and the one side got bunched up, he figured, the other side would hang flat to compensate. Dylan went to the basement to get the roll of screen, making a note to himself to just leave it in the porch for a couple days. He carefully cut two new pieces and stapled one to each side.

"There you go!" Dylan said cheerfully to Loup, fully aware of the déjà-vu feeling. And—

Froot Loup obligingly stepped through. The screen on the one side bunched up so much it poked out the screen on the other side.

Dylan studied the problem again. After a few minutes, he went into Rev's study for her letter opener and proceeded to undo what he'd just done. He cut four new pieces and stapled two pieces to each side—overlapping pieces.

"That's a good idea. Less likely to bunch, yeah?" Rev said from the couch.

"You think?"

THAT AFTERNOON, DYLAN had a scheduled interview with Social Services. But since Froot Loup was still following his every move, they were afraid she'd run after them all the way to Sudbury. Keeping her in the porch when they left wouldn't work since they'd so thoughtfully made the screen into a sort of two-way doggy door for her. And they both agreed that tying her up while her new mom abandoned her would be too traumatic.

"Can we use your answering machine to make it a conference call?"

"Maybe," Rev replied. "If we ask her to call us, and if I leave the machine on, it not only records, which would be good for you in any case, but if I have the volume up, we both could hear her."

"But could she hear us?"

"Oh. Right. She'd hear you if you pick up, but I think that cancels the recording. Plus, she couldn't hear me. And I couldn't hear her. It'd be just like a regular phone call," she finished lamely. And decided she was still a bit stoned.

"I wonder if she could call your number and my cell at the same time," Dylan said. "That would work, right?"

"I don't think she can do that. They're two different numbers."

"Oh. Right." Definitely still stoned.

"She could probably put her phone on speaker phone though. Then we could all hear each other. If one of us was there instead of here," she added as an afterthought. "Which sort of defeats the purpose."

"Not if it's me who stays here," Dylan said. "You're not that important. To Froot Loup," he grinned.

"You're suggesting that I drive into town, to the Social Services office, just so the three of us—no, that's just too stupid." She got up and went to examine her answering machine.

"Guess what? It has a speaker phone setting," she called from the kitchen. "I've just never had occasion to use it," she added, anticipating the need for defence.

Dylan joined her in the kitchen, then went back to the porch to get the phone number. He joined her again in the kitchen, and dialled the number. "Hello, Ms. Bricker, please. Dylan O'Toole."

"One moment, please."

"Ms. Bricker."

"Hello, Ms. Bricker. This is Dylan O'Toole. We have an appointment a little later today, but I'm afraid something's come up and I can't easily leave the house. Would it be possible to do the interview by phone?"

"Certainly. Would you like to do it now or would you rather call back at ... two o'clock?"

"Now is good, if that's convenient."

"It is."

"Okay, thanks," he made frantic handwriting motions to Rev, who went back into the porch to get his big notepad and a pen. "I have you on speaker phone, my friend and colleague Chris Reveille is here with me. She's investigating, in an unofficial capacity, the recent break-in at the egg bank and the subsequent illegal fertilization."

"The Susie Davenport thing?"

"Yes, you know her?" Rev spoke up.

"The shelter and Social Services have some overlap in clientele."

"Right. Of course."

There was a pause on the other end. "So am I to understand you consider Social Services a suspect of some kind?"

"Well," Rev replied, "it occurred to me that with the parent licensing legislation, the demand for Social Services services may decrease"—she was momentarily distracted by the intrigue of pondering 'Social Services services'—'Social Services social services' in fact—"which could lead to funding cutbacks, and, consequently, staffing reductions. Last hired, first fired—maybe somebody's trying to save his job?"

"Well, it would be *her* job. So she wouldn't have the equipment—"

"A used condom and a turkey baster—"

"Eew."

"Agreed. But people have done much worse to keep their jobs."

"True enough. But the reduction in need could result, instead, in a decrease in caseload. That's what we're all hoping for. Praying for. Desperately."

"But it's not your call."

"True enough. The powers that be prefer to have ten seriously overworked burned-out-in-a-year staff instead of twenty happy I-have-a-life staff. Go figure."

"Yeah, it's the have-and-have-not hierarchy over the share-the-wealth co-op. No news there."

"True enough."

There was another pause. "Did you want to speak with Elisha? She's our last hire."

"If she's available, sure, that'd be good."

"Elisha! Got a minute?"

They heard Ms. Bricker explain the situation to Elisha, who said 'Eew'. Then asked when the eewness was to have occurred.

Rev gave her the window of time she had been given.

"Monday to Friday, I go straight home from here. And I stay there until morning. So it couldn't've been me."

"You've got someone to vouch for that?"

"Husband and two kids."

"Okay, good, thanks, I'll cross you off the list."

"Thank you, Elisha. Mr. O'Toole, what questions can I answer for you?"

"Does Social Services have an official stance on the new legislation?" Dylan had a list of questions on his big notepad. In a stunningly unexpected display of preparation.

"No, but I can tell you that most, if not all, of us are in favour of it. We see broken kids every day. Kids who didn't get what they needed at a critical stage in their development. These kids go through life, aggressively, belligerently, thinking the world owes them something.

"And indeed we do. But we can't give it to them because that critical window of time has passed: we can't go back and flush from the fetus the chemicals that interfered with its development; we can't go back and provide the baby with the nutrients required for growth; we can't go back and give the child the safety and attention that would have led to a secure personality. Every year, millions of the people we've created so carelessly are starved, beaten, or otherwise traumatized. Thousands die. And that doesn't count the ones still walking around."

Part way through that extremely well-put explanation, Dylan started making frantic mini recording gestures to Rev, who went rummaging in his jacket pocket, but returned too late.

"Are you concerned at all about abuse of the system?" he asked, still madly scribbling about critical windows and the walking dead. Rev turned his recorder on and set it by the phone.

"Yes, of course. The new law opens the door for all sorts of abuses. We were quite concerned about who would be designing the screening process. But most of us are satisfied with the result. We continue to be concerned about who administers the screening process. In the wrong hands, it could go very wrong very quickly.

"But look around: it's not as if the current situation is abuse-free. Why do you think we exist?"

"Why do you think the current abuse occurs?" Dylan asked. "You're referring to child abuse? By parents?"

"Yes. There are a number of reasons for child abuse. I could write a book. In fact, I have." Dylan scribbled a note to himself. "But I think the bottom line is that we don't value parenthood. I'm going to pull up a quote ... here we go. 'Abuse and neglect in various forms will continue until we as a society value parenthood; until we regard parenting as a privilege, rather than as a by-product of sexual intercourse, a route to adult identity, or a route to social assistance.'"

"That's from your book?"

"Yes, but I'm quoting Katherine Covell and R. Brian Howe. They've done some good work, you should look them up."

"Actually, I've already come across them, but not that particular bit, thanks."

"There's this idea in our society that having kids is a good thing. Always. Well, it's not."

"You're right," Rev spoke up. "Someone tells you they're pregnant, and you're supposed to say beam, and gush, and say 'Congratulations!' I tend to say instead something like 'Do you want it?' or 'And is that a good thing?'"

"Bet that goes over well at the baby showers."

"Actually I don't get invited to baby showers anymore. Not since—never mind."

Dylan glanced at her. He'd ask later. He was sure it would be good.

"People do not like their unexamined beliefs challenged," Ms. Bricker continued. "We see that a lot here. They can get as violent with us as they are with their kids."

"No surprise there."

"Which explains why," Dylan was catching up, "everyone thinks *not* having kids is such a bad thing. I mean, we're—people like us, people without kids—we're irresponsible, we're immature," he looked at Rev for confirmation.

"We're selfish," she added with a nod.

"I assume you're going to check out one of the parent license classes?" Ms. Bricker asked.

"Yes, we are, thanks."

"Good. I'm pulling up something else ... that might frame the experience for you ... here we go. A group called Invest in Kids did a survey a while ago, and they found that only 34% of 1,645 parents knew that the experiences a child has before the age of three will greatly influence their academic achievement. Only half knew that emotional closeness strongly affects a baby's intellect."

"Wow."

"And—I use this one a lot—only 18% knew that a six-month-old infant can*not* consciously manipulate its parents."

"So much for daddy who diddles his baby girl," Rev recalled some horrific news item, "because she was acting like she wanted it."

"Indeed," Ms. Bricker said.

"Is there anything else—"

"We already legislate to some extent what parents can and cannot do," Ms. Bricker said. "We already say to some parents you can't raise these kids. This just pulls it back one step to the point of preventing the fuck up in the first place, rather than making us all try to fix the fuck up later. Which is, in most cases, as I've indicated, impossible. That language was off-the-record," she added.

"I'll change it," Dylan assured her. "The point is a good one."

"Have you spoken to any drug rehab counsellors yet? And you might want to talk to Don, he's one of our on-site counsellors. Child psychologist, actually. Does a lot of work with the parents who pass through here."

"I'd like to speak to both of them," Dylan said.

"I'll transfer you," she said. "Unless you have any further questions for me?"

"No," Dylan said, having exhausted his list of two. "Thank you for your time.

"No problem," she said.

They listened in amazement then, as not just one, not just two, but several people demonstrated knowledge of phone magic. Don wasn't in, according to Cindy, but Andy, in drug rehab, was, according to Rick.

"Andy Nesbitt, what can I do for you?"

"Hello, I'm Dylan O'Toole, I'm writing a series of articles on the new parent license legislation, and Ms. Bricker, of Social Services, suggested that I speak with you."

"Oh, sure, what did you want to know?"

"Oh—well, I'm not—"

"The legislation will put you out of a job, yeah?" Rev stepped in.

"I wish."

"But without drug addicted parents, we won't have drug addicted kids."

"Woh. First, a lot of drug addicts *don't* have drug addicts for parents. Second, the legislation is actually *increasing* business, because people have to get clean before they can become a parent."

"Oh, right." How did she miss that? She stroked him and anyone like him off her suspect list.

"So you think the legislation is a good thing?" Dylan asked.

"I do. But not because it keeps me employed. Have you ever seen a crack baby?"

"No."

"Give me your email address, I'll send you a link to a video."

"Okay," Dylan provided his address, then asked a follow-up question. ""What about—I've heard that many an addict has straightened out once they had a kid. What's your response to that?"

"My response is you don't create a little human being to be your personal rehab program."

"So why *do* you create a little human being?" Rev asked. Curious.

"You got me," Andy confessed. "Maybe when I think of a good reason, I'll create one. Any other questions?"

"Not at the moment, thanks."

"I'll send you some literature. There's some good information out there about the economic costs of drug abuse during pregnancy. Very utilitarian, but hey. The video should give you some idea of the human costs. It's criminal. I mean, literally, yes, but also—well, you'll see."

WHEN THEY RETURNED to the porch, it was full of blackflies and mosquitoes again. Froot Loup was nowhere to be found, but was, of course, the culprit.

"Froot Loup!" Dylan called, and the little wolf came running.

"Hey, she came! When I called her! When I called her name!" Dylan was delighted. Then remembered why he'd called her.

They watched carefully as Loup stepped through the door. The halves didn't fall nicely onto each other. More bunching, more gaps. More sighs.

Rev went back into the cabin for the stapler and the scissors. Dylan pulled the roll of screen from behind the couch. He cut a small piece of screen and stapled it to cover the gap Froot Loup had left.

As the little wolf obligingly stepped through again, they stared at it intently, as if it were a piece of modern art in the National Gallery, then walked from side to side, considering it.

"Here," Rev said, pointing to a gap visible only from the left. Dylan cut a triangular piece of screen and stapled it over the opening, on the first layer.

"And here," she said, having walked around to look at it from the right. Dylan cut and attached another piece of screen.

She crouched to get the low view. Okay, that was a mistake. Dylan helped her up. Since her knees obviously refused to do so.

Then they went outside and looked carefully at it again, adding a piece here, and another piece there.

Loup walked through to join them outside.

Dylan added another couple pieces of screen. They went back inside, Loup kind enough to follow. Rev pointed and Dylan added another piece.

"There. Done, yeah?"

"Yes," Rev agreed. "It is very 'Violin and Candlestick'."

"It is, isn't it," Dylan said. "Only without the violin. And the candlestick."

17

'm up for a walk," Rev said, getting her jacket. "Wanna come with
to get the mail?"

"Sure," Dylan replied, going to the closet as well.

Rev's mailbox was at the intersection half a mile up the road,
which was as far as the rural delivery route went. She didn't mind
the walk. Especially since she made it only once a week. Because, as
was the case with email and voicemail and, well, everything, she
thought, most communication sent her way was garbage. When she
wanted to go for a real walk, she went into the forest.

"Loup!" Dylan called when they were outside. She was at his side
in an instant.

"She can come, right?"

"I doubt we can stop her. Should be safe enough."

It was indeed, safe enough, since Loup chose to trot along beside
them—thirty feet into the bush. She kept her eyes on them, and they
on her. It was almost like she was stalking them.

"That's probably a really good habit for her to get into," Rev said.
"Staying off the roads altogether."

"She seems to come by it naturally. Fear of all things human?"

"Perhaps. Or fear of assholes who engage in drive-by hunting."

"What?"

"Every fall we get a couple guys who just cruise around in their
pick-ups, rifles in their laps, looking for an easy kill."

"Seriously?"

"One year, I saw a guy just parked, waiting. Turns out his buddies were in the bush on their ATVs scaring the deer out onto the road."

"So he was just sitting there waiting to pick them off. How sportsmanlike."

They heard a vehicle then—a considerate slow-moving car instead of a zooming, dust-raising ATV—or a rifle-bearing pick-up—coming up behind them, and they turned to see the silver SUV of one of their neighbours. They stepped off to the side of the road, nodded, then carried on once it had passed. Dylan noted that Loup had stopped when they had stopped, freezing into an alert position, and then had resumed moving when they had. He smiled.

A minute later the vehicle came at them again.

"Must've forgotten something," Dylan said.

Rev stared at it, noting its slow speed. She looked up the lane, then turned, and looked down the lane.

"Well, I'll be fucked!"

Dylan turned to her, confused.

"That's the third time I've seen her do that. She's getting her fucking mail!"

"But isn't her mailbox just at the corner? Right beside yours?"

Rev nodded. Now it was Dylan's turn to look to his left and then to his right. "But that's only, what, 400 meters?"

Rev nodded again. "It's bug season."

"Yeah, but," he lifted his arms, the mesh of his bug coat falling in folds, "there are bug jackets. Twenty bucks at Home Hardware."

Rev resumed walking. Stomping, actually.

"Here I am rationing my trips into town, fully aware of the relationship between fossil fuel emissions and climate change, and one neighbour drives in three times a week—once to get her hair cut, guess she hasn't figured out the whole scissors thing yet, once to do her grocery shopping, because god knows she needs a lot of food, and once to get the Saturday paper—"

"Because god knows she's got to be informed about the world—are they the ones who go RVing every year for a couple months?"

"Yup, and get on a plane without a moment's thought, to Ireland, or Australia, or Alaska—they're retired—"

"But aren't they retired *teachers*?" Dylan asked.

"Yes! So they should know better! And now another neighbour gets in her car and drives the 400 meters and back to get her mail. Because of the bugs."

"So we have them to blame for climate change—the hurricanes, the droughts, the rising temperature— You know, they moved the point of no return from 2020 to 2015. We're at 1.6 degrees."

Rev was quiet. Most scientists, the people who engage in evidence-based reasoning, agreed that the point of no return was a rise of 2 degrees.

"And if we knocked on their doors—" Dylan suggested.

"They'd have no idea what we were talking about."

"We could connect it to higher food prices. And higher gas prices."

"If higher food prices mattered, they'd be eating less. And if higher gas prices mattered—"

"Right."

"This is why we need to legislate shit!" she turned and screamed after the car. A hand appeared out the window and waved at them.

"YOU KNOW," DYLAN SAID once they were back, "we should put something on Loup. I mean, if she goes off trotting on her own— *when* she goes off trotting on her own," he corrected, "what if someone shoots her?" He couldn't bear the thought.

"You mean a collar?"

"Not exactly a collar, I meant something to, I don't know, identify her as off limits, I guess. A brightly collared bandana or something."

"Ebay."

"LISTEN TO THIS," DYLAN said from his lounge chair on the porch. Rev was beside him on her couch working on some questions. Loup was in the corner gnawing on her shoe. "Westman says that the licence requirement would define parenthood as a relationship rather than as a biologically determined state."

"That's exactly what it would do," Rev agreed. "Fucking—well, intercourse—is a biological state. Parenting is something altogether different. Actually, so is fucking," she added. Then said, "Pity parenting is the default consequence of intercourse. And fucking."

"It sure challenges intelligent design," she added a moment later. "At the beginning, yeah, it's good to wire together a biological drive, especially one that can feel good, with replication. But without natural predators, that's the kiss of death for any species. Unless they're intelligent enough to voluntarily limit their production. Which we're not. Apparently."

"Well, most people aren't," she continued. "Intelligent enough," she clarified. Then clarified further, "To control their own biology rather than be controlled by it. I mean, even on the small stuff."

And then a few more moments later, "Which means, actually, the way it's set up *is* intelligent."

"WHAT IF SNEEZING released spores that became human beings?" she asked half an hour later.

"Antihistamines would be big business," Dylan murmured, focused on his laptop.

"Hm. Do you think they'd be available over-the-counter? And covered by health plans? Or would they be shrouded in sin? And available only on the black market?"

"Hopefully, they'd be mandatory," he said. "Or people really would be finding kids in the cabbage patch."

A LITTLE WHILE LATER, Rev went out onto the lake in her kayak, and Dylan went into the forest on his bike. Froot Loup ran along beside, under forest cover. She was clearly delighted, and it occurred to Dylan that this was the first time he'd taken her into the forest. It was the first time he'd gone biking since the day he'd found her. The day she'd found him. The forest was clearly her home, he realized, glancing over at the pup, happily making her way.

WHEN THEY RETURNED, Rev saw Froot Loup riding in the little basket—how she fit was beyond her—actually, now that she was closer, she saw that basically just her back end was in the basket. The rest of her was holding onto—hugging, actually—rather possessively—the moose leg that was set across it.

"She found it and insisted on carrying it home," Dylan explained, as he disembarked. "She wouldn't let me help. Moose legs are heavy. Did you know that?"

"No. Never had occasion to carry a moose leg, myself."

"She had to keep setting it down and resting, poor thing. So finally I picked her up, leg and all, and put her in my basket. That worked."

Froot Loup grinned at Rev. She had a moose leg!

Rev frowned as she got a close-up look at the leg.

"We want to encourage this sort of thing, remember?" he said.

"Yeah ... it's just that it's not moose season. And this leg is—relatively fresh."

"Oh. So what does that mean?"

"Well, it could have died naturally, in which case it might be diseased," Dylan reached to take it away from Loup, "but look at the end. That's a clean cut."

"Which means it was hunted illegally?"

"Wouldn't be the first time," Rev said, then exploded. "Goddammit, why do men want to kill so badly?"

"Some men," Dylan qualified, but quietly because he knew she knew.

He carefully lifted a still grinning Loup out of the basket, Loup making sure she had a good hold of her leg, Dylan actually supporting most of its weight. She started toward the porch, half-carrying, half-dragging, her moose leg.

"No!" Dylan and Rev shouted simultaneously.

Loup turned to look at them. Then slowly lay down where she was. She watched as they went into the house. She considered the situation, then headed again toward the porch. They were sure to be there, and she wanted to be with them.

"No!" they said again to her, from inside the porch.

So she lay down just outside the door and started gnawing away.

NEXT MORNING WHEN they entered the porch, they weren't at all surprised to see her curled up on her red comforter, Dylan's shoe tucked beside her, her moose leg between her paws. She smiled at them when they entered.

Rev stood, coffee and pizza in hand, took in the situation, then simply said, "Mosquito netting."

"Of course! It'd be soft and hangey. Instead of stiff and bunchey." Dylan turned on his laptop and went straight to Ebay.

THE PHONE HAPPENED to ring when Rev went in for coffee refills. Dylan couldn't hear the conversation.

"You know the neighbour with the silver SUV?" she handed Dylan his refreshed coffee mug and settled back into her couch with her own refreshed mug.

"The one who drives 400 meters to get her mail?"

"Yeah. She and her husband have invited us to dinner."

Dylan read her face. "And that's a bad thing because ... "

"Because in the ten years I've been living here, they've not once invited me to dinner."

"Ah. But now that there are *two* of us."

Rev glared. At the couple-obsessed world. Solos, especially solo women, simply didn't count. She was invisible. Until there was a man by her side.

"So why don't you go? Just you? Make them feel uncomfortable in the way only you can." He grinned at her. Challenging.

few days later, Dylan was invited to attend a parents' support group. Word had gotten about, apparently, about his article. Articles. Book.

"Wanna come?" Dylan asked Rev, as he got ready to go. Notepad, pen, mini-recorder …

"I dunno. Are they going to talk about what color their babies' poop is?"

"One can learn a lot from the color of poop."

"No doubt. But … Froot Loup probably isn't ready to be left alone yet. First time you drive away, I should stay here with her, make sure she doesn't run after you."

"Oh god, do you think she would do that?" Dylan was alarmed. Then he had another thought. "Do you think *she* wants to come?"

"Well, she's probably far more interested than I am in the color of poop," Rev said, "but I think wolves might agree with cats about car rides."

"They might, yes. And, in any case, I agree that she's not ready for any more traumatic experiences just yet."

"Speaking of which," Rev said, "do we want to tie her up when you drive away? So she doesn't run after you?"

"That in itself might be traumatic."

"As would being hit by a car on the highway."

They thought about the dilemma for a bit.

"How about this," Dylan said. "I drive away, but then turn around and come back in five minutes. She'll see that. I do it again, but return in ten minutes."

"Might work. If she understands you're always going to come back—"

"And if wolves tell time like dogs do, ten minutes is the same as ten hours, so no matter how long I'm gone—"

"Okay, but what if she runs after you, you turn around, and she figures she made that happen. By running after you."

They gave the problem some more thought.

"Maybe the parents' group would be willing to meet here," Dylan suggested.

"Not keen on that. And we're going to have to deal with this sooner or later."

So Dylan got in the car, Rev sat down beside Froot Loup, who was sporting her new neon pink bandana, and spoke reassuringly to her as she anxiously watched Dylan back out. One point three seconds after he was out of sight, she raced after him.

"Shall we revisit the tying up idea?" he said after he'd pulled back into the driveway and gotten out of the car. Froot Loup trotted circles around him, then wove in and out through his legs.

"I don't think so. It occurred to me that that would feel exactly like she's caught in a snare, and the exactly wrong thing to do when that happens would be to struggle and try to escape."

"So we could use this as a snare lesson, then!" he said eagerly. "Teach her *not* to struggle. That's something we should teach her in any case. This might be the perfect opportunity—"

"Yeah, but I'll bet that lesson would be best taught by you. You're her mom."

"Yeah."

They thought some more.

"And," Dylan said, "even if she does decide that jumping into the car is the lesser of two evils—"

"Three if you count running after you all the way to Sudbury. Assuming the other evil you had in mind was losing her mom again—"

"—what do I do in Sudbury? It's too hot to leave her in the car."

"Plus she might freak out at that in any case and tear up the—everything."

So Dylan went inside and called the parents' group. Rescheduled his visit for a couple weeks hence.

"OKAY, SO LET'S TEACH Loup not to struggle when her neck is in a noose," Dylan said the next day. "And actually," he was thinking out loud, "we should go one step further and teach her to bark when she's caught. So if that ever happens, we can find her and rescue her."

"Good idea," Rev said. Then changed her mind. "No, bad idea. She'll bark the whole time she's tied up then while you're away. And to reinforce the snare lesson, I'd have to let her loose."

"Right. Okay, that won't work."

"What if we teach her not to walk into a snare trap in the first place?" Rev suggested. "We could do that, right?"

"But then when we tie her up when we leave—"

"We'll be completely undoing the lesson. That won't work."

A few minutes later, Dylan tried. "What if—if I understand snare traps correctly, the idea is they're set so the animal walks through and gets caught around the neck. So what if we use a harness here. Do you think she could distinguish between being grabbed around the neck and being grabbed around the chest?"

"Maybe. So, what, we introduce her to the whole harness thing first, and then a couple weeks later introduce the snare thing?"

"If she's not leaving the cabin much anyway, she won't need to know about snares right away."

"Right. And if we get a harness that, I don't know, feels as different as possible from a wire loop ... "

They thought it through and decided it was a good plan. "Ebay?" Dylan asked. Rev nodded.

And a week later Froot Loup had a cute little pink harness. That was lined with pink faux-fur.

OVER THE COURSE OF that week, they put the harness on her from time to time just so she got used to it.

Dylan also decided to teach her to "Stay!" Not only would it be useful when he did leave, but, he figured, there may be other times they wouldn't want her to go to where she wanted to go. So whenever he left the porch, he said "Stay!" to her and at the same time put his hand up like a crossing guard, since, as he'd learned online, wolves respond more to gesture than to voice. He rewarded her with pizza whenever she didn't follow him.

He quickly realized it was a hard command to teach, so he decided to start instead with "Sit!"

"Sit!" he said to her, simultaneously pointing to the ground at her feet, then gently pushing down her rump, forcing her to sit.

"Good Loup!" He gave her lots of praise and a chunk of pizza. Which she stood up to eat.

A few minutes later, "Sit!" Dylan said again, pointing to the ground again, then pushing down her rump.

"Good Loup!" He ruffled her fur, crooned to her, and gave her another chunk of pizza.

He waited five minutes before the next repetition.

And then ten minutes.

"Sit!" Dylan said after another ten minutes, pointing to the ground. After a few seconds, Froot Loup slowly set her rump onto the floor and hoped for some pizza.

"Wow," Rev said from her observation post on the couch, "that took all of five repetitions."

He repeated the procedure throughout the day. Next day, more repetition, but sometimes with a pizza reward, sometimes not. Always with over-the-top praise though, full of warmth and affection. By the third day, his praise was the only reward she needed. She sat whenever he told her to, no hesitation, pizza reward or not.

"Stay!" was harder because there was little he could do to make her understand what he wanted. It didn't have the hands-on possibility that "Sit!" had. First, they had Rev gently hold onto her, but that seemed to distract her more than anything. So Dylan anticipated when Loup would stay anyway. She'd stopped running out of the porch and around to the back door, for example, every time he went into the house to answer the phone, having figured out on her own that he'd come back. So Dylan started saying "Stay!" to her, and putting up his hand, whenever that happened. Which, since Rev went outside and called her landline number with her cell phone, happened to happen a lot. And whenever Dylan returned, he brought a chunk of pizza to reward Froot Loup for staying.

Moving the lesson outside was a bit harder. But the phone ring helped. First Dylan told the little wolf to sit, which she did. Then the phone rang. Dylan said "Stay!", put his hand up, and walked into the house. "I'll be back" he called back to her. Loup stayed put, for the fifteen seconds it took for Dylan to return with a chunk of pizza. "I'm back!" he said to her, as he gave her the pizza. Once they'd successfully lengthened that to a minute, they cut out the phone ring half the time. Then they started cutting out the pizza. And lengthening the time. They also changed the location, sometimes doing it at the back of the cabin, sometimes at the front. By the end of the week, having worked on the lesson a dozen times throughout the day for about five minutes at a time, Froot Loup was staying put for up to half an hour while Dylan went inside.

"Do you think she's learning that she's supposed to stay here all the time?" Rev wondered aloud.

"I don't think so. I'm making a big deal of saying 'Stay!' and we're not reprimanding her whenever she leaves the property. Which she hasn't really done ... " he trailed off, realizing Rev could be right.

"Maybe just to be sure she understands it's okay, we should reward her when she wanders around? Not in an obvious way, but maybe you could—"

"Okay." So they started paying attention to her when she wandered around, giving her a smile, a kind word, a handful of kibble, just to let her know it was okay.

Then they decided to take it to the next level.

"Sit!" Dylan said to the little wolf, pointing to the ground, and congratulating her when she did so. "Stay!" he said, putting his hand up, then "I'll be back." He got into the car and turned the ignition. Loup got up, but didn't take a step. Dylan got out of the car. "I'm back!" he said to her, and gave her a chunk of pizza, scratching her behind her ears and telling her what a good little wolf she was. He repeated the exercise. Again. And again. Eventually Loup stopped getting up when Dylan turned the ignition. So he started backing out. Just twenty feet, then he pulled back in. "I'm back!" he said, putting his arms around her. Repeat. Repeat. By the end of the week, he was able to drive right to the end of the driveway, and Loup stayed put. Watching, anxiously, but still sitting.

"So you're ready to try driving out of her view?" Rev asked.

"Yeah. But I'm thinking, in order not to undo everything we've achieved so far, that we should have her harnessed and tied. It's like forcing her rump down. Giving her a bit of help to do the right thing."

They'd already put a clip onto the end of a twenty-foot long rope and fastened it to the shed entrance. They figured Loup would want to wait at the driveway, and twenty feet would enable her to curl up in her den if she wanted. Though truth be told, she had yet to do that, preferring her corner in the screened porch.

"Just out of sight at first?"

"Yeah, then we'll see how it goes."

Rev sat beside Froot Loup and tried her best to act as yet another surrogate mom, saying "Stay!" and telling her that Dylan would be back—in his words, "I'll be back", since there was no point in confusing her with the grammatically correct pronoun—as Dylan backed to the end of the driveway, then drove out of sight.

Froot Loup immediately got to her feet, let out a whine, and pulled on the harness.

Dylan returned.

"I'm back!" he said to her as he got out of the car and gave her a chunk of pizza. "How'd it go?" he said to Rev.

"She got up, whined a bit, and pulled on the harness a bit."

"Could've been a lot worse."

"Yup. Again?"

"Again."

They repeated the sequence until Froot Loup stopped pulling. Over the next few days, Dylan increased his time away, and by the end of the week, he was able to remain out of sight for half an hour.

Froot Loup continued to sit up when he left, and she cried, but she stopped pulling to run after him, and eventually, after a few minutes, she sat back down, watching the end of the driveway. Once she even lay back down.

"So this is going well."

"It is indeed," Dylan said. "Do you think she might stay without the harness?"

"She might. But why make it that difficult for her? She doesn't seem to mind the harness. She's not pulling anymore to get loose and chase after you. And the risk is too great if she does."

"That's true."

"Plus, learning not to struggle when she's in the harness might transfer to learning not to struggle when she's in a snare."

"Are we good or what?"

They would have celebrated with pizza, but there was none left.

19

Next morning, they worked in companionable silence for a while, both of them glancing often at the sparkling water. Loup had started lying out in the sun, beside the porch. She was glancing often at the squirrels that ran chittering from tree to tree.

"So," Rev asked after an hour, "who's on your schedule for today?"

"Today I interview the politicians and the lawyers. Wanna come?"

"Actually yeah. The conversation with the lawyer might be interesting."

FROOT LOUP SAT UP WHEN Dylan and Rev came out the back door. Dylan put her harness on, then clipped it to the long rope.

"I'll be back," he assured her, scratching her ears and giving her a few long strokes. He confirmed that the rope was long enough for her to continue to lie in the sun, or move into the shade, or go into the shed. He looked around, then moved his bike out of entanglement reach. Then he filled her dishes in the shed with fresh water and kibble. The he brushed a bit of dirt off her moose leg. Rev waited in the car, not impatiently.

"Stay," he said to the little wolf then, again scratching her ears. And, again, "I'll be back."

Her eyes were anxious, but she nodded. No. Did she? Dylan

looked at Rev. "Did you—"

He headed to the car. "Stay," he said again. And once more, "I'll be back."

Rev backed the car out of the driveway.

Loup cried, just a bit, then howled. Just once.

Dylan howled back. Just once.

"IF I'VE LEARNED ANYTHING as a politician," Ross Girard, Sudbury's MP, said to them, "it's that change doesn't happen by itself. You have to make it happen." They were having lunch—apparently lunch was a moveable feast among politicians—at one of Sudbury's finest restaurants, The Cantonese House.

"By legislation?" Dylan asked, nodding a thank you to the waiter who placed a plate in front of him.

"'Fraid so. Even if that legislation is just for incentives. Rather than, as in this case, for permits."

"Like subsidies for the oil companies," Rev offered. Dylan's plate looked better than hers, so she reached over and helped herself to a forkful.

Ross nodded, missing her point. "People generally do whatever they've always done. Parents will raise their kids the way they've been raised. It takes someone very unusual to evaluate—to step back and take a look at what they're doing and say hey, this isn't good, or this isn't good enough, I can do better, I'm going to do it differently, I'm going to change."

"I'm curious," Dylan said, "how much is this costing the taxpayers?"

"The Department of Licensing Parents is expensive, yes," Ross said, "but a study at Western put the financial costs of child abuse in Canada at more than $15 billion. Social services, $1.1 billion. Judicial services, $600 million. Health services, $222 million. Education services, $24 million."

The guy had his talking points down.

"You know," he said a few minutes later, "I was on the committee that reviewed the cloning legislation."

"Is that legal now too?" Rev turned to Dylan. "We were away for what, eight months?"

"No, it's not legal now." Ross said. "Stem cell research has been legal for a while, and the use of surplus embryos from IVT, but reproductive and research cloning is not. But it's a fine line."

"And we crossed it?"

"A little bit, yes. Stem cell cloning is legal now, but still not the cloning of human beings." He sipped his glass of water.

"But where I'm going with this is, we were making legislation to control cloning. We didn't want people creating their own little army."

"Someone in Defence raised that possibility?" Dylan asked, somewhat incredulously.

"Actually, yes."

"Of course they did," Rev said dryly.

"But my point is that we were all set to control cloning. To legislate what you can and cannot do with regard to the creation of humans. And rightly so, I believe. So you see the inconsistency? Why should the creation of human life by one method have oversight and by another method be laissez-faire?

"We wouldn't allow some guy in the lab to clone a copy of himself. We wouldn't allow cloning just for fun. And we certainly wouldn't allow it to happen accidentally.

"We had quality controls in place. We said that cloned human beings shall not exist in pain or be severely compromised with respect to basic biological or biochemical functioning.

"We had screening standards in place. Rigorous screening standards. People would have had to submit, and have approved, a detailed plan regarding responsibility for the cloned human being. We weren't about to allow some fool scientist to create it and then just leave it on the lab's doorstep one night when he leaves.

"Thing is," Ross Girard, MP, was winding up for the final pitch, "*we can already create human life*. Kids do it every day. We would not accept such reckless creation of life if it happened in the lab. Why do we condone it when it happens in bedrooms and backseats?"

Dylan slipped his mini recorder onto the table and pressed record. "Um, that was great—could you say it all again?"

20

o who did you line up in the way of lawyers to interview?" Rev asked as they got out of the car in front of The Fancy Pig, one of Sudbury's drinking spots, not terribly surprised that they'd agreed on this location.

"It's a surprise."

"You got Alan Shore?"

"Close." He opened the door, Rev walked in, and stopped immediately.

"Jesus, you became a lawyer too?" She was looking at Dim's twin brother, Assaracus, who was grinning nervously at her from his seat at the bar.

"Hello to you too. Ms. Reveille." He adjusted his bowtie.

Dim, short for Dmitri, was one of Rev's ex-students—all of whom she'd insisted call her by her name rather than by the uterus-identifying prefix, 'Ms.' He'd been in her grade ten all-boys class the day she taught them how to put on a condom, and when he showed up some twenty years later as the only lawyer in town when they'd needed one—when they were arrested for their addendum to the Right-to-Life billboard—he'd thanked her for that lesson, as it had enabled him to avoid paying so much child support that he would never have been able to afford law school.

Assaracus—Ass, for short—was the student who had reported her and gotten her fired.

"When I called Dim," Dylan said cheerily, pleased to have masterminded the reunion, "he suggested his brother here, who happened to be in town for another matter. So he was in your class too?"

"Yes." Rev said. Then told him about the role he'd played in her illustrious teaching career.

"Bummer."

"Yes, well, the little Ass always was a stickler for the rules."

"Assaracus," he adjusted his bowtie again. "Assaracus Stevastianos Kosta."

"Pompous little shit."

"A round of Frosty Fuddbuckers!" Dylan called out to the bartender.

"Oh, I'll just have water," the little Ass cleared his throat.

"Bummer," Dylan said again.

"You were supposed to be teaching us English," the little Ass said self-righteously to Rev, fastidiously folding a napkin to put under his glass.

"Pompous little shit." She got up, took her Frosty Fuddbucker, and went to sit at the other end of the near-empty bar.

"Bummer," Dylan said yet again. He sighed, then put his recorder on the bar.

"So, Ass—aracus, what do you think of the new law that says people have to become licensed before they can become parents?"

"Oh, I love it. The more laws, the more work for me, right? In fact," he leaned in to confide in Dylan, who leaned away, "I'm waiting for there to be a law against lying. To anyone. Think how much business that would generate!"

"Right, and what about *this* law, in particular? Do you think it's a good one?"

"Oh, well, a law's a law."

Dylan stared at him. Then tried again. "As Rev pointed out to me earlier, we've got all sorts of laws about ending life. How many kinds of murder are there?"

"Oh, lots. First degree, second degree, and involuntary manslaughter. Depending on whether it's premeditated, accidental, or reckless. Then there's infanticide, and suicide, and abortion, and euthanasia—

and there alone, we distinguish between active and passive, and voluntary and coerced, in which case it wouldn't be euthanasia—"

"And yet, we've got nothing about beginning life."

"Not true. I'm afraid Ms. Reveille is mistaken about that," he smiled forgivingly in her direction.

"Pompous little shit."

"There's wrongful life. In wrongful life suits, a child and/or the parents can sue a doctor and/or a hospital if they failed to provide information during the pregnancy about a disability. The argument is that had the parents known, they might have decided to abort."

"So what happens if they win? Do they—does the kid get killed?" That can't be right.

"No, they're awarded compensation for damages. For the expenses of round-the-clock personal care. For example."

"Oh. Okay, so that implies that we already think children have a right to be born healthy or at least free of avoidable defects," Dylan said.

"I suppose."

"Which means that the new law for biological parentage, which insists on certain genetic standards, isn't all that new. In theory."

"It isn't all that new in practice either. Did Ms. Reveille give you that impression?"

"Pompous little shit."

"For years, judges have been ordering women not to have any more kids. Mostly drug addicts."

"Just the women?" Dylan asked.

The little Ass didn't respond.

"So this whole licensing thing just takes it out of the hands of individual judges," Dylan thought aloud. "Hopefully making it more consistent across the board."

"That would be a good outcome, yes. Consistency is achieved when people follow the rules, when they do what they're supposed to do."

"Pompous little shit."

"And actually," Dylan continued to think aloud, "licensing should *decrease* the number of wrongful life suits. Drug addicts and the like wouldn't be allowed to be pregnant, so you wouldn't end up with severely debilitated people would have cause for such a suit."

"Oh. I hadn't thought about that."

"What about lawsuits by those who think they should have passed the course and didn't?" Dylan asked. "Do you anticipate many of those?"

"No, not really. As I understand it, the course is free and people can take it as often as they want. Frankly, anyone who fails more than once likely won't have a case. I'll gladly take their money though and fight for them, because that's their right, and I'd never deny someone something to which they have a right."

"Pompous little shit."

21

hall we stop by Sobeys so you can get a couple Sara Lee cheesecakes?"

"No ... hey!" She pointed out the window at a little shop called Delightfully Delicious Delectables. "That's new!"

Dylan pulled into the next parking space, and they walked back to the little shop. As they entered, they saw that it was primarily an ice cream shop, but it also had the obligatory-for-tourists fudge counter, as well as a bakery counter. No cheesecake, alas, but—

"An eggnog cheesecake milkshake, please," Rev said triumphantly.

"Really? They have that?" Dylan scanned the flavour board. He'd made them cheesecake milkshakes once, rather serendipitously, when they were on the road, but hadn't thought to repeat the endeavour.

"And I'll have a bluegreen milkshake," he told the counterperson.

"Really? Bluegreen? That's not even a flavour." She looked at the board again—how could she have missed such a blatant category mistake?

"Which makes it all the more intriguing."

"It could just taste like water," Rev said.

"Don't be silly. Water isn't bluegreen anymore. Maybe it tastes like sky and grass!"

They paid for their milkshakes and left the shop, the counterperson having been remarkably uninterested in their banter.

"Well?" she asked once Dylan had taken a sip.

They traded.

"Hm. Yours is definitely eggnog cheesecake."

"It is, isn't it. And yours is—blueberry mint?"

"I think so. Though it could be sky mint. We've never actually tasted sky, so we can't really know, can we?"

"A dubious epistemology."

"At best," he agreed cheerfully, and took another sip of his blue-green milkshake.

"YOU SAID WE NEEDED more kibble?" Rev asked, once they were back in the car.

"Yeah, and I'd like to buy her some toys—think she's okay?" He'd been worrying about her since they left.

"I don't know," Rev said, unable to utter baseless platitudes of re-assurance, "but that reminds me, we also need more pizza."

AS SOON AS THEY TURNED into the driveway, they saw the frayed rope. Dylan went immediately into frantic mode. How did they not anticipate that? When they left, they should have parked a few hundred meters up the road and waited for five minutes. Just in case.

"Froot Loup!" he started calling as soon as he opened the car door. "Loup!" He stood in the small yard, uncertain as to which way to go first, where to start—"Loup! I'm back!"

Froot Loup came running at full-speed from around the corner of the house and leapt into Dylan's open arms. He caught her, held onto her, hugged her, crooned to her. "See? I told you I'd be back!" She licked his face. Thoroughly.

Rev smiled.

"What a good little wolf!" He started dancing with her, singing "I've got sunshine on a cloudy day ... "

He set her down when they'd finished the verse, then, with Loup close to his side, he walked toward the porch, which was where Rev had gone, having noted the direction Loup had come from. "So I wonder what she—"

Loup's blanket, the one that used to be Rev's blanket, had been pulled onto Rev's couch, from the corner where she, Rev, had put it. Dylan's shoe, somewhat soggy, was tucked in. Beside the moose leg.

WHILE DYLAN DEALT WITH the porch—the mosquito netting had worked fabulously—and fed Loup, Rev unloaded the car. Half an hour later, they were in the porch, as it had been when they'd left, with the evening essentials. Pepsi, pizza, and a joint. And the sun wavering through the trees, glittering on the lake.

"Hey, I wonder if Loup wants to play!" Dylan said once they'd finished the joint.

"Oh yeah." She'd actually been trying for fifteen minutes to remember what was in the bag sitting on the kitchen table. "What did you buy for her?"

Dylan went into the kitchen for the bag. The one with 'THE PET STORE' and pictures of dogs and cats all over it.

"I thought it best to get realistic toys. Things that might help her develop survival skills." He held up a red rubber three-round-tiered Kong toy.

"Yeah, that looks a lot like something she'd find in the wild."

"I wanted to get a ball, but also a chew toy. I thought this would work as both. You know, like a reversible jacket."

"You know, I actually had one of those. It was pink on one side and purple on the other." She got lost for a moment trying to imagine turning it inside out.

"Come on, Loup, let's play!" He went outside, Loup following.

Rev watched as he threw the Kong. Loup also watched. Dylan walked across the yard and picked it up. Rev watched as he threw it again. Loup also watched. Again. Dylan walked back across the yard and picked it up.

"Ready?" Dylan said to Loup, waving the Kong excitedly. Rev watched as he threw it yet again. Loup also watched. Yet again. Dylan walked across the yard and picked it up.

"Maybe she'd be more interested in chasing it into the water," Rev suggested.

"Good idea!"

Dylan threw the Kong into the water. And they all watched $14.99 sink to the bottom of the lake.

He returned to the porch, Loup on his heels, and pulled another toy from the bag. A lime green octopus. Dylan squeaked one of the legs and Froot Loup pounced, grabbed it—and a bit of Dylan's finger—just a little bit—and proceeded to tear off each of the eight legs. Then disembowel the head.

"Well. I hope *she's* around next time you meet an octopus in the forest."

Dylan reached into the bag for the third and last toy. It was a fluorescent orange and yellow and blue parrot. Froot Loup watched intently as Dylan wound it up, doing so with his knuckles, keeping his fingers tucked away safe, then set it on the floor. The parrot flapped its wings lamely, just once, before Loup pounced on it, then trotted through the screen door with it to the middle of the yard. Where she proceeded to bury it. For later.

"SO WHAT DO YOU THINK of the possibility that the new law will reduce crime?" Dylan asked a while later. "Which would, then, free up a lot of money for other purposes. From the police force, the judicial system, the prison system. It's an argument Westman makes. And something I was going to ask the little Ass about, since he's an officer of the court, but—"

"My first thought," Rev replied, "is that incompetent parenting isn't limited to the lower classes, which is, I presume the connection he's making to crime."

"He is making that connection, yes. Though I thought your first thought would have been something endorsing my thought about the futility of my asking the little Ass what he thought about ... " Dylan gave up.

"I chose not to voice that thought."

"Really? You can do that?"

She grinned over at him. And thought again how glad she was he'd decided not to go to Argentina.

"I think rich people are fucking us over a lot more," she said, "and a lot more seriously, than poor people. Sure, the petty criminals are the ones with the guns, but they're killing us one at a time. Actually, mostly they're killing each other. It's the guys managing the subsidies and monopolies that are killing us, wholesale. They're fucking up the planet. Poor people don't have enough power to do that."

"And you're suggesting that powerful people, rich people, have had bad parenting?"

"It's a thought. My business ethics classes, which were for business students, were almost always, and exclusively, full of self-interested people who were no different from the drug dealer on the street. Their prime directive was profit. Not making the world a better place."

"And you attribute that view to bad parenting?"

She thought about that. "No, maybe not. My brother went into business. And we had the same parents. Though," she added, "we didn't have the same parenting."

She tried again to sort through it. "My business ethics classes were almost always, and exclusively, full of men. So maybe I attribute it to being male. A certain kind of male."

"The street criminals that clog up our judicial systems and fill our prisons are also predominantly male," Dylan observed.

"See?"

"And yet, parenting is predominantly done by women."

22

ev set her work aside. Once she got to a certain point, she let the material percolate. It was just as effective as paying conscious attention to it. More effective, actually. Solutions appeared—well, not out of nowhere—out of the coffee pot of her brain, into which she'd spent hours carefully pouring all the right stuff.

"Time to get the mail?" Dylan asked. Loup's ears went up. She had learned what 'time to get the mail' meant.

"Well, actually, I was thinking time for a long kayak, but sure, I'll come with you to get the mail."

They got their bug jackets, while Loup waited at the back door. As soon as they got to the end of the driveway, she disappeared into the bush, trotting along beside them in what Dylan called 'stealth mode'.

Their neighbour's silver SUV crawled by.

"Do you know that when her husband goes away, she locks the door?"

"You don't lock the door at night?"

"Well, no, actually, but I don't mean at night. I mean whenever."

"What's she afraid of?"

"Everything. She watches a lot of tv."

"Ah."

"You know," Rev said, "I can't even imagine what my life would be like, what *I'd* be like, if I didn't know what I know from reading. If my entire worldview—my beliefs, and therefore my opinions, and therefore, my behaviours—was informed only by what the producers in Hollywood choose to broadcast. Their choices being primarily dictated by their advertisers. Which is to say by Corporate America."

"Hm."

A few moments later, they passed the only other house between Rev's cabin and the mailboxes. Mr. Delaney, who lived about halfway, was outside refilling his bird feeder.

"Good day, sir!" he called out, presumably to Dylan.

Rev stopped. She looked at him. "'Good day, sir?' Wait a minute, you're *not* mentally delayed?"

He stared at her, puzzled.

"Every time I walk by, and you're outside refilling," she nodded at what he was doing, "you tell me you're 'feeding the little birdies'."

He was silent.

She worked it through. "You thought *I* was the village idiot?" she exclaimed. "All this time, talking to me like I was six ... And why did you think that?" she asked pointedly.

He was still silent.

"Well fuck you!" she shouted, then resumed walking. "Sir!"

"HEY, CAN YOU—AREN'T you supposed to be working on your article? Articles?" Rev said to Dylan later that evening when she walked out into the porch.

"Yeah, but this is far more enjoyable," he said, continuing to brush Loup with the brush he'd apparently also bought at the pet store. She sat before him, absolutely still. "Such a pretty wolf," Dylan crooned to her, running the brush through her red-silver coat again and again, turning her into a glistening beauty. "Such a pretty wolf ... " She fixed her rapt gaze on him.

"Okay, so when you're done there, can you help me with this?"

"Sure," he said, putting the brush down. Loup watched sadly as he got up and sat in his chair. Rev passed him a single sheet of paper from her couch.

"This is ... ?"

"Raquelle's resume. She, Brittany, and Susie are applying for coparenting licences. They're planning to move in together once Susie's delivered. Raquelle's going to be the primary income-earner, Susie's going to be the main stay-at-home mom, and Brittany's already got a flexible, part-time job at the library, so she's going to be a bit of both. They're hoping that between the two of them, they'll have enough to support the three of them. Plus their kids, six in all."

"Do you think they can do it?"

"Well, I think it's the best possible arrangement. None of them could do it on their own—you can't work full-time and look after a kid. Unless there's a daycare at your workplace. This way, none of them will have to pay for childcare. Which would probably reduce their income to below sustenance in any case. And they'll have just one rent, one electricity bill, and so on."

"Yeah, but three adults and six kids—on one and a half—"

"Hopefully, the fathers will pay child support, but they're not counting on it. Which is why Raquelle has to get a really good job."

"It's sort of a non-gender-aligned polygamy arrangement," Dylan said, thinking it through. "Back when we were in Utah, I was surprised you didn't say anything about that. Polygamy."

"Gender alignment aside, I think polygamy is a good arrangement. If you're a woman into the whole kids thing. It's gotta be incredibly exhausting being on high alert twenty-four hours a day, seven days a week, having to attend very closely every second, because the moment you relax, for just an instant, your child could be—dead.

"I remember one time, I offered a friend, a new mother with a toddler—I said I'd look after the kid so she could have a bath. Without locking the kid in the bathroom with her. A long, luxurious bath. I figured I could manage for an hour not to kill the kid."

"Hm."

"She nearly wept with gratitude. She didn't take me up on the offer, but she told me that just knowing that she could have a whole hour to herself, that she could relinquish that responsibility for just an hour— And, well, Grandma's got stuff to do these days. So co-wives? They're co-moms."

"Yeah, but what about the harem thing?"

"Well, again, it means they don't have to be available all the time. To the husband."

"Hm."

"What I don't get is how any man, any ordinary non-CEO-type man, can make enough money to support several adults and all those kids. Which brings me to that," Rev nodded to Raquelle's resume. "A lot depends on Raquelle getting a good job. Hence her request that I help her with her resume."

"I take it she doesn't know your employment history."

"Hence my request that you help me with her resume."

"But you know my employment history."

"Yes, but remember that study we read about how men overvalue and inflate on their resumes, and women do just the opposite?"

"Yeah ... and you think—"

"You're the one who suggested I ask Anita for pay."

"Right, okay ... "

While Dylan started to read the resume, Rev opened her laptop and started pecking away. A few minutes later, she cried out, "Hah! Go to 'resumes r us dot com'."

"There."

"Okay, click on the Sales Rep resume, 'before' and 'after'."

"Woh. 'Sales rep for food processing equipment and storage racks,'" he read aloud. Then, "'Served as a commissioned sales representative for state-of-the-art food processing equipment and storage rack systems with weekly sales of $10,500 achieved by developing strong customer rapport, identifying opportunities, and selling products from inventory.'"

"Which basically means 'sales rep', right? See? That's what I mean. We need to turn Raquelle's resume into an 'after'."

Dylan was still reading. "Did you see the top? Where there's just his name on the 'before' version?" Dylan read the 'after' version aloud. "'A seasoned professional with practical experience in and solid understanding of a diverse range of business management applications, including market analysis, sales and marketing, team-building, and quality assurance. Demonstrated ability to select, train, and retain self-motivated, customer-oriented employees. High-caliber presentation, negotiation, and closing skills.'"

"Which basically means he's got a degree in business. Which he already said—'B.B.A.'!" Rev said with frustration.

She continued to browse the site. "All those years, when I just said something like I had ten years' teaching experience, I should have been saying that I had 'ten years' experience with multi-faceted curriculum design and delivery'."

"And that you had 'interpersonal management skills focused on optimizing the performance of multi-leveled participants'," Dylan said, then added, "'And engaged in formative and summative evaluation using multiple criteria designed to assess, provide feedback, and identify opportunities for supplemental multi-faceted curriculum design and delivery.'"

"You know," Rev said, "teachers should be getting six-figure salaries."

23

ylan!" Rev shouted from outside. She'd just come back from kayaking.

He looked up from his laptop, having already returned from the forest.

"Loup's poop is all yellow!" She was staring at a pile of it.

"Maybe she ate your buttercups."

"I don't have any buttercups. What a preposterous idea," she muttered as she continued to check the yard for more poop. Loup had been doing her business in the forest, so clearly something was amiss.

"Could be giardia," Dylan called from the porch, having done a quick google. "Or elevated billirubin. Which indicates a liver problem. If wolves are the same as dogs in this respect. Let's see if it goes back to brown in a day."

"Let's see if someone will come out and give her some vaccinations," Rev one-upped him once she was inside.

So they called around. Yes, the wolf should definitely have a number of vaccinations if she was to continue to be in close proximity to Dylan and Rev. And yes, bringing her by car was likely to increase the trauma of what would likely proceed to be a traumatic event. So a house call was arranged. Even so, there was some concern about what would happen and, consequently, agreement all round that a muzzle would be brought and likely used.

SEVERAL DAYS LATER, JUST before two o'clock, Froot Loup was lying in her corner of the porch, gnawing on Dylan's shoe, when she suddenly became alert and sat up. Rev looked at her curiously.

"Wow," Dylan said, looking at his watch. "By her standards, we must be totally deaf."

"What, you mean—" Rev stopped as she heard the car turn into her driveway. "Ah."

They heard a car door close, then "Hello ... " a woman called out.

Froot Loup ran out her door before they could stop her. Dylan's shoe still in her mouth.

"Shit. We should have—" They both rushed out after Loup and around the corner of the house to the driveway.

"Oh, you are a little sweetheart. And I'm so very sorry about your mom," the woman was on her knees on the grass, rubbing Froot Loup's belly. "And is this your shoe?" she tentatively picked up Dylan's shoe, clearly testing Froot Loup. Froot Loup did not lunge and tear it out of her hands. Instead, she wagged her tail. "It *is*? It's a really good shoe," she set it back on the ground, passing the test Froot Loup had given her.

Dr. Theresen looked up to Dylan and Rev. "We're good," she said, "but if you could just hang back a minute ... " She continued to rub Froot Loup's belly, then gradually extended her touch, crooning to her as she surreptitiously gave her a full body exam. Loup pulled away a bit when she got to her paws, so she didn't insist, but came back again and again to the paws until Loup stopped pulling away.

She gradually worked her way up to Loup's head, carefully, cautiously, then started scratching her ears. "Oh, that feels good, doesn't it?" she continued to croon and managed to get a good look inside each of them. She also let her hand fall onto Loup's lip every now and then.

"Rev—it is Rev, yes? Could you get the black bag from the front seat?" she asked. "And Dylan, you're the one who found her, right? Could you come join us now?"

Dylan crouched down beside them, and Froot Loup squiggled over to him. *Two* people to give her belly rubs!

"Could you continue with the fully body stroking?" she said to Dylan as she opened the bag Rev had set beside her. "We'll do the shots now, while she's all relaxed. She seems in good shape," she said, as she prepared the syringes. "No lacerations or parasitic infections as far as I can tell. She's got a beautiful coat. Did you actually manage to bathe her?"

"The lake," Dylan said.

"Ah. That would make it easier. Still, that was smart thing to do. I wouldn't be surprised if she'd had a few cuts and scrapes that you probably cleaned out for her." She made the first injection, while Dylan continued the belly rub and took over the crooning. Froot Loup didn't even notice.

"Okay," she said a minute later, "she's covered for the standard things now, parvovirus, distemper—I've also given her a rabies shot, of course, and one for Lyme disease and giardia, given her lifestyle. They're annuals, most of them, so they won't help her once she's on her own, but at least she'll be good for the first year."

"Super, thanks," Dylan continued the belly rubbing.

"Now, I'd like to look into her mouth if she'll let me." She rummaged in her bag for a doggy treat. "How would you like one of these?" she offered the treat to the little wolf. Froot Loup took it eagerly. "No problems chewing. You've noticed nothing?"

"No, she's been the perfect little wolf," Dylan said. Rev smiled.

"Okay, let's take a look," Dr. Theresen slipped her thumb under Loup's lip and lifted to take a good at her teeth. "My, what lovely teeth you have," she couldn't resist.

She was able to get a good look around, Loup even opening wide for a look at her tongue and throat. She flashed her light into each of Loup's eyes, gave Loup another treat, then closed her bag.

"So, what are your plans for her?" The examination was over, and the four of them were lounging on the grass.

"Whatever Loup wants," Dylan said. "I mean, we're providing food and shelter and snuggles, but we're not tying her up. When, if, she wants to leave, she's free to do so."

Dr. Theresen nodded.

"Do you think she'll leave?" Dylan had to ask. "When she reaches maturity—will she just become wilder and wilder and then disappear one day?"

"I don't know. I know we have this idea that wolves are pack animals, and that's true, but the pack is all kin. If Loup doesn't have any kin, I don't know whether she'll want to join a pack. Whether a pack will even *let* her join."

"I guess that's where the phrase 'lone wolf' comes from," Rev suggested.

"There are a few wolf preserves in the province. You could call them. See what they think."

"Good idea."

"But you do know, of course, that they're predators. Do any of your neighbours keep pet rabbits or chickens? Any farmers with livestock?"

Dylan looked to Rev. "None of the above. Frankly, we're more concerned about Loup's predators. A lot of guys around here are into the whole hunting thing."

"That explains your bright bandana," she crooned at Loup, giving her a few more strokes. "I suppose it's possible she might end up basically on her own, but come hang out here during the worst of the hunting season. I've heard moose do that. Hang around near buildings once the gunshots start. Or when Loup's natural prey gets scarce, she might come begging for a bit of kibble."

"Or a Meatlovers' pizza."

She burst out laughing. "Is that what you've been feeding her?"

24

H m," Dylan mumbled to himself as he read something on his laptop.

"What?" Rev had to ask.

"There's this couple—they were denied a licence to parent because they wanted to produce a second child to create a bone marrow donor for their first child."

"Really? But the Director, what was her name? She didn't mention motive as being among the criteria."

"She didn't, no. We briefly talked about it with Andy. The drug guy."

"Oh yeah," Rev remembered. "So—what does this mean?" she nodded to his laptop.

"That it's gone horribly wrong already?"

"Are you sure it was the Parent Licensing Agency—Board?—that refused a license? Not some NRT clinic? Have you interviewed anyone in NRT yet?"

"Not yet. They're next month. I think."

TWO HOURS LATER, REV spoke. "So what *would* be an acceptable motive?"

Dylan thought for a bit. "I don't know. I know people often have a child in an attempt to fix their relationship."

"Which is just using someone."

"Creating them first and then using them"

"Gotta be a special place in hell for—why else do people have kids?"

"Well," he said, "we already discovered, and rejected, the 'because it's expected' and 'to prove one's manhood, womanhood, or adulthood' motives."

"I think a lot of women do it because they're bored with their lives."

"Also not acceptable."

"Or because being a mom, having your kids listen to you, is probably the only authority they'll ever be granted. But, again, not acceptable. What other motives are there?" Rev wondered.

"I Imagine a lot of people have kids simply because all their friends have kids."

"Or they do it to carry on the family name."

"To carry on the family genes."

"To produce an heir for the family business."

"To produce another pair of hands to work in the field."

"To have someone to take care of you in your old age."

"To have a playmate for an existing child."

They thought some more about why people have kids.

"It's a do over!" Rev exclaimed. "A desperate attempt to redeem one's fuck-up of a life!" Then added after a moment. "From a species-level point of view, *that'd* be an acceptable motive, yeah?"

25

S o do you think this is enough?" Dylan walked into the porch holding half a dozen wire clothes hangers he'd turned into loops. "For our don't- struggle-when-you're-caught-in-a-snare lesson with Loup?" They'd decided that since she could get loose, and more, since she'd started going off on her own a bit at dusk, they'd teach her about snares sooner rather than later.

Rev considered the question. The concept of 'enough' was slowing her down considerably. That and the joint they'd had half an hour ago.

"I thought we'd put them all over the yard," Dylan said, "then we'd teach by example. I'll crawl into the loop, get my head stuck, struggle—"

"Then strangle yourself to death? That'd show her."

Dylan thought a moment. "Okay, no, I'd struggle, and instead of strangling to death, I'd exhibit signs of great distress."

"I'm sure you would."

"And then you'd come to the rescue?"

"That would teach her that if we don't telepathically know she's in a snare trap in great distress, she'll die."

"I should have thought this through before I got stoned," he said, slumping into his chair.

"What if you bark?" Rev suggested. "Once you're in great distress. And then I come to the rescue."

They thought about that.

"Didn't we already think of that and decide no?"

"Do you remember why we decided no?"

"No."

"Me neither."

They thought about it a bit longer.

"What if we teach her instead not to step into the snare?"

"That'd be a much better lesson," Dylan agreed.

"But I don't think we should put the snares here. That'd be like planting landmines. This is supposed to be a safe place for her, right?"

"Right. I'll go put them in the forest." He got up, picked up the wire loops, and went outside to get his bike. Froot Loup followed him.

He came back to the porch. "Froot Loup will come with me. And she'll see where I put them. So that won't work. I think you should go hide them in the forest." He set them on the table.

"Okay." Rev got up, got onto Dylan's bike, and pedalled off into the forest.

While she was gone, Dylan played with the loops, making each one a perfect circle.

"SO I'VE BEEN THINKING about our snare lesson," Rev said the next day, still stiff from her three-hour bike ride through the forest—on a bike she could sit down on and a bike whose pedals she could reach, but a bike on which she couldn't do both at the same time—and still slightly amazed she'd found her way back. Never mind that she'd ended up making a new trail to achieve that goal. Pretty much beside the old one, but she'd find that out later. "And I'm thinking we should make the snares out of the same wire that snares are actually made. Out of."

"But my loops look the same. Don't they?" Dylan asked. He thought he'd nailed the whole wire loop thing.

"But wolves' eyesight isn't that good. Especially relative to their other senses. And relative to us. That's why they walk into the snares in the first place, right?"

"You're right. So you're thinking clothes hanger wire smells significantly different from snare wire?"

"Could be as different as chocolate and cheesecake. For all we know."

"Because we're glakh," he agreed.

Rev waited.

"My word for 'can't smell a damned thing'. Much better than 'nose-deaf' or 'scent-blind'. The other possibilities I was considering."

"Fish probably don't have a word for water," Rev mused.

Dylan considered the relevance of that for a few moments, then gave up.

"I remember reading somewhere," he said, "—Bob liked to hang his head out the window when I took him for a car ride—"

"You took him for car rides?"

"Of course!" Dylan was indignant. How can you not take your best dog friend for a car ride? "I read somewhere that for dogs, the air rushing by was 'a symphony of scent'."

"Cool. But it assumes an essentialist language."

"A symphony of scent? Glakh?" Dylan was lost.

"No, my idea that Froot Loup will distinguish between clothes hanger wire and snare wire. It assumes her words are for what things are. It makes more sense for wolves to have a functionalist language. To have words for what things do. Not for what things are."

"That would require fewer words," Dylan agreed. "And given her comparative cognitive abilities ... Or were you thinking of her comparatively limited vocalization abilities?"

"Both, I suppose. Though I'll bet wolves' howls have a lot more distinguishing subtleties than we recognize."

Dylan thought about learning how to howl. It might be easier than learning Japanese.

"So you're thinking a loop made out of a clothes hanger wire and a loop made out of snare wire would both be, what, 'predator'? 'Thing that can kill'?"

"Maybe even 'thing that can kill me'. I suspect their worldview is very subjective."

"I wonder if that's also because of their relatively lesser cognitive abilities."

"So the stupider a person is, the more self-centered they are?

That's interesting."

"It is, isn't it."

THAT AFTERNOON THEY WENT into town to buy snare wire. And pizza. And kibble. Froot Loup was going through a lot of kibble.

"This is truly nasty stuff," Dylan said, as he sat on the floor in the basement—they didn't want Froot Loup to see what they were up to—with the wire and wire cutters. And thick workgloves.

"It is," Rev agreed.

A while later, he asked, "Do you think this is enough?" He'd made a dozen loops, each attached to a long bit of wire so Rev could wrap them from low, wolf-neck-high branches.

"I think so. She may need more than a dozen repetitions, but we can just reuse what we've got, right?"

So Rev went upstairs to put on her bug jacket, thoughtfully taking the loops with her, and the bag of butcher bones they'd bought, then jogged into the forest.

AN HOUR LATER, DYLAN biked up the main path, Loup trotting at his side. He stopped where Rev was waiting.

Loup went immediately to the baited snare about ten feet off the side of the path.

"NO!" Dylan screamed just as she stepped through the loop Rev had hung from a bush just in front of the bone she'd tossed onto the ground.

Loup stopped instantly, cringing at the sound of his anger.

Dylan walked toward her, saying "STAY!" and then wiggled the wire hanging loosely around her neck. She looked at it, smelled it, then whimpered.

"Back up," he said to her—he'd considered this earlier and decided 'Back away' might sound too similar to 'Stay'—and gently pulled her backwards out of the snare. He praised her and gave her a chunk of pizza from the bag full of cut-up pizza chunks he'd brought with him.

"Maybe she remembers," Rev said, having noted the whimper.

"I hadn't thought of that. That'd make this easier."

But Loup still wanted the bait. A fresh bone? That still had meat on it? Who wouldn't?

"No!" Dylan held the wire to her nose. "Stay," he said, and gave her another chunk of pizza. Then to Rev, "So do we let her have it?" We don't want to teach her she can't have any food she finds in the forest."

"I don't know. Maybe 'Eat only what you kill' is a good lesson."

"No, I think wolves are scavengers as well as predators. Loup might have to be, to survive on her own. No. Stay," Dylan continued to hold her back with commands. She was doing very well, given. But he realized he hadn't brought enough pizza.

"Good point. But they often put more than one snare at the same bait. I think we should teach her to avoid altogether any food near wire smell." Rev thought a moment. "I'll hide a few bones *without* snares nearby. So we can teach her to distinguish."

"That's a good idea."

"Okay, the next one is on the right just before the fork," Rev said, and Dylan and Loup continued on their way.

"NO! STAY!" She heard a few seconds later, as she trotted behind them, and threw a bone a few feet in on the other side off the path, noting a landmark.

She caught up to Dylan and Loup. "Did she step through again?"

"No, this time she stopped in front of it."

"Fast learner."

"It might have been my 'NO!' though, instead of the smell of wire. We have to get her to smell the wire and stop on her own accord."

They carried on to the next practice snare.

ON THE WAY BACK, REV nodded to the boulder at the side of the road. "Bone without snare off to the left." But Loup was already there.

"CAREFUL!" Dylan called out. He'd added that word to their repertoire. He leaped off his bike and grabbed Loup. "Careful, careful," he said, but Loup was already hanging back, sniffing the bushes around the bone. "Good Loup, careful," and when she'd made a circle and determined there wasn't any wire around, Dylan let her get to the bone.

"Did it work?" Rev caught up.

"I think so," Dylan said, impressed. "She actually hesitated. Seemed to understand. We'll have to do this again though. And again."

"Of course."

A FEW WEEKS LATER, after several more sessions with baited and unbaited butcher bones, when Dylan and Loup went for their daily ride-and-run, Loup led Dylan straight to all the real snares the hunter-asshole had set. He dismantled every one of them.

26

And so they decided they could leave Loup alone again. Not even harnessed and tied. She'd doubled her weight and had been taking off on her own, usually at dusk, but she always came back within a couple hours.

"So shall we go to the parents' group tomorrow?"

"Sure," Rev said. "But why don't we go for a long walk before-hand, with Loup. Tire her out, so she'll be content to just lie around waiting here for us."

"Excellent idea."

SO NEXT DAY, THEY headed off into the forest, Loup in her pink bandana trotting in the forest alongside them in stealth mode.

"Have you been to the top of the ridge?" Rev asked.

"Don't think so," Dylan replied.

"Let's go there. You'll like the view. And it's not as difficult a climb as it sounds," she added, mostly to herself.

The path was overgrown, and it was slow-going, but despite the added stress on her knees, she preferred such trails. They were more likely to be dirtbike- and ATV-free.

They passed through a large section of maple trees on the way that Rev called 'The Emerald Cathedral' for the way the sun broke through and illuminated the bright green leafery. In the fall, it became 'The Golden Cathedral'. Unfortunately, she had yet to see 'The Scarlet Cathedral' since that transition happened during moose season.

"God damn it!" Rev said vehemently once they reached the top.

"What?"

She nodded.

Dylan looked out at the beautiful view, nothing but trees for miles and miles—and, smack dab in the center, a huge red-and-white Canadian flag flying from what must be one of the tallest trees.

"That's new. Looks like it's at Hull's place."

"Someone lives out here?" Dylan said incredulously.

"No, that's part of my anger. It's just his hunt camp. So he's there only what, twice a year? I've never even met him. But that'll be there for the rest of my life."

"And every time you walk through here, you'll—"

"It'll be visible from the lake too. Every day I go kayaking." She hadn't been out for a couple days, which explains why she hadn't yet seen it.

"Ah." It was the boat all over again.

"I wonder if he's there now," Rev said, and resumed walking. With intent. To do any number of things, many of which Dylan amused himself imagining.

HALF AN HOUR LATER, they came to his hunt camp, a roughly-put-together shack with an outhouse, woodpile, and shed. An ATV was parked out front. They walked around to the back to find him fiddling with the gas generator. Maybe he was finally giving it a tune-up that would make it so she didn't hear it, from her house miles away, whenever he turned it on.

"So, Merle, is it?"

He looked up from the generator and smiled at her.

"I'm curious," she launched right in. "Why the sudden need to proclaim to everyone that you were born here?"

"What?" He wiped his hands on a rag, squinted at her, still smiling at her.

"The Canadian flag," she nodded to the tallest tree. "You've made sure we all can see it. Whenever we're out anywhere on the lake."

It dawned on him then that she wasn't flirting with him. He looked around, confused, then up at the flag. As if he'd forgotten it was there. As if, quite possibly, it got there one drunken night. "It's just a flag."

"It's a symbol! It stands for something. You're sending a message, and I'm asking why. Why are you shouting at me that you're Canadian? Every time I go out on the lake. For two whole hours."

"What?"

"What if I flew the Darwin fish flag in your face all day every day. Or the rainbow flag?"

He didn't get any of it.

"I don't even notice it any more," he said, shrugging. Then turned back to tinker with his generator.

"SO I'M THE ONE WHO suffers," Rev said, half a mile later. "Because I pay attention to things and what they mean, I'm the one who suffers."

"And me too," Dylan said. "Sometimes. A little bit. I pay attention," he added unconvincingly.

Loup ran ahead joyfully. She wasn't bothered at all about what things meant. Except maybe the pile of bear scat she'd noticed a while back.

"It's bad enough that business has permission to contaminate the commons with their messages," Rev continued, "but if every individual does it—"

"I read a sci-fi novel once where hologram ads popped up around you wherever you went."

"Yeah, I read that one too," she shuddered.

"And there's one where satellites or something are allowed to project advertising so there's a perpetual golden arches in the sky."

"What if his neighbour put a mural on her garage door of Hothead Paisan bashing in some guy's head, so good ole' Merle had to see it all day, every day, whenever he was home. I wonder if he'd get it then?"

27

Froot Loup emptied her water dish as soon as they returned, so Dylan refilled it, and also filled her food dish with kibble. Sprinkled some Froot Loops on top for dessert.

"I'll be back," he told her, once they were ready to go, making sure the knot of her bright pink bandana was tight. She watched them leave.

Rev glanced in the rear view mirror just before she turned out of sight. "She lay down," she said to Dylan, who relaxed a little. But he turned around several times and scanned the forest beside them all the way to the highway. No Froot Loup.

THEY PULLED INTO THE parking lot at the community center and entered the building. There was a sign in the lobby indicating that the parents' support group was in the lounge. Arrows helpfully pointed the way.

The lounge was full of people, an assortment of couples, single women, and single men. Chairs were arranged in a circle, but most people were standing around a table of refreshments, chatting with each other.

A woman with a hostess thing going for her broke away and approached Dylan and Rev as soon as they entered the room.

"You must be Mr. O'Toole?" she asked, radiating warmth and

support. Rev hated her instantly.

"Yes, Ms. Andrews? Thanks for allowing us to attend your meeting."

"Please," she gestured to the table, "help yourselves to coffee and muffins, we'll be starting in a few minutes."

Rev got coffee and muffins for both of them while Dylan got his mini-recorder out and belatedly checked the battery.

"Everyone, if I could have your attention? I think we're all here—perhaps we could begin?"

People made their way to the circle of chairs.

"We have two special guests this evening. Would you please welcome Mr. Dylan O'Toole, who is writing a series of articles on the new parent licence legislation. He expressed interest in what real parents think about the new law, so I suggested he attend one of our get-togethers. And with him is—"

"Oh, sorry, everyone, this is Chris Reveille."

Ms. Andrews was clearly waiting for more.

"I'm investigating an illegal fertilization at the egg bank, and it occurred to me that with the new legislation mandating parent education, a little business such as yours, that provides parent education, might be in trouble."

"Oh, this isn't a business. Second," she smiled with modesty so fake, boobs all over L.A. sagged in defeat, "I'm not here to teach anyone anything. Being a parent is all about finding your own way. We're all here to help each other."

One of the women nodded. A few of the men pointedly did not.

"Sort of like the blind leading the blind," Rev commented. "In that case then, I'm here out of morbid curiosity."

"I see," Ms. Andrews smiled. Tightly.

"But it's not like that," she recovered, "Parenting is a lot like life. Messy, out of control, full of flaws. We live and learn as we go."

"Trial and error?"

"Trial, yes, definitely trial," she smiled ruefully, as if recalling her own difficulties as a parent and inviting others to smile at their difficulties as well. "But there are no errors," she made eye contact with several parents in the group. "That's how we learn. You have to be free to stumble and fall."

"Would you allow that same freedom to airplane pilots? Surgeons? Set them free on a learn-as-you-go basis?"

In the uncomfortable silence that followed, one of the men spoke up. "I think the new law is wrong. It goes against our natural instincts. To have a family. To have kids." Several people in the circle nodded. Certainly Ms. Andrews nodded.

"You say that as if following your instincts is a good thing," Rev replied.

"Well—isn't it?" he said, as if he'd never even considered the opposing view. Any opposing view.

"But if that were the case, we'd never have firefighters going into a burning building to save people. Because instinct tells us not to run into fire. Most of us," she added, looking at him.

"Okay, yeah, but," he missed the insinuation of her addition, "that's good."

"So what you're saying is that sometimes following your instincts is good and sometimes it isn't." He'd also missed the point of her counterexample.

"Well, duh." Was she an airhead or what.

"So how do you decide? When is it good and when not?"

"If you're saving somebody's life, then it's good," he said, as if speaking to a child.

"Then why not just use that as your standard? Appealing to instinct is redundant. Since you're going to trump it anyway whenever, well, probably whenever you want ... " It was hopeless. Simply hopeless.

"What I don't get though," another man spoke up, "is that, I applied for custody for my kids, okay? And now I have to—" he pulled a rumpled piece of paper from his pocket, "I have to show that I have 'the ability to properly and effectively raise the child, knowledge of child-rearing techniques, sensitivity to the feelings of others'—what the fuck is that all about? 'A lifestyle,'" he continued, "'and other personality qualities which would be useful for the child to emulate and identify with'—you've got to be kidding. 'Commitment to the child's education, health, and friends—'" He looked helplessly around the circle. Apparently he thought they could help him get all that. Before his upcoming court date. "Why do I have to prove this shit now when I didn't have to before? When we had our kids?"

No one had an answer.

"I have to 'demonstrate my fitness' and 'prove my competence'!" He shook the paper in his hand. "And yet, *she's presumed* to be competent." The tone in his voice made it clear he was talking about his wife. The bitch.

Every one of the single men present grumbled their agreement. Ms. Andrews opened her mouth to say something, but someone else beat her to it.

"You want to talk about double standards? Try adopting a child! We're on our third adoption," she reached for her husband's hand, "and every time—you want to talk about jumping through hoops? I'll bet what you had to do to get custody is nothing compared what we've had to do!" The woman looked at her husband for confirmation. "It's not our fault, it's only because—" she broke off before she revealed which of the two was infertile. And probably because her hand was hurting.

"Okay, but what I don't get, about the new law and having to take that course, is what right does someone else have to tell me how to raise my kids?"

"*Your* kids?" Someone from the circle spoke up. "Do you own them? Are they your *property*?"

"No, I mean yes, but—"

"Other people have that right because what *your* kids do affects them." Clearly someone's kid had pissed off this person—who was *not* Rev—in a big way.

"What I don't get," someone else spoke up, a heavily-made-up woman, "is the implicit assumption that bad kids are due to bad parenting."

Someone snorted. The woman glared at him. "I think some of the blame has to be put on the schools. After all, they have my Janey for eight hours a day."

"I think you've got a point. I struggle with the influence of my kids' friends. She is addicted to her cell phone, forever texting her friends."

"And tv. My god, if I could just take that thing to the dump."

"What's stopping you?" Rev asked. Everyone seemed to think she'd asked a rhetorical question.

Ms. Andrews tried to end the interview portion of the evening. "Perhaps we could—"

"I think it's a great idea," someone else spoke up. "The course. Jack and I, we looked very closely at our friends who'd had kids, how their lives had changed, before we decided that yes, having kids was something we wanted to do, and as soon as I became pregnant, we started going to prenatal classes, and once Jenny was born, we continued going to classes, reading books—"

"And coming here," Ms. Andrews said warmly.

"Oh, yes, but in all honesty," she confessed, "I'm here not so much for education as, well, I was hoping to find some support. My Jenny was born with CMT. She's spending her entire life in a wheelchair. And I love her dearly, but," the woman hesitated, then decided to carry on, "sometimes I want to push her wheelchair down the stairs, I swear to God." She looked around the room, begging for someone's eyes to say they understood, they'd feel the same way. And they'd come look after Jenny next time she felt that way.

"What I worry about most," another woman spoke up, "is the long-term. My Ally's turned out to have colic. I knew that was a possibility, but they say that when it does, it usually goes away after a couple months. It's been eight. Months. Eight months of inexplicable crying. Ally won't remember this, I know that children usually don't remember anything that happens to them before the age of three. But I will. I'll remember how she made my life hell. I'll remember that for the rest of my life. And I know with my head it's not her fault, she's not to blame, but even so, it's—it's getting harder and harder to feel warm and affectionate toward her. And I'm afraid I won't be able to find my way back to that. When she was born I wanted nothing more than to snuggle her every second of the day. Now—"

"Now you want to throw her down the stairs."

"I do," she whispered, "some times. So I keep my distance. Literally, physically, as well as emotionally. And what if I stay this way. What if I'm cold and distant and a teenaged Jenny won't understand why, and then she'll—"

"If I'd had a choice," the first woman resumed, "between this zygote with cystic fibrosis and that zygote without—only a masochist would choose the one with."

"You don't choose. You take them both. You accept what God gives you," Ms. Andrews said.

"That's a pretty passive way to go through life," someone who hadn't yet spoken said.

"Passive?" Rev couldn't help herself. "It's irresponsible! Not to make choices."

"And you've all made the choice to attend this group," Ms. Andrews said, beaming.

"YOU KNOW WHAT THEY should've done instead?" Rev said, once the meeting had adjourned and they were back in their car. "They should have removed the regulations for foster parents and adoptive parents and people seeking custody. Implemented a lottery system. Or a first-come first-served system."

"'Imagine some drunk stumbling up and saying 'I'll take that cute little blond-haired girl over there.'"

Rev glanced over at him.

"That's how Roger McIntire described the current system. Lack of."

Rev nodded. "The shit would've hit the fan. *Then* we should have introduced the idea of prerequisites. For all parent-wannabes."

"It's indefensible, isn't it. Our belief that biological parents are *necessarily* competent parents. A belief we maintain in the face of overwhelming evidence to the contrary." He looked out at the land, less bleak now in the middle of spring, the almost-summer.

"At least adoptive parents have chosen to have kids, made a conscious choice to be responsible for them," Rev said. "If anything, the double standard should have gone the other way."

"Agreed. It would have also counteracted the tendency, when the kids are genetically related, for parents to see them as ego-extensions and/or private property. Both of which would, perhaps, increase the potential for abuse."

28

"H ome?" Dylan asked hopefully, worrying about Loup.

"Not quite," Rev replied. "I brought Raquelle's resume. Was hoping to drop it off." She looked over at him.

"Okay."

"SHE'S NOT HERE," PAT said to Rev at the shelter's door. "She said she was going to the park."

"The one at the end of the block?"

"Yeah."

"Okay, thanks."

Rev went back out to the car to tell Dylan.

"Would I freak her out if I came along?" he asked.

"I don't think so. You'd be with me. She's pretty level- headed."

"THERE SHE IS," REV nodded to Raquelle sitting at a picnic table in the middle of the park. Two other young women were with her, all of them keeping half an eye on a bunch of kids playing in the large sandbox nearby.

"Hey, Rev," Raquelle called out to her. "Everyone, this is Rev. She's the one I was telling you about," she said cryptically. "We were just talking about why we had kids."

Torn between academic curiosity and personal disinterest, neither Rev nor Dylan responded. But then Raquelle scooted over, clearly making room for them to sit. So, they sat.

"To be honest, I had some concern," the freckled one offered. "I wasn't sure, but ... I don't know, there came a point ... As soon as I saw her ... No, even before that ... I love her—more than you can possibly imagine. I'd do anything for her," she ended simply, smiling broadly.

"Yeah, but that's just the drugs talking," Rev said.

"No, I don't take drugs. I'm not—" she looked at Raquelle and the other woman with alarm.

"Oxytocin," Rev clarified. "The so-called 'cuddle drug'. It's made by your pituitary gland. What happens is the high levels of estrogen during pregnancy—you know your estrogen levels shoot up, yeah? Well, that increases—that increases the oxytocin levels in a woman's brain. Especially near the end of pregnancy. In fact, oxytocin is what triggers contractions. That's why pregnant women are advised not to take it. It could trigger a miscarriage. But it also triggers feelings of joy, warmth, affection, love—"

The other woman, the one with the black lipstick, spoke up. "So can you, like, *buy* oxytocin?" she asked. She had put two and two together.

"Yeah, but you don't need to now," Rev said to her. "Right?"

"Oh, yeah." And had gotten five. She rested her hand on her big belly.

"Which is why I think a lot of women like being pregnant," Rev added. "They get addicted to the feel-good oxytocin."

Black lipstick guiltily looked away.

"Anyway," Rev continued, "so the higher the levels of oxytocin in your body, the more strongly you bond with your newborn. They've shown that mothers with high oxytocin levels are more likely to hold their babies, and play with them, and talk to them in that annoying baby talk voice. So all that mother love? Just the drugs talking."

"And women whose bodies don't produce it?" Raquelle asked, intrigued. "Or don't produce enough of it?"

"They don't bond with their babies. They're the ones who realize what ugly little shits their kids really are. And then kill them. We call it post-partum depression. Instead of low levels of oxytocin."

All three of the young women looked concerned. And rightly so.

"And since oxytocin is released during breastfeeding, and, actually," she added, "whenever the nipples are, um, stimulated—"

"So *that's* why … " Black lipstick again.

"That's why it's important that women breastfeed right away. Doing it during the first hour causes oxytocin to shoot off the chart in both the mother and the baby. So bingo. Mega mother-baby bond."

"I wonder—my mother never—"

"Oxytocin also," Rev continued, letting Raquelle follow her wondering thought on her own, in private, "enables a mother to recognize her baby's smell, and vice versa. Which means they'll be able to find each other after the birth."

"Should they be separated on the ice floes," Dylan added, recalling a scene from *Happy Feet*.

Rev nodded. "It has evolutionary value, obviously, for all species. But here's the thing. The mother's brain is actually reorganized by oxytocin. Which means that all that maternal behaviour becomes hard-wired. Oxytocin causes women to be more caring *in general*, more sensitive to other's feelings, more eager to please others—"

"So, can people be tested for oxytocin deficiency?" he grinned at her.

29

Anosmic," Dylan said a few days later during their morning-on-the-porch.

"What?"

"The word for nose-deaf. We already have one. It's anosmic."

"I like glakh better."

"So do I," he grinned.

He'd also looked up Hothead Paisan. And understood why she was Rev's role model.

ABOUT AN HOUR AFTER that, out of the corner of his eye, Dylan saw a quick movement along the length of the porch.

"What was that? Did you see that?"

"Yes," Rev said, sitting up. Marten? Baby bear?

"Where's Froot Loup?" Dylan stood up, ready to protect her from—everything. "Froot Loup!" he called anxiously, moving to the door. "Loup!"

Just before he opened the door, Rev on her feet beside him, they saw what exactly they had seen. Froot Loup ran by with a bunny rabbit in her mouth. Head held high, she was prancing. So happy, so proud.

It took a moment for the terror to turn into relief. "Baby's first kill," Dylan said, fondly.

He went back to his laptop and cued Queen's "We are the Champions" in time for her third victory lap.

"Good Loup," Dylan went out outside to praise her achievement, as she threw the bunny rabbit, now mercifully dead, they hoped, into the air.

"That's a beautiful bunny rabbit. Good choice," he crooned as Froot Loup resumed trotting around the cabin with it. "And you caught it all by your little self."

"And killed it. All by your little self," Rev added, dutifully, beside him. "And will now tear it to pieces. All by your little self."

'No time for losers,' Froot Loup had rounded the cabin again and threw the bunny rabbit into the air. Again. "Cuz we are the champions,' she shook it thoroughly. 'Of the world!' She threw it into the air one more time. Then carried it triumphantly to the porch.

"NO!" Rev and Dylan shouted at the same time.

Froot Loup looked at them, understandably a little confused, but then just trotted off to her den in the woodshed. Or the nearest patch of sun. Frankly, Rev didn't want to know.

N ext day, when Rev stepped outside, she was hit in the head with a muskrat. A dead muskrat. But still. Froot Loup had apparently made another kill.

"Good kill, Loup," Rev said, gushing and giving Froot Loup the impression she'd just won the Olympic Gold for the muskrat throw. She was sticking to their agreement to reward any behaviour that would enable her to return to the wild and survive. Flinging a dead muskrat in Rev's face wasn't such a behaviour, but hopefully Froot Loup understood it was the behaviour just prior to that that Rev was praising.

Alas, three days later, Dylan was hit in the head with a dead otter.

At least they thought it was an otter. Hard to tell with the head missing. But it was clear she was upping her game. She herself was, after all, getting bigger by the day.

"We have to catch her at the moment of the kill," Rev observed, "so she understands more precisely what behaviour we're reinforcing here."

Dylan wiped otter gunk from his chin. "You think?"

31

So," Rev said to Dylan a few days later as she came from the kitchen into the porch, "You'd called the local high school to set up an interview with the principal and some of the teachers?"

"I did, yes. I thought end of June, they'd be available."

"Uh-huh. Good idea," she said, her eyes twinkling. Dylan didn't know her eyes could do that. "But—get this. The principal just called back. The school's closed. Now. For an impromptu celebration. Apparently there's dancing in the street."

"Seriously? At this moment?"

"Seriously. At this very moment." She held up her car keys.

FROM THE MUNICIPAL parking lot a block away, they heard Kool and the Gang's "Celebration" blaring, and as soon as they rounded the last corner, they saw what must have been every teacher in the district, from grade one to grade twelve, in a sort of a parade that just went up one side of the street and down the other, forming an endless circle of celebration. Once Rev and Dylan got over the shock of seeing dancing teachers—certainly none of the teachers at any of the schools they'd taught at had ever danced—they wove in and out of the merrymakers, resuscitating their disco moves. Badly. But enthusiastically.

"No more lying about the grades just to keep your job!"

"No more giving a pass just because a kid knows his name!"

Two people were swinging each other around.

"No more spending half the day trying to get their attention!"

"No more spending the other half trying to keep it!"

They continued to swirl and shout "No mores ... " at each other.

Rev and Dylan made their way up the street, stopping to approach a weepy prematurely-grey woman. "My daughter's in teacher's college, and she's going to be okay!" she said to them, holding out her wrists so they could see her scars.

A few meters further along, they approached another person, crumpled against a streetlight post, rocking back and forth. "If I can just hang on for a few more years, I might never be told to fuck off by a six year old again!" the woman looked up at them. "Is that not cause for celebration?"

"It is," Dylan assured her.

"This is weird," Rev said, looking around her in wonderment. "All this repressed—I thought it was just me all those years."

"We can start assigning homework again!"

"We can get through our carefully prepared lessons again!"

Further along, a few carried signs. Nicely done in colourful crayons and paints on bright Bristol board. "Totalitarian? Utopian!" "This is a solution, not a problem!"

Dylan saw someone from the local television station interviewing a principal—he could always tell who the principals were—they were the ex-gym teachers—so he tore himself out of the groove he was getting into with KC and the Sunshine Band's "Boogie Shoes" and hustled over with his mini-recorder to piggyback. Rev was close behind. She made it a point never to miss a chance to see a principal make a fool of himself.

"Teachers are required to study full-time for at least eight months before the state will allow them to teach, allow them the responsibility of educating children for a mere seven hours a day, and that, only once they become six years of age," the man was saying. "And many say that we have set the bar too low, that our teachers aren't qualified enough, they don't know what they're doing, they're not doing a good job.

"But we haven't set the bar as high—in fact we haven't set a bar at all—for parents. Someone can be responsible not only for a child's education, but for virtually everything about the child, for twenty-four hours a day, until that child is six years of age. That is, for the duration of the critical, formative years—and he or she doesn't even have to so much as read a pamphlet about child development."

Dylan and Rev exchanged a glance. An articulate principal was like a boxer able to do long division.

"How many children have been punished because they couldn't do what their parents mistakenly thought they should be able to do at a certain age? 'Remember this, do that, don't do that?' How many have been disadvantaged because they grew up on junk food—for their bodies as well as their minds? How many have been neglected, wasted, because their parents didn't notice the seeds of some talent? And how often have parents undermined a girl's attempt to be strong and independent or a boy's allegedly sissy interests?"

"But won't this mean, eventually, lay-offs and closures?" the reporter interjected. "Surely the number of children entering the schools will decrease."

"What it means is that we'll be able to lower the teacher-student ratio. Which will mean more one-on-one attention. Which will mean the quality of education our children receive will increase."

Several exuberant teachers passed by behind him and made silly faces into the camera.

"But—"

"It'll also mean—do you have any idea how much more expensive it is to educate a disabled student? Students with learning disabilities require far more resources, if only because of the need for a severely reduced teacher-student ratio. And who pays for that? You, me, and the other students. Why do you think we had to cut music, art, and phys-ed? Because we had to hire ten new teachers to deal with the twenty new students who are so retarded, because their mothers drank so much while they were pregnant, or had the kids on a McDonalds diet for the first six years, that we'll be lucky if they can read and write by the time they graduate. From high school."

"What about the criticism that the schools should have been

teaching parenting skills all along?" the reporter asked. "That it should have been a mandatory course, and if it had been, we never would have gotten into this mess with licensing."

"First of all, I want to go on record as saying I don't think it's a mess. Certainly, no licensing arrangement is going to be perfect. The question is whether, all things considered, it will be more right than wrong.

"Second, students don't really learn what we teach them."

"Damn it!" Rev said. "Now he's gone and gotten himself fired. And he was doing so well."

"This is especially true for courses we make mandatory," he continued. "Force someone to do something—force them to come to school, force them to take a course—that achieves nothing.

"Truth be told, our schools are next to useless for well over half of our students. They come to us unprepared, they don't want to learn, they don't pay attention, they don't do the homework. It's hopeless. It's *been* hopeless. Until now.

"As Roger McIntire notes, 'We already license pilots, salesmen, scuba divers, plumbers, electricians, veterinarians, cab drivers, soil testers and television repairmen'," he looked straight into the camera. "'Are our TV sets and toilets more important to us than our children?'"

"And now he's gotten himself reinstated," Dylan grinned.

THEY TURNED THEN AS the volume of the crowd noticeably increased, and saw that another group of people had entered the street from one of the side streets.

One of the newly arrived headed straight for one of the nearby teachers. "Hey, jackass, have you taught my son to stop swearing yet?"

Another of the newly arrived confronted another one of the teachers. "When are you going to stop letting your classes watch tv all day?"

"When am I what?" the teacher replied, astounded.

"Shonna says you just let them watch tv all day."

"Right ... and Shonna never lies."

The woman opened her mouth, but the teacher beat her to it.

"Have you really started a boob job fund for her?"

"I'm looking out for my baby's future!" Shonna's mother protested. "*Someone* has to," she added with disgust.

"Right ... " the teacher simply folded his arms.

"And you!" Another enraged parent pointed at another surprised teacher. It was rapidly becoming the worst parent-teacher night ever. Or the best.

"You *never* assign homework!"

The teacher rolled her eyes—

"Yeah, she does," another parent came to her defence, then said smugly, "but *my* boy always gets it done in class."

—right into the back of her head.

They watched then as another parent approached yet another teacher, this time swinging. The teacher put his "Stupid parents breed stupid kids" sign up in defence. It got broken in two. They started to walk down the street.

"This is Jeannie C. Riley's 'Harper Valley PTA'," Dylan said. "Only inside out. Times ten."

"Yeah ... you know, I always identified with the mother. What happened?" She asked, puzzled.

"Nothing. It's the mother who's the radical, telling it like it is, exposing the hypocrisy of the teachers, remember? All the teachers in the song are clueless preachy judgemental conservatives."

"Which makes me wonder why I ever thought to become a teacher."

"*To Sir with Love. Room 222. Welcome Back Kotter.* Teaching is, or at least can be, or at some point became ... a radical act. We both saw that."

"Which explains why I was so successful. At getting fired."

And why I quit, thought Dylan.

"I think we were part of a new generation," he said, then couldn't believe he'd just said that, but went on anyway, "and there weren't enough of us at any one school at any one point in time. And then the generation after us was like the generation before us—"

"So we just keep going around in a circle? It's hopeless," she looked out at the street, which had become a free-for-all. "Absolutely hopeless."

"And yet—" Dylan nodded at the few teachers who were still dancing. That, or limping.

A THIRD GROUP THEN entered the street, close to where they were. Another group of parents, it seemed, this one in favour of the teachers. Or in favour of the legislation. Or both.

"Our children are our future!" One held up a sign.

"And yet," Rev commented, "we have allowed idiots to make them. And raise them. Which begs the question: who have the real idiots been?"

A few of them spotted Dylan standing there with his mini-recorder still in his hand. They came over and started talking.

"We endorse the new law," one said.

"In fact, we welcome it," another added. "We've taken courses on our own, without being forced to do so, we've bought books, and read them, over and over ... "

"And we resent paying for other people's kids," someone pushed his way closer to Dylan, who obliged by holding his recorder up to him. "If they can have however many they want, when we limit ourselves to two, they should pay for them, not us. In fact, we're not going to do it anymore," he looked around and received many nods. "You want to make a third new person, you're on your own. *You* pay for its food and clothing, *you* pay for its healthcare, *you* pay for its education. No more mother's allowance, no more income tax deductions, no more free education up to grade twelve."

"But that would be penalizing the kids for the parents' actions," Dylan said.

"Which is why this contraception vaccine should be mandatory," someone called out.

"And the antidote available only to those who are licensed!"

THE NEW GROUP HEADED for a relatively empty section of the street, and Rev and Dylan walked on, through the various clumps of people. A man looked pointedly at her unshaved legs as she walked by. Just as he opened his mouth, Rev said to him, "You know, you could look handsome if you fixed yourself up a bit. Lost a bit of weight, did a little something to your face." He closed his mouth.

THEY CONTINUED TO WEAVE in and out along the street, but then stopped as two parents approached another teacher. The parents' distress was palpable, and they were curious—

"Ms. Bevan, we know you're trying," the mother looked around her nervously, "but Patrick is an Evan Charein waiting to happen. Can't you stop the other boys?" She was begging.

The teacher, presumably Ms. Bevan, looked—empty. "No," she replied. The defeat in her voice was equally palpable. "Keep Patrick at home," she added. Insisted.

"But then he'll be arrested for truancy and sent to some detention center," the mother said. "Where he'll just get beaten up anyway."

"We want him at school," the father said. "We want him to learn."

"Then home school him."

"But—isn't that just for Christians?"

"Convert."

"But we don't know chemistry or—"

"Bring him to my house Tuesday nights," she said quietly. "Seven o'clock."

"But—"

"Biology is Monday nights at Mr. Ballow's house," she glanced around nervously. "Literature, Wednesdays, Ms. Crickson." She quickly wrote her phone number on a piece of paper and pressed it into the woman's hand. "Call me." The parents looked at her, as if they might persist, but then just nodded, and hurried away.

"What was that all about?" Rev asked the teacher. "Who's Evan Charein?"

The woman sighed. "A kid who kept getting bullied until he finally showed up at school one day with a gun and started killing the boys who had been doing it. The police arrived and one ended up killing Evan. Had to. He was the one with the gun. When the officer later found out the whole story, he killed himself. Figured he'd shot the wrong kid."

"Jeezus Christ," Dylan muttered.

"Can't the bullies—can't the students who are beating up Patrick just be expelled?" Rev asked.

"First, they're not just beating him up. They're—facebooking or tweeting—I don't know. Second, the principal at our school believes that every child has a right to an education," she sighed.

"An inalienable right?"

"He doesn't know what that means."

"How about framing the situation as competing rights. Surely he understands the concept of competition."

"He does. But he doesn't get that being constantly afraid for your life isn't exactly conducive to learning. Or teaching."

"Sounds like you should have a gun," Dylan said.

"Oh, I do."

There was a moment of silence.

"So why don't you shoot the boys?" Rev suggested. Reasonably enough.

"Because I'm a teacher who's scared shitless. Not the sniper from *Flashpoint*."

"So—what are you doing at your house—Tuesday nights?" Dylan asked. "Extra tutoring?"

"I'm part of an underground school," she looked around again nervously.

"Really? But—one night a week?"

"With keen students, we can cover a whole week's work in an hour. And then some," she smiled.

"Yeah, I guess I believe that."

"Is he gay?" Dylan asked. "Patrick?"

"No," she sighed again. "Just smart, sensitive, and small."

"You know 'bullying' is like 'domestic violence'," Rev said as they moved away. "It sounds so—it sounds like it's just spitballs and taunts at recess, calling a kid 'Dumbo' because his ears are big. We need new words for posting videos on the internet showing kids in forced and humiliating sexual situations," she guessed. Right. "If Steve Jobs had done something like that to Bill Gates—"

"Not to mention the beating up part."

"Yeah, well, we *have* a word for that. Which makes it all the more appalling that schools don't automatically expel kids for assault. And have them arrested."

"Scuffles are part of growing up," Dylan shrugged.

"Are they?"

"Well, for boys."

"Only because we allow it," Rev said. "If it's harder for males to be non-violent, because of testosterone or the Y chromosome, that doesn't mean we should condone it."

They walked on.

"And I wouldn't call several guys beating one guy to a bloody pulp a 'scuffle'."

"Nor would I, no."

THEY WALKED ON, toward a sort of soapbox corner.

"What can be more important than parenting?" Another of the 'pro' parents was shouting out. "It's at the heart of what makes us what we are, biologically, socially, intellectually, emotionally— And what can be more important to us, individually and collectively, than what we are?"

Just then a fourth group rounded the corner. Parents against the legislation, presumably.

"What I was going to say," one of them said to the shouting out woman.

The two of them looked at each other. Confused.

Then someone started singing "Every child is sacred." To the tune of Monty Python's "Every sperm is sacred."

Hopeless, Rev thought again. Absolutely hopeless.

WHEN THEY CROSSED THE side street, they stopped, their attention caught by as they looked left then right—"Are they doing what I think they're doing?"

Dylan nodded. "'Doin' it in the road.'"

"And are we to assume that those are their kids?"

Dylan nodded. "All eight of them."

Not at all interested in the view, they walked on.

"THIS IS LIKE DEMONSTRATIONS against abortion," Rev said a few moments later. "They cry 'No abortion!' but no one steps up to take responsibility for the kids they won't let us abort."

Dylan looked over at her, confused.

"They're saying everyone should have the freedom to be a parent, but are any of these people willing to step up and take over from or even help the incompetent parents, the ones who find out to late they're in way over their heads? Or, of course, become competent parents themselves? I doubt it. They want rights, but not the responsibilities that go with them. The legislation just makes sure that those who claim the former can deliver on the latter."

"Perhaps we should have made licensing as simple as prove maturity and prove knowledge," Dylan suggested.

"No, they'd still object. 'We have the right to be immature! And ignorant! And we have the right to replicate our immaturity and ignorance, and squirt and spew it all over the rest of you!'"

"Spew?"

"I don't know, I've never given birth."

"Yes, but—spew?"

"SPEAKING OF WHICH," REV said a few minutes later, after they'd turned around and started heading back, "what if all males had to have their DNA on file with the government. And all newborns had to have their paternity established by law. And all males discovered to be fathers had their wages garnished at the source—to support the mother of the child for six years, assuming she would be the one to be with the child 24/7 for the first six years and could not therefore obtain employment and therefore income of her own—and the child for 18 years. *And* condoms and vasectomies were illegal.

"Do you think men would champion the right to life as vociferously as they do now? Would the meaning of sex for men change from casual relief, pleasure, and/or conquest to—something else?"

"DO YOU HAVE KIDS?" A woman stomped up to Rev as they were leaving the scene.

"What?"

"You don't, do you," she challenged. "You know, people like you are the reason we have to wait until 70 now to start collecting our pensions."

"What?"

"It's because of people like you who haven't done their duty!"

'Duty?' Rev mouthed at Dylan.

"There aren't enough people paying into the system now," the woman carried on, "so they've taken our pension benefits away. Five years' worth."

Rev was suddenly up to speed. "Are you saying that my kids were supposed to pay for your living expenses?"

"*My* grandkids will be paying *your* pension!" the woman shouted.

"And that's the *least* they should do for me," Rev shouted back, "for all the damage they will have done, to me, up to that point. Watch *The Age of Stupid*. They will have fouled my water and smogged my air. They will have used reduced our fossil fuel reserves even more, increasing the cost of my food. And they will have fucking moved in next door."

"DID YOU NOTICE ANY trend?" Dylan asked Rev as they approached their car.

"No teachers against the legislation?"

"Yeah, but also more men than women against the legislation."

"Hm," she pondered that as she unlocked the doors. "They're also more vocal about contraception and abortion."

"I wonder if that's a male thing," Dylan said. "The focus on rights, rather than responsibilities."

Rev sighed. "I think you're right. I wish we had some data for this, I'm thinking it's because in general women see responsibility where men see power and status. That would also explain why women less often than men seek political office, for example. And CEOships. And, of course, men think they're entitled to—well, to everything, but certainly to power and status. Hence their outrage.

"Having a kid," Rev continued, "for a woman, is a big responsibility. She sees dirty diapers, sleepless nights, and no more me-time. It's interesting that it's the right *not* to reproduce that's been sought by *women* through time.

"Men see—well, I don't know what they see. You tell me. The chest-swelling 'father of two' label? An audience for their every word of wisdom? Their own private cheering squad? Evidence of their virility—narrowly and mistakenly measured by offspring? And why is virility important anyway? The need to have progeny, especially *male* progeny ... "

"Yeah," Dylan said, reaching into the glove compartment for their stash of parking lot and parking meter coinage. "I've always noticed how people, especially men, who have never shown any interest in babies, or children, or the development from one to the other, who've never shown any interest in spending time with kids, who, in fact, have *avoided* kids all their lives, never giving them a second glance, and who, furthermore, have nothing but contempt for those who do look after kids—suddenly say they want kids."

Rev snorted. "They don't want kids. They want their wives to have kids so they can say they're a father. Because that means they're a man. Go figure the logic on that."

"Yeah, that's my take. It's not so much wanting kids as wanting to 'have kids'. Because having kids confers some sort of maturity, respectability, stability." Dylan had a 'been there' feeling.

"Forget for a moment that any immature, unstable, unrespectable person can reproduce," Rev said drily as she pulled out of the lot. "It's weird. The license says maturity, therefore kids. Most people think kids, therefore maturity."

"But," Dylan was still thinking, "having kids does say 'I'm putting someone else before myself'. Isn't that a sign of maturity?"

"Oh please. That 'someone else' is just an extension of the parent's ego. So they're really just putting themselves first. Kids are a great camouflage for selfishness. I can't tell you how often I saw some adult assume right of way for himself because she had kids with her. If they really wanted to put someone else before themselves, they'd help out in a soup line or sign up for CUSO."

"How can having kids say you're *not* selfish?" she wasn't done yet. "You're imposing another human being, your spawn, on the rest of us. Without our consent."

"Maybe it's the taking on of responsibility that makes becoming a parent the rite of passage to respect and maturity."

"So I should show up at NASA and take over the next launch? Think I'd be applauded? Congratulated? Would someone throw me a launch shower?"

"AND, BUT," REV SAID, once they had finished their errands and were on the highway heading back home—Dylan smiled at her tendency to just pick up a discussion, often days later—"if men *had* been the ones primarily responsible for parenting all this time, we'd already have mandatory parent education. Hell, in men were in charge of kids, there'd be Ph.D. programs in Parenting."

Dylan thought about it. "I think you're right. History shows that anything women do is automatically undervalued. Look at bank tellers."

"They're mostly women."

"Yes, but initially they were men. And the position was highly valued. After all, they were handling money. Then when women became tellers—"

"It miraculously turned into low-level clerical."

Dylan nodded.

"That would explain why men don't want women to become truck drivers."

"Or electricians, or plumbers, or CEOs, or philosophy professors—"

"So if men did the parenting, it would be a high-paying, high-status job."

It took a few more miles.

"Maybe that's the route we should have gone," Rev said. "We should have somehow made men the primary parent. Then all the standards of the licensing program would have been met. Voluntarily. Eventually," she added.

"It's a thought," Dylan said. "In Sweden, people who take parental leave get 80% of their income for the duration and their job is essentially held for them. And their children have access to subsidized preschool, and their grandparents get state-sponsored care."

"Wow."

"Even so, initially, most of the leave was taken by the mothers, not the fathers."

"The fathers' income was higher," Rev guessed at the reason.

"Exactly. So then they set aside two of the thirteen months specifically for fathers. It wasn't mandatory for men to take paternity leave, but the family lost a month of subsidies if he didn't."

"And?"

"Soon more than eight in ten men took leave."

"And? Did it increase the level of parenting? Did it make parents more competent?"

"Hard to say," Dylan confessed. "Because of the self-selection factor. But it's worth looking into, isn't it?"

"Unfortunately," she sighed. It was a very heavy sigh.

32

"Puppies!" Dylan cried out, seeing the sign at the side of the road. "Pull over, let's go see the puppies!"

"But—we've got Froot Loup—"

"I know, I just want to cuddle them. Puppies are pure joy. You *have* to cuddle them. It's a rule."

"Oh well then, far be it for me to break a rule," Rev muttered as she slowed, then turned into the driveway. Dylan didn't even wait for her to turn off the ignition. He leapt out of the car and practically ran to the low-fenced enclosure that held almost a dozen puppies. He carefully stepped inside, then just as carefully eased down onto the ground. In a second, he was covered in puppies, and grinning like an idiot.

A woman came out of the house. "Hello!"

"Hi," Rev said. "My friend wanted to stop and cuddle the puppies."

"So I see. Are you interested in adopting?" They walked over to the enclosure.

"I don't—"

"These aren't all from the same litter," Dylan said.

"No," the woman replied. "They're rescued pups from up north. I'm part of the Puppy Rescue Network. Have you heard of it?"

"No," Rev replied.

"Oh, you're just a sweet little snookums, aren't you, a liddle-widdle snookums," Dylan said to a pudgy black-and-white puppy stumbling over him.

"I don't think he has either," she answered for him, seeing as his brain had clearly gone off-line.

"There are several areas that have a real problem with unregulated dogs. There are packs of them wandering the streets, and they just keep reproducing."

""Why not spay or neuter them?"

"Can't catch most of them."

"Hm."

"In many places, they simply cull them twice a year."

"They shoot the ones who keep reproducing?" Rev was interested in the idea.

The woman looked at her with narrowed eyes. "They don't target in particular those who have puppies."

"What are you doing with my shoelace, you little fluffibuns ... "

"So there are a few people who try to rescue the puppies," the woman continued. "Whenever someone knows of a new litter—typically they hear mewling from someone's shed or under someone's porch—they go and get the puppies, take them inside, make sure they're looked after, and then when they're old enough to make the trip, they get them to people like me, a little further south, and we put them up for adoption. So if you were interested ... "

"I'm afraid we've already got—"

"Are you a little sweetheart?" One of the puppies was licking Dylan's face. "You are? Are you sure? A little sweetheart?"

"A house visit is required, of course. We make sure the adopting family knows how to care for dogs, knows what's involved. I went to one house once, and my god the place was a dump. Garbage all over the place, bust open bags, chicken bones! I saw chicken bones! Empty cases of beer stacked beside the garage. A thick chain, just a few feet long, attached to a post. I refused to give them a pup. Couldn't get away from that place quickly enough. Oh, and you'd have to sign a form agreeing to spay or neuter the dog."

" ... a little baby belly, yes, you've got a little baby belly too, all squishysoft ... "

"Another time, I did a visit to an elderly person in an apartment. Who insisted he adopt one of the German Shepherd pups. There was no way he could give it the exercise it required. I met a large dog once who'd been raised in an apartment. First time the dog went for a walk in the forest, he actually stopped at a fallen tree across its path and whimpered. He couldn't jump over it. He hadn't developed the coordination and physical confidence to negotiate his way— having spent his entire life to that point in a small apartment with barely enough room to turn around ... "

"So is it working?" Rev asked. "The Rescue Network?"

"Yes," she replied. "It's taking time, but yes. There are fewer packs roaming around full of often sick and injured dogs. And fewer culls."

"Many of these will grow up to be little dogs," the woman continued.

"Liddle widdle eensy teensy dogs ... "

"We should be able to place all of them, I think. It's really difficult to get a small mutt. Look in any newspaper for a puppy and all you'll see is labs, huskies, shepherds, rotties, and then poms, shih tzus, and chihuahuas."

"That's interesting," Rev said. "Why is that?"

"Well, I think it's because it's mostly the owners of small breeds that spay and neuter their dogs. They're the ones acting responsibly. It's always the big dogs you see on the short chains, or in the too-small pens, or—the guy who's most likely to want a Rottweiler is the guy who no way is going to get him neutered."

"And this little piggy went to the market," Dylan was playing little piggy with one of the puppies' paws.

"Are you sure you don't want to adopt?"

W hat the—"

Her mailbox was bashed in. As were the three other boxes beside hers. She stepped up to take a closer look.

"The Turners have been at it again."

Dylan looked at her quizzically. Loup waited patiently, hidden in the bush.

"Every now and then, they get drunk and drive around in the middle of the night with a baseball bat and bash everyone's mailbox."

"Why in—" he shook his head in total incomprehension.

"Let's go." Instead of turning back to the cabin, she headed further down the road.

"Where?"

"To their house. This mailbox cost me $50. Plus shipping. Another $30. Plus the time it'll take me to get this one off its post and put the other one on. Which will be five hours. So let's say $250."

"Five hours?" he strode along beside her. Loup trotted along beside him.

"Yes. Because first I'm going to have to go back and get my screwdriver and my new mailbox, three weeks from now, when it arrives, and then walk back out here. Then I'll realize that when I stained the post, I got some stain in the screws, so I won't be able to unscrew them. The holes will be full of gunk. So I'll have to walk all way back to my cabin and get a hammer and prybar. Then walk back out again.

"Then by the time I get the damn thing off with my hammer and prybar, I'll have buggered the holes so much, I'll have to replace the piece of wood the mailbox sits on. So then I'll have to walk back to my shed, and it'll take me a good fifteen minutes to go through my leftover wood bits to realize that the bits I have that are the right thickness aren't long enough or wide enough, and the ones I have that are long enough and wide enough are too thin. So then I'll have to drive out to the highway, to the lumber store, to get a new piece of wood. That'll take over an hour. Half an hour each way, and at least fifteen minutes at the lumber store. Then when I get back, I have to saw the 8 foot piece I bought to the right length.

"Then when I walk back to my mailbox, I'll realize that they gave me the wrong thickness. Because they weren't listening. After all, I probably just want it for some artsy craftsy thing, maybe I'm going to embroider 'Home, Sweet Home' on it and hang it in the bathroom, so really, any thickness will do. So then I'm going to have to drive back.

"This trip will take close to two hours because I'll have to argue that I should get a refund even though the piece of wood I'm returning is already cut. But of course no one heard me tell the guy what thickness I want, because, like the guy I was talking to, no one was listening to me. So I lose the argument. And make a note that next time I should write the measurements on a piece of paper and make a copy. So then I come back, cut the second piece of wood to the right length, and go back out to my mailbox.

"Then I realize I've got a Phillips screwdriver and Robertson screws. So then I have to walk back to the cabin to get my Robertson screwdriver.

"You've done this before." Dylan noted.

By this time, they were at the Turners' house. Rev knocked on the door. Dylan covertly gestured to Loup, camouflaged among the trees and scruffy bush beyond the driveway, to sit. She did. Dylan smiled.

"So plus the gas and the wood and taxes ... " Rev was muttering to herself.

After a long time, one of the Turner boys answered it.

"Pay up, Justin. $400 to replace my mailbox."

"What?"

"My mailbox."

"Oh that," he shrugged, grinning with what he no doubt thought was charm. "We got drunk last night."

"Yeah. And stupid, immature, inconsiderate, irresponsible, and violent. That's rather my point. What's yours?"

"We were drunk," he repeated. Without the grin this time.

"I got that. So?"

Dylan was enjoying himself.

"Now it's time to pay up. For your behaviour while drunk. For your choice to get drunk."

"Hey, I have the right to do whatever I fucking want!" he was starting to get with the program.

"And who told you that?"

He started to close the door.

"$400, Justin, pay up." Rev had put her foot in the door.

"I don't have $400."

"Hm. What to do," she looked around, feigning thought. "I know! I'll take your bike instead. That'll cover it."

And before he understood her—before he believed her—she'd walked over to his Honda 100XR dirt bike, straddled it, flipped up the stand, kicked it to life, and drove out of the driveway.

"Cheers, mate!" Dylan said, and strolled after her, Loup silently escorting him.

WHEN DYLAN GOT BACK, Rev was in the porch. He joined her.

"The way you were talking about them, I was picturing them seventeen, eighteen. Justin was in his thirties."

"Yup."

"And he's home this time of day, midweek? I mean, what does he do? For a living?"

"I don't think he has a job," she said.

"So how does he afford all the gas—he's the one that zooms around all the time, right? Annoying the hell out of everyone who lies here?"

She nodded.

"So how does he pay for all that gas?"

"Well, I guess you and I pay for it. Unemployment, welfare, disability."

"He's disabled?"

"One story is that he's actually mentally delayed."

Dylan snorted.

"The other is he hurt his back at work. Probably showed up drunk."

"So his back's too messed up for any job. But it's up to dirtbiking all day."

"Apparently."

I didn't know you had a tv." Dylan plopped himself down beside Rev on the couch in the basement rec room. He had the makings of a joint in his hand.

"Well, I don't watch it much. For obvious reasons. Good idea," she nodded at his hand.

"So whatcha watchin' now?" He saw then why he hadn't known about it. It was in a closet, which she'd opened. He'd always assumed there was other stuff in that closet. And there was, he saw now. As he rolled a joint.

"You also have snowshoes. And cross-country skis." He nodded to the open closet.

"Yeah. Tried 'em both when it became clear I couldn't run any-more through the deep snow—" she had half her mind on what she was watching.

"You used to run in the deep snow?"

"Best workout ever."

"But ... "

"But it's hard on the knees. Turns out so is snowshoeing and cross-country skiing."

"Kayaking's easy. On the knees. Because you don't use them to paddle." He giggled, clearly imagining just that.

"It is," she reached out to accept the offered joint.

"Biking's not." He and Loup had spent the afternoon in the forest.

"It is. Not."

He pondered whether that meant she was agreeing or disagreeing with him.

"So, back to my initial question—" Dylan had clearly forgotten what his initial question was.

"*Alphas*. It's new. Thought I'd check it out. It's about smart people."

"And it's on tv?" Dylan was incredulous.

"'Marcus can see twenty moves ahead,'" one of the characters was saying, "'and doesn't understand why others can't. So when what they do harms him, he believes it's intentional.'"

"Yes!" Rev shouted.

Dylan turned to look at her.

"I too—and many, many others, it's not an alpha trait—or maybe it is—maybe I'm an alpha!" She waved the joint. "Because I can think ahead too! I can imagine the likely effect on others of my actions, and I work through the ethics of my behaviour. So when what someone else does affects me, I can only assume that either they don't care about others, and so haven't bothered to think ahead about the effects of their actions or work through the ethics of their behaviour, or they do, and have, and consider what they've done to be morally acceptable. Or I must assume that, unlike me, they can't imagine the effects of their actions or they don't comprehend the ethics of their behavior."

She'd lost Dylan at 'can think'.

"Which means, in short, that either they're inconsiderate, egoistic, irresponsible, lazy assholes or they're idiots.

"And so when I point out that what they're doing does affect me, invariably they respond with aggressive defensiveness. Because, of course, I'm implying they're either assholes or idiots!"

A few moments later, when she'd exhaled, she added, "Pity they don't just apologize for their thoughtlessness and ask me to help them work through the ethics of their behavior."

A SHORT WHILE LATER, when *Alphas* was over, Dylan reached for the remote and flipped through a few channels, stopping at what was possibly a rerun of *Queer as Folk* since the scene was a drag queen show.

"You know, I've never understood drag queens," Rev said. "Why would you emulate the very worst of what it means in our culture to be female? Why would you voluntarily spend hours putting on make-up, and doing stuff to your hair, and then torturing your body by wearing high heels and girdles. And over-emoting about trivial things ...

"And I hate drag queen *shows* even more," she said. "They're saying 'Let's be entertained by idiot women who accept these constrictions, this superficial way of living ... '.

"What would men think of drag king shows?" she looked at Dylan. Somewhat incredibly, for an answer. "What would their response be to a parade of women making fun of *them*? Of the *worst* of them? Walking around a stage in pants down past their cracks, baseball caps on backwards, taking big steps from side to side, suggesting their package is so very huge, grabbing it every now and then—why do they do that?" She spat on the floor.

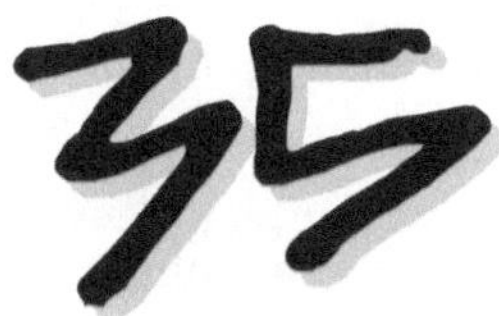

35

"Tell me again why we thought the egg bank break-in had something to do with the new legislation?" Rev said the next morning.

"Because the legislation says, essentially, that the state can say who can and cannot have children. And squirting your stuff all over a bunch of petri dishes full of eggs says 'Nuh-uh!'"

"Hm."

"Are you thinking it *doesn't* have to do with the new legislation?"

"Well none of my leads are leading anywhere. Which, come to think of it, makes them not-leads." She was still a bit stoned. So that intrigued her for a while before she found her way back. "None of the people or groups we thought might have motive didn't. Do."

"So … " Dylan was no help at all. Apparently he'd used up the day's lucidity with his opening explanation.

"So it might, but only indirectly. Maybe the crime is fallout from the rise of other coparenting arrangements, as allowed by the new legislation. Combined with the decrease over the years of the number of women getting married."

Dylan didn't follow.

"If men are less apt to become married, and less apt to be coparents, but are still wanting to replicate—"

"But parenting and replication are separate."

"Tell that to all the guys at the mall."

"Oh yeah."

"So ... " he prompted a while later. He needed Rev to connect the dots for him. Pretty little polka dots, he imagined.

"So I was thinking that our original thought was right. That it was the action of someone's estranged husband, someone's beloved but stymied self-replicator."

"So ... "

"So I'm going to go to the egg bank to find out whose eggs beside Susie's were squirted on. Tomorrow," she added.

That afternoon, Dylan called out to Rev from inside the cabin, "I'm going into the bush with Loup."

"It's the weekend," she called back.

"And … ?" He stepped into the porch, helmet in hand.

"The ATVs and dirt bikes will be out in full force, using the trails as a racetrack. You can hear them from miles away, so you'll have time to get out of the way, but I wonder if we should encourage Loup to stay off the trails altogether when she hears engine noise."

"Good point." Dylan took his helmet off. Loup looked disappointed.

"But they have—didn't you say there was a snowmobile club trail near here?"

"Yeah."

"Couldn't they just use that?"

"Yeah."

He sat down and opened his laptop. A few minutes later, he said, ""You'd think 279,000 miles would be enough."

"Apparently they need more."

He stared at her, surprised at her apparent resignation.

She sighed. "I wrote to my MP, my MPP, the snowmobile club, and MNR, asking for signs to be put where the snowmobile trail intersected any other trail, especially the main trail we all—we all used to—walk on, indicating that said other trails were *not* part of the club trail system."

"And?"

"I was told that everyone had a right to use crown land trails. I wrote back and said that that wasn't strictly true since the forementioned 279,000 miles of appropriated crown land have signs saying 'Permit Holders Only'."

"And what did they say to that?"

"I'm still waiting for a reply."

Dylan's brow furrowed. Was this the boat request thing all over again?

"So then I asked whether signs could be put up at least reminding drivers that they were at that point going onto a multi-use trail, please exercise extreme caution, and slow down for pedestrians, skiers, snowshoers, cyclists, etc."

"And?"

"They agreed, but said I'd have to pay for the signs."

"You'd have to pay for signs to be put on crown land. Signs urging safety."

"Yup. $200 each."

37

The egg bank was in a tall building a block from the hospital. Just as the elevator began its ascent, a nicely-dressed man squeezed in. He nodded to Dylan, then glanced at Rev.

"And why aren't you smiling today?" he asked her, cheerfully.

She glared at him. "Because I'm thinking."

"Go ahead," Dylan said. Prodded actually, though with seeming casualness. "Ask her what she's thinking."

FIVE MINUTES LATER, THEY were back in the elevator, going down.

"I can't believe I actually thought they'd release the names to me," Rev said.

"And I can't believe you said their intent to install better locks was like implementing chastity belts."

THEY DECIDED TO WALK to the hospital. When Dylan had called one of the local gynaecologists, Dr. Temmers, she was so happy to have received his call that she went ahead and set up a meeting for him with several people in the field.

They made the mistake of entering through Emerg.

Rev looked at the line-up: three kids with runny noses and not a Kleenex in sight, two drunks with what could only be called injuries due to intoxication, and one skydiver. Ex-skydiver.

"See that's what I'm talking about ... " she said, wondering whether there was less stupid behaviour in countries without a government healthcare plan.

Dylan herded her toward the directory on the wall, and then to the nearest staircase, passing, of course, the elevator, at which stood ten people needing to go up one floor. They walked up to the fifth floor, and found the East Wing Meeting Room.

"Referral from your family doctor, please," a harried, tired woman at the reception desk called out when she saw them.

"I don't have a family doctor. I don't have a family," she added, by way of explanation, "so why should I have a family doctor? I have a personal physician."

"We're here for a meeting," Dylan explained, pulling Rev down the hall to Room 516.

"Dylan O'Toole?" one of them asked as they appeared in the doorway.

"Yes," he replied.

"Hi, come in," she said, gesturing to the two empty chairs.

"I'm Dr. Temmers, we spoke on the phone," she said, then introduced the other three people sitting around the large table, chatting amiably. He introduced Rev, and they sat down. They waited politely while he set his mini recorder on the table, in the middle, and pulled out his pen and notepad.

"So what do you think of the new legislation, the part that addresses the biological parenting?" He started the interview.

"We couldn't be happier with it," Dr. Temmers said. "At first they were defining parenthood as starting from the moment of birth. So we lobbied hard—"

"'We' meaning—?"

"The entire medical community. We're the ones who understand how critical the prenatal period is. A woman who takes drugs while she's pregnant is actually giving them to the developing fetus."

"And not just the prenatal period," a woman in a white lab coat spoke up. "I'm Dr. Verish," she introduced herself again, suspecting quite rightly that Temmers' introduction hadn't stuck. "V-E-R-I-S-H," she said to Dylan, who made a note. "I'm in NRT. Along with Dr. Cedare, C-E-D-A-R-E" she nodded to the fourth woman, on her right, "geneticist."

"And NRT stands for ... " Dylan felt stupid. Not for the first time in his life.

"New Reproductive Technology. So-called artificial insemination, fertility treatments, that sort of thing."

"'So-called' because ... ?" Rev hadn't missed that.

"Because the line between natural and artificial is arbitrary. And it's in the way of advancement. Sexual intercourse is, should be, so yesterday," she said.

"And your comment about 'not just the prenatal period' means that ... " Dylan said.

"It means that drugs, for example, also affect the quality of the ova. And sperm. Let's not put the blame totally on the woman. Yes, she's solely responsible for the uterine environment, but drug-using men aren't *required* to impregnate a woman. And non-drug-using men aren't required to impregnate drug-using women. They make a choice. They're equally responsible."

"So ... "

"Garbage in, garbage out," Dr. Verish said. Succinctly.

"So you don't think mandatory genetic screening is going too far?"

"No," Dr. Temmers said, "it's not going far enough! The uterine environment can be affected by drug use, yes, but it can also be affected by diet. Food is, after all, just drug delivery."

Dylan looked confused. Rev looked intrigued.

"If we expand the definition of drugs to include all chemicals— and that's what proteins and vitamins are, essentially."

"Even water—" someone else interjected. "Dr. Ellitts," she said, then spelled it for Dylan. "I specialize in prenatal surgery."

"And exposure to various substances, that has an effect as well, of course," Dr. Temmers continued, "and exercise, which transforms chemicals from one form into another—"

"Or not—"

"Detrimental effects can result in pain, injury, and illness. In short, all of these things seriously affect the person's nature, and their quality of life. So there should be more rules, rules about what the pregnant woman can and cannot—must and must not—eat, drink, do—"

"But it's her body," Rev said.

Dr. Temmers nodded. "And if she wanted to keep full control over it, she shouldn't have started growing another body inside of her body."

Rev thought about that for a moment, then conceded with a nod. "Fair enough."

"Think of it this way," Dr. Verish spoke up. "If we had artificial wombs—and we should by now, there's no reason we couldn't, except that instead we funded sending a man to the moon in a penis-rocket—"

"—and we funded Viagra—"

"Right. And Cialis. And Levitra. One wasn't enough. If we had artificial wombs," she continued, "what do you think we'd do if someone sprinkled a bit of cocaine into it, which messes up their neurological development? We'd arrest the guy. Charge him with assault causing grievous bodily harm or some such.

"Same goes if he poured some in some caffeine, which would reduce the amount of iron and calcium the fetus got. Or suppose he did *not* pour in some vitamin B12, for example, which the body uses to process and repair DNA strands.

"A horticulturalist pays a lot of attention to growing the very best. He develops and refines the additives, monitors the plants very carefully, adds another drop of this or that to the soil, prunes back the leaves just another centimetre, increases the humidity in the greenhouse just a bit, and on and on, to grow the best rose, for example, the one with the most vibrant color, the healthiest petals, the highest proportion of petal to leaf, or what have you, I don't know exactly.

"And yet many pregnant women by and large continue to eat and drink and behave as they did prior to being pregnant. Which, look around, is awful. We are overweight and unfit. Canadians in their twenties and thirties are pathetic compared to Swedes in their fifties.

"Being pregnant should be like training for a marathon. For the months up to the race, you watch what you eat and drink, you figure out the perfect mix of carbs and sugars and proteins and you stick to it, you figure out the perfect training schedule, how many miles how many times a week, how much and what kind of weight training, and so on."

"And now," Dr. Temmers said, almost triumphantly, "there is absolutely no need to shrug and accept that she's doing the best she can. Now, with the vaccine, pregnancy is fully chosen, so we are justified in expecting, demanding, the very best."

"If men were the ones to be pregnant," Dr. Ellitts spoke up, "you can bet every one of them would have a team of specialists. They'd have their own nutritionist, massage therapist, trainer. Just like our professional football players."

"You got that right," Rev said.

"What about the concern that mandatory genetic testing will lead to an increase in abortions?" Dylan asked, "Of fetuses deemed substandard?"

"I think most of us would object to the word 'substandard'," Dr. Temmers replied, "but we would not object to that increase in abortion. In fact, many of us in the medical community believe infanticide is not altogether a bad idea. Obstetricians deliver many babies that, frankly, we hope don't make it past the first hour." She looked nervously at the mini-recorder.

"I can make that anonymous," Dylan said.

"Thank you," Dr. Temmers said, then finished her thought. "But we're obliged to go to extreme measures to see that it does make it, rather than just let—and I hate to put it this way—let nature take its course."

"But there's a lot to be said for putting it that way," Dr. Ellitts said. "I know why you object—it sounds like you're saying nature has the right of way, that we shouldn't interfere with nature. Which sounds uncomfortably close to endorsing some sort of divine law. But miscarriage often occurs because something's not going right, and if it didn't occur, the organism would be so disabled it would not survive. It's only our extreme measures, typically involving multiple surgeries during infancy, which is very difficult, for everyone, and then lifelong assistance, that make such disabled human organisms survive. But I think our goal, as humans, should be more than mere survival."

"So you'd support a sort of advance directive for birth, like we have now for death? No heroic measures—"

"Yes! I hadn't actually considered it that way, but yes, that would be a very good thing. Hopefully, however, with the new legislation mandating prenatal screening, we'll catch those cases now in utero."

"What we're talking about has been standard from the beginning for those requesting NRT assistance," Dr. Verish said. "All potential donors must complete a questionnaire providing information about their health and the health of their first-degree relatives. Any indication of serious genetic anomalies or other high-risk factors disqualifies a potential donor from participating in the program. Tests for HIV and other infectious diseases are also done."

"So when a woman becomes pregnant with the assistance of, essentially, the state, she gets premium sperm" Rev said. "But otherwise—"

"She could always ask her husband to ... " Dylan trailed off.

"There is no doubt that the effects on the mother—the inconvenience of changing her lifestyle—are far less severe than the effects on the child who is to be born," Dr. Temmers said.

"And don't forget that for her, it's temporary. Nine months. For the child-to-be, it's permanent," Dr. Ellitts added.

"Perhaps this makes that clear." Dr. Temmers slid a sheet over toward Dylan and Rev. It contained a few photographs, accompanied by a paragraph of text. They looked at it. The photographs were horrific. The text was equally so: "The use of certain drugs during pregnancy, both illegal and legal, can cause, in the newborn, excruciating pain, vomiting, inability to sleep, reluctance to feed, diarrhea leading to shock and death, severe anemia, growth retardation, mental retardation, central nervous system abnormalities, and malformations of the kidneys, intestines, head and spinal cord." Dylan made a note of one of the citations, a book by Deborah Mathieu called *Preventing Prenatal Harm: Should the State Intervene?*

"But what you're doing, what the legislation mandates, is just correction, right? Just the withholding or removal of defects, not enhancement."

"Yes," Dr. Cedare finally spoke. Pity," she added. Then explained. "We could use a little more intelligence, no?"

"No," Rev replied. "History's full of brilliant people screwing the rest of us." She looked to Dylan for confirmation and received it. "What we need is more thinking, about the big picture, the picture that goes beyond the here and now and the me. Is there a gene for that?"

W hen they got home, Loup wasn't there. They weren't completely worried, since she had started taking off on her own at dusk for a bit, but it made them realize that she was growing up.

SO THE NEXT DAY, they went back into town for a crate and a leash, and the day after that, they drove to the wolf sanctuary just outside Timmins. Well, actually, the day after the day after that, they drove to the wolf sanctuary just outside Timmins. It took much of the day to get Loup into the crate. They ended up putting not only the red blanket and her shoe and her moose leg inside—which had Dylan teary-eyed—but also covering the cage with the blanket from her den. They decided to leave the blanket on once they'd lifted the crate, Loup inside, into the car. Dylan had read somewhere that that made car travel easier for many dogs.

They didn't talk much during the drive. They just listened to Brian Eno's "Ambient" which Dylan had burned onto a CD specifically for the drive. He'd remembered it had a particularly soothing effect on Bob.

As they approached the sanctuary, a 15-acre enclosure, Dylan started to change his mind. Not that his mind was made up in the first place.

"I don't think I can do this," he said. "I don't think I can leave her—and just walk away."

"But she needs a pack. She'll be happier."

"We don't know that."

"No, we don't." Rev's mind hadn't been made up either. On the one hand, Loup hadn't flung a dead animal at them every time she came back from being out-and-about at dusk. On the other hand, Loup hadn't flung a dead animal at them every time she came back from being out-and- about at dusk.

"Maybe we can just see," Dylan suggested. "Maybe we can just leave her here for a couple hours, tell her we'll be back, and see how it goes. Ask what happened while we were gone. Whether she sat in the corner and cried or romped non-stop with the other wolves."

"That's a good idea."

"And then if she likes it, maybe we can treat it like a summer camp. Bring her here every now and then for a couple weeks, so she can play and have a good time, but—"

"I'm not sure they'd—"

"—her home would be still be our place. She'd always come back—home."

They'd reached the parking lot. It was just a large, open expanse of dirt, with a barn-like building in the corner, and chain link fencing visible along the edge of forest.

"But she might get shot or trapped out in the forest at our place," Rev said. "Here she's safe."

"And fenced!"

They got out, and Rev opened the back hatch.

"Hey, Froot Loup, that wasn't so bad, was it?" Dylan crooned to her as he took the blanket off. They'd already put her harness on, back at the house, and he stood there with the leash, talking to her, making sure she was calm before he opened the crate, reached in, and hooked it onto her.

She stepped out of the crate and jumped down out of the car. She looked around curiously. Then her nose twitched, and she turned into the breeze. Her ears twitched. Suddenly a howl rose from the distance.

Dylan reflexively turned to where it had come from, but then turned back to look at Loup, expecting, and not quite wanting, to see eagerness on her face. At the same time, Loup looked up at Dylan, as if for—an explanation, permission? Another howl joined with the first one. Loup leaned against Dylan's legs. Then very slowly she lay down, almost cringing. Her ears were back, flat against her head. They both saw that.

"We've got the screen thing all figured out," Rev said. "Be sad to waste that accomplishment."

Dylan grinned.

"And she knows about snare traps."

"She does, yes," Dylan reached down and started petting her. "We can build a fenced enclosure for during hunting seasons. Can't we?"

A man had come out of the nearby barn and was walking toward them as quickly as his limp allowed. He was a burly man, wearing a flannel shirt and worn jeans. He looked at them, and at Loup.

You brought a wolf here?" he asked, angrily.

"Yes, we thought—this is a wolf sanctuary, isn't it? We thought—Loup needs—"

They both felt stupid. They should have called. What were they thinking?

"Wolves are pack animals."

"Yes, that's why—"

"They form packs *with their own*. All the wolves here—they're all siblings and offspring of the original pair, Tracks and Hen."

"Oh."

So stupid.

"That howl you heard? That was a warning for members of other packs to stay away."

"Oh."

So very stupid.

He scratched his head. "Why don't you put her back in your car, then come into the barn. We'll talk."

Loup went eagerly back into the cage, back into their car. They both saw that, too.

"I'll be back," Dylan told her, smiling broadly. "Good Loup, I'll be back."

ONCE INSIDE THE BARN, the man gestured to some bales of hay, then lowered himself slowly onto the only chair.

"I blew out my knee playing football," he explained, as if he'd been injured in the line of duty rather than in a line of scrimmage.

They just nodded, then told the man Loup's story.

"So," Rev said, seeing that in the course of telling Loup's story, Dylan had turned into a pile of regret and apology, "we know wolves are pack animals and we were thinking it's cruel not to let her join a pack. So we brought her here," she finished lamely.

"Wolf packs rarely adopt a wolf. Usually they kill it."

So very incredibly stupid. A mushy pile of regret and apology. Guess who was going to get an entire MeatLovers' pizza tonight, she thought.

"Some wolves are solitary," the man said. "It's not unheard of. If she has a large enough territory, with sufficient prey, she may not feel a need to be part of a pack. It sounds like the land around your cabin might suffice. It wouldn't be anyone else's territory. Plus she's getting kibble at your place."

"Yeah, should we stop that?" Rev asked. Not mentioning the Meat-lovers' pizza.

"Well, if you do, then she'll have motivation to hunt further. Which increases the risk of her coming across competition. And since it won't be someone from her own pack, since she doesn't have a pack ... " It sounded like he thought they shouldn't've rescued her in the first place. But it wasn't exactly their idea, Rev remembered. Loup trotted after Dylan on her own accord. What was he supposed to do?

"What about a mate though? I mean, are we depriving her— should we get her spayed?"

"I hate to suggest anything that'll reduce the wolf population even further, but in this case, that might be a good idea. The onset of sexual maturity is another trigger for dispersal. Leaving the birth pack."

And getting killed, Dylan thought.

"And when does that happen?" Rev asked.

"Somewhere between one and three years of age."

The man thought a bit.

"Have you tried taking her back to where you found her. If that's part of her pack's territory, it's possible she'd recognize scent markings. Or someone in the area might recognize her. As kin. As part of the pack."

"Would they accept her now that she has human scent all over her?" Rev asked.

And cherry cheesecake scent, Dylan thought.

The man shrugged.

"If she'd had any siblings," Rev tried again, "wouldn't they have been with her at the time?"

"Yeah, probably," the man said.

"What about dad?" Dylan asked. "Would he care?"

"The whole pack should care! So I'm thinking maybe—" he couldn't bring himself to say her full name— "maybe Loup's mom was a lone wolf herself."

39

What was that all about?" Rev had slammed down the phone just as Dylan entered the kitchen the next morning.

"Guy up the river a bit. He's got early Alzheimer's and gets dizzy. He's looking for a babysitter. Someone to cook and clean for him. So he doesn't have to move into a home."

"And he called you?" Dylan said with disbelief. As far as he knew, she had no babysitting experience. And absolutely no aptitude whatsoever for—any of that.

"I'm a middle-aged woman," she said in a dangerously flat voice. "By definition, that's what we are, that's what we do, that's what we're for, don't you know that?" She was seriously pissed off.

"But doesn't he know—I mean, you used to be a philosophy professor. You write for the LSAT. Didn't you turn down a job in Princeton writing for the GRE?"

"Yeah, but he doesn't know that."

"How can your neighbours not know that? You've lived here for what, almost fifteen years?"

"Because I don't go around announcing it and—"

"And they never ask. Because they never suspect. Because, after all, you're just a middle-aged woman. They just assume you're—got it. Bloody hell."

DYLAN ADDED A PIECE of the Chocolate Eruption cheesecake they'd bought on the way back from Timmins to her breakfast plate, which already had on it the requisite piece of cold pizza, and poured their coffee.

The phone rang again.

"What, did he forget he just called?" Dylan asked. Then giggled. Rev smiled, her anger gone in a poof. She hoped Dylan never went to Argentina.

"For you," Rev said, a moment after she answered it, and handed Dylan the phone.

"Hello?"

"Hello, are you Dylan O'Toole? You're writing an article on the new parent licensing legislation?"

"I am, yes, and I am, yes."

"I'm Yvonne Dennison. Dr. Verish suggested I call you. I'm a surrogate. She's my doctor. For the surrogacy."

"I see. Of course," he said then, realizing that surrogates would use NRT services. "And ... "

"She thought you might want to know a bit about what surrogates typically have to go through."

"Oh—yes, I would, thanks for calling," Dylan started miming writing on a notepad. Rev looked at him like he'd gone insane. As did Loup. Who helpfully took her shoe to him. His shoe, technically. The other one. Since the first one was now just a memory of leather and lace. And yes, Loup was in the kitchen.

"Could you hold on a minute while I get a pen and my notepad?"

"Okay."

"Remind me never to play charades with you!" Dylan said to Rev, as he went into the porch to get his pen and notepad.

"Yeah, like that would ever happen."

He grinned.

"Why don't you put her on speaker phone? That way you can have both hands free. For making notes."

"Good idea." He picked up the receiver. "Hi, Yvonne? Can I put you on speakerphone?"

"Okay."

Dylan proceeded to disconnect the call. He stared at the phone, which was emitting a dial tone.

"So that wasn't how you did it before," Rev pointed out.

"It wasn't, no."

"I think you needed to press the speaker phone button *before* you hung up."

"You think?"

The phone rang again.

"Yvonne? Sorry about that. Let me try again." Dylan pressed the speaker phone button then put the receiver back into its cradle. "Yvonne, are you still there?"

"Yes."

"Okay, go ahead. What was the process for becoming a surrogate?"

"I had to have a medical exam, of course, and genetic screening, but what kind of surprised me was the psychological evaluation. They wanted me to be sure I knew what I was in for.

"Plus, I had to sign a contract, saying I wouldn't smoke, or drink, or use drugs, or do anything 'deemed to be dangerous to the well-being of the unborn child'. That would have been a breach of contract. There are a lot of attachments about the risks of pregnancy that I had to read and sign. And I had to keep all my appointments—medical, psychological, counselling. And do anything else 'deemed necessary'."

"Could you possibly send me a copy of the contract? It would be helpful, I think."

"Okay," she replied.

"Where do we live?" Dylan turned away from the speaker to ask Rev. He'd entered the address once into the Ebay system then forgotten it.

"R. R. #2," Rev said into the speaker, adding the postal code.

"You've got that?" Dylan asked, took her phone number in case he had to call back, then ended the call.

"'Anything else deemed necessary'," Rev repeated. "That's a lawsuit waiting to happen."

"HEY, LISTEN TO THIS," Dylan said after they settled in the porch to work, Loup's blanket, shoe, and moose leg back in her corner, along with a newly empty pizza box she was currently tearing apart, "Dr. Verish sent me an email. An addendum. I think I was supposed to see this before Yvonne's call."

Rev looked up from the LSAT question she was working on.

"'Something else you should know,'" Dylan read aloud, "'is that when someone comes to us, essentially asking for assistance to become a parent, she has to sign a statement indicating that she has received, read, and understood not only information outlining the risks, responsibilities, and implications of donor insemination, but also the sperm screening and medical test results.'"

"Would that women were required to provide such informed consent for 'unassisted' reproduction," Rev observed.

"'The Royal Commission also recommends that counselling be provided,'" Dylan continued, "'addressing information about alternatives such as living without children, exploration questions related to values and goals that patients may wish to take into account when making their decisions.'"

"Again, we should be requiring that of reproducing-by-intercourse parents as well."

"So until now," Dylan summarized, "children born as a result of assisted insemination or *in vitro* fertilization have been privileged to a higher standard of care in their creation than children born as a result of coitus."

"Nicely put. Is that in your article?"

Dylan was tapping away.

"I wonder if that's been targeted by the disability lobby," Rev said.

"How so? I mean, why so? I mean, what exactly?"

"The notion that we have the right to reproduce as we see fit only if we can do it on our own. If we need medical assistance—"

"But those seeking *in vitro* fertilization aren't disabled," Dylan said.

"No, I guess not. Nor are those seeking fertility treatments. But they could be. I mean, it's all a matter of definition, isn't it."

"So is the double standard justified because those seeking assistance are using societal resources?" Dylan tried again. "The regulations are in place to see that such resources are not misused?"

"But people reproducing on their own are also using societal resources. Most notably the healthcare system. We're *all* using societal resources. Roads, schools—"

"So the double standard has, has had, no justification whatsoever?" Dylan tentatively concluded.

"You could put it this way," Rev said a minute later. "Prior to the legislation, to *not* have a double standard, the IVF people would've had to go ahead with people with diseases and disabilities of all kinds. Helped them create, and pass everything on to, new human beings. And people who object to the legislation couldn't object to that."

Dylan tapped away.

Rev returned to her work.

"Oh, this is interesting," he said a moment later, "I have to use this somehow."

She waited.

"'Furthermore,'" he resumed reading Dr. Verish's message, "'all NRT clinics must be licensed. That is, a license is required to perform insemination at any site other than the vagina, even if the recipient is the social partner.'"

"Whereas," Rev articulated the point Dr. Verish was leading them to, "when the vagina is the site, it's 'anything goes'."

"Until now."

THEY SPENT THE REST of the day in a leisurely fashion, recovering from the previous day's ordeal. After they did a bit of work (a very little bit), they puttered around, then went for a walk, (a very short walk since it was the weekend), then, since it was already evening (admittedly irrelevant), they rolled a joint and watched a scifi movie.

A few minutes in, Rev snorted. "Right. The aliens want to meet with them, and they're sending a bunch of men. Women are the ones with superior linguistic skills. They're the writers and translators. Women are the ones who always want to dig deeper with 'But what did you really mean?' Men run as fast as they can from any psychological investigation. Women are the ones with extensive mediation experience. Marriage used to be all about alliances between tribes and the kids run to Mom to settle disputes. And speaking of disputes, women prefer a win-win outcome. Men love a win-lose outcome. So *women* are the ones who should be on the first contact team. *They* should be our diplomats."

"Like you have any diplomacy," Dylan snorted, handing her the joint.

"Men have the weapons," he said a few seconds later, exhaling.

"They will be but slingshots," she replied, and inhaled.

TWO HOURS LATER, THEY were watching a tiddlywinks game. On the Twiddlywinks Channel. It was the eighth-finals.

Two men sat at a table, several tiddlywinks in front of each of them, but their attention was on the little pot in the middle. They were not smiling. They were concentrating.

"Hey, I used to—"

"Shh!" Rev hissed. "This is *important!*"

Definitely stoned, Dylan thought.

The people in the bleachers surrounding the table on all four sides clearly agreed. They were absolutely quiet. Respectful. The player in the red uniform focused, thinking very hard about his next move.

"The squidger!" Rev shouted to him helpfully. "You have to pick up the squidger!

"Squidger," Dylan said, then giggled. "Squidger." He giggled again.

After a few more very long tension-filled moments, the player picked up his squidger. Rev and Dylan cheered.

"Okay, now flip your wink into the pot!" Rev said encouragingly.

The player studied the table, concentrating.

"The pot's in the center of the table," Rev shouted.

Just as he was about to flip his wink, he stopped. Silence.

He pulled a squidger cloth from his pocket and cleaned the squidger.

Then he studied the table again, leaning to the left and to the right. Then he got up from his chair and took another look at the table.

"He's gotta be careful not to go offside," the commentator whispered.

"He does," the other commentator agreed, "but he's gotta take a good reading of the distance and angle of orientation involved in this next shot. He might not get another one."

Rev didn't care. She'd fallen asleep.

Satisfied, the player returned to his seat, and stared at the pile of blue and red winks in front of him. A pile of green and yellow winks sat in front of the player in the yellow uniform.

"For our viewers, Jim," the commentator whispered, "does it make any difference which wink he chooses? They are, of course, all the same size, but they are different colours."

"Well, Joe, that's a really good question. Different players will give you different responses. As will their coaches."

Everyone was quiet as the player made his shot. A groan rose from the crowd as the wink fell short of the pot, followed by several cheers.

"Let's watch the replay of that shot, Jim."

The shot was replayed. In slow motion.

"Oh, see that? It fell short."

"Yeah, that's a shame."

The shot was replayed again, this time from a different angle.

"Yes, it definitely fell short, Joe, no doubt about that call."

The player in yellow flipped his last wink. It landed on the red wink that had fallen short. Even louder groans and cheers rose from the crowd.

"Oh, he's been squopped!" Jim cried out. "That's gotta be humiliating."

"Squopped," said Dylan. And giggled. "His squidger got squopped," he said and erupted into uncontrollable giggles. Rev woke up.

"Yes, and that's game," the camera cut to a clock. "Let's hope the crowd keeps it together. We don't want a repeat of the riot that occurred yesterday."

"We're going to cut to a commercial while the referee tallies up the tiddlies—" Dylan erupted into giggles anew, while several fans were on their feet in the bleachers, shouting and shaking their fists.

The commercial was for a complete set of twiddlywink player cards. Twenty-five in all, a different serious-faced player, in close-up, on each card. Rev fell asleep again.

"Well, Joe," they were back on the air and the referee had declared the player in yellow to be the winner, "this is a real shame. A real shame. And I don't think any one of us saw this coming, Cody out of the quarter-finals. If anyone could've made that last shot, Cody could've. He's one of the best players in the league."

"And one of the highest paid too, at $5.2 million last year," Jim said.

"You know, he even had a twiddlywinks scholarship to Princeton."

After ten more commercials, five for beer and five for big trucks, the program resumed. Joe was in the locker room interviewing Cody.

"You know, I've dedicated my whole life playing twiddlywinks," Cody said, clearly disappointed with the outcome of the game. "And I gave it 120% today. You can't give more than that."

"Do you think your opponent just wanted it more today, Cody?"

"No, Jim, I don't think so," he replied.

"Now, Cody, you lost the squidge-off today, how did that impact your game, can you tell our viewers?"

"Well, certainly there's some loss of confidence when you lose the squidge-off, but I just kept focused, kept my strategy on, and played the game." He gave a reluctant-hero shrug.

"And what about the condition of your squidger," Jim asked. "I noticed you used your squidger cloth several times during the game."

"Yeah, I like to keep my squidger clean," Cody said.

"Squidger squopped." Dylan giggled.

A LONG WHILE LATER, during which they did a great deal of nothing and then went outside to look at the stars, there was a loud bang. Like a rifle shot.

"Where's Loup?" Dylan was already on his feet. Normally, although she took off at dusk, she was always in her den at night (and yet, they'd both noted, she was always in the porch in the morning when they got there). Dylan always went out to the shed to say goodnight to her.

"Froot Loup!" he screamed frantically, running around the corner of the house.

And then another bang.

"It's fireworks!" Rev ran after him. "Dylan, it's just fireworks!"

But he was already out in the shed, where he found Froot Loup in her den, shaking and whimpering. He cautiously crawled toward her, crooning. Then had a thought, took off his shoe, and led with it.

"It's okay, Loup, I'm here." She was terrified. But not aggressive. At least not toward his shoe. When he got a little closer, he started stroking her, trying to calm her down.

Another bang.

"God damn it, who the fuck is setting off fireworks?" he turned to shout-whisper at Rev. "At a lake! In the fucking forest!"

"It's the July weekend. They do it. All part of the woo-hoo. Is she okay?"

"Yes. I mean, she's not hurt, but she's shaking like crazy."

"I had a friend once whose dog was all undone by fireworks. They actually ended up having to sedate her every time."

"Yeah, I've heard about stuff like that. Bob was okay with it. Froot Loup obviously is not." He continued to pet her and crawled closer to curve himself around her as best he could.

"Want me to bring out a couple pillows?"

"That'd be good, yes. Thanks."

When she returned with the pillows, Dylan was singing to her. A little wolf lullaby.

U m, Rev?" Dylan's eye was caught by movement in the grassy area just in front of the porch.

"That's not a wolf, is it?"

A fluffy black and white creature had appeared out of nowhere and as soon as it saw Froot Loup, it flattened. And as soon as Froot Loup saw the creature, she flattened. They faced each other, on their bellies, about twenty feet apart.

"I've never seen wolves in black and white. Or in fluffy. So I'm going to go with 'no'."

"Flaker!" They heard a woman's voice calling. "Flaker—" She rounded the porch and came to a sharp stop. "Is that a wolf?" she said quietly, seeing Dylan and Rev on their feet inside the porch.

"Yes."

"Is Corn Flake in danger?" She looked anxiously at her dog.

"We don't know," Dylan said, equally quietly, slowly coming out of the porch.

Rev followed. "Corn Flake?" she whispered to the woman. "Seriously?"

"Is Corn Flake," Dylan couldn't help grinning, "acting like he's in danger?"

"I'm not sure," the woman said, studying him. "He flattened like that when he saw a bear. Made himself very small."

"So he's telling Froot Loup not to eat him," Rev suggested.

"Froot Loop?" the woman said to Rev. "Seriously?"

She turned back to Corn Flake. And Froot Loup.

"But with the bear," she said, continuing to speak quietly, "his ears were back. And he pointedly did not make eye contact." She continued to look carefully at her dog.

"Well, he's certainly making eye contact now," Dylan observed.

Flaker was staring at Loup. Intently. She was staring back. With curiosity. And interest.

"He's an Australian Shepherd. That's how they control the sheep."

"With a staring contest?" Rev laughed quietly.

"Yeah, sort of," the woman also laughed. "I'm Kit," she said, by way of introduction, but not taking her eyes off the scene unfolding before them.

"Dylan."

"Rev."

"We could get a chunk of pizza," Dylan was madly thinking about what to do. He did not want this to end badly. And he suspected it could. It could end very badly. "That would distract Loup."

"No, I think introducing food—Flaker can be very competitive when food's involved."

"Okay, no on the pizza."

"Do you think he's getting ready to herd Froot Loup?" Rev too had been thinking.

"I don't know. Maybe?" Kit replied. "What would your wolf do if Flaker suddenly ran at her?"

"We don't know."

"Okay, that's a good sign," she said then, as Corn Flake wagged his tail. Tentatively. His incredibly fluffy plume of a tail. Kit's tense shoulders relaxed a bit.

"And that's an even better sign," Dylan said, as Froot Loup wagged her tail. Equally tentatively.

Corn Flake crawled forward on his belly a few inches. Froot Loup did the same. Flaker crawled forward again. Loup also moved forward.

"Oh please," Rev said.

"I've never seen anything like this before," Kit said, as they continued to crawl toward each other in incremental stages, tails still wagging.

"So he herds sheep?" Rev asked.

"Well, no, he herds huskies. Apparently. He just got kicked off a dogsled team. Kept trying to herd his team-mates. When they were all harnessed up."

"But he's not a husky. What was he doing on a dogsled team?"

"One of my colleagues has a team. It's a motley crew. Flaker doesn't have the mass, the weight, of a husky, but he has the stamina and the speed. Like huskies, he was born to run."

"After sheep."

"After sheep," she agreed.

"So when he got kicked off ... "

"I couldn't bear knowing that every time Mike harnessed up the team, Corn Flake had to watch and not be part of it. He was left behind. Every day. Broke my heart."

"So you adopted him."

"I did," she smiled.

By now, Corn Flake and Froot Loup were an inch away from contact. They leaned toward each other. Tails thumping, they nuzzled each other's muzzle, then exchanged a cautious lick.

"Aaaww," they all said. Well, two of them. Rev uttered another "Oh, please."

A threshold seemed to have been met. Dog and wolf both got to their feet then and proceeded with the standard canine and, presumably, lupine, meet-and-greet.

"SO YOU MENTIONED YOUR colleague—you work with a dogsled outfit?" Rev asked Kit, as the five of them were sitting on the grass, eating the last of their pizza and drinking Pepsi and water.

"No, I work at the detention camp."

"There's a detention camp around here?" Dylan asked.

"It's sort of an Outward Bound for young offenders, right?" Rev looked at Kit.

"Pretty much."

"So what do you think of the new parent licence thing?" Rev asked. Surely Kit would have an opinion.

"I think it's about time!" she said with no hesitation at all. "Most of the kids we get? They're fucked up because their parents are fucked up. End of story. They never had a role model for all the social contract stuff. You know, you do shit, you pay for it. Accept the consequences of your actions, your behaviours, your choices. *Think* about the consequences of your actions, your behaviours, your choices."

"But you like your job?"

"I do. I'm not sure how long I'll last though. Burn-out's common. Sometimes I just wanna go to the parents and say 'You broke it. *You* fix it!'"

Rev glanced at Dylan—he should quote that—but he was busy giving belly rubs to Flaker and Loup. She made a note to herself.

"And the schedule's wicked," Kit continued. "Adds to the high turnover. But yeah, I like my job."

"Not a nine to five, I take it," Rev said.

"No. Some days are nine to five, but some are twelve hour shifts, and there's a lot of overnighters. And then once a month we go out with the kids on two-week trips. Plus there's a lot of overtime extras at a moment's notice, to drive a kid to court or to a doctor's appointment, whether I'm on call or not," she grimaced, "all for the lovely income of minimum wage."

"And Flaker can go to work with you?" Dylan asked, rolling around on the ground. Literally. "That'd be cool."

"I thought he could," Kit said. "They're okay with him coming on the trips, but they're giving me grief about the twelvers and over-nighters. I don't like to leave him alone that long in the house. And I don't want to leave him tied. I have a fenced in enclosure now, but—"

"Why don't you bring him here?" Dylan said, looking to Rev for agreement, and getting it. "How often is it?"

"An unpredictable number. We get our schedules for the month just a few days in advance. We never know. It really messes it up for those with families."

"Hence, also, the high turnover."

She nodded.

"Well, how about you let us know your schedule when you know it, and we'll see if we can accommodate Corn Flake on the twelvers and overnighters?"

"You'd do that? Thank you, I'd love that!"

"I think they'll love it too," Dylan said, nodding at the two of them now rolling over each other on the grass. Loup had found her pack. Sort of.

The next day, they were scheduled to check out the parent licensing course and sit in on a few classes.

"I'll be back," Dylan assured Loup as he checked that her bandana was securely knotted, then joined Rev in the car.

"You know," he said, reaching for his seatbelt, "we might have our solution for hunting season."

"Keep Loup in Kit's enclosure with Flaker." She'd had the same thought.

"We should definitely get her spayed," Dylan said then.

"Yeah. It would be difficult to find adopters for a litter of wolf-dog hybrids."

"Corn Flake might already be neutered. Given his lack of humping attempts—"

"Even so."

THE SUDBURY DEPARTMENT OF Parent Licensing had converted one of the out-of-business stores in the downtown into the education center. They were directed to a small waiting room, while whoever had been scheduled to give them the show-and-tell was located.

"Listen to this," Dylan said to Rev as he was flipping through some of the literature on the table. "Robert Hawkins, a clinical child psychologist, describes a good parent as someone who is an astute

observer of behaviour, sensitive to his child's spoken and silent messages, and able to make conscious and rational decisions about what to
teach his child, drawing on a large repertoire of sound behavior-
modification techniques."

"Yeah, the guy at the garage is all that."

Rev stood up then and went to the other side of the room to look
at the bulletin board that covered the entire wall. She expected it
would be covered by happy, cheerful babies and toddlers, but
couldn't help herself. She had to investigate anyway.

"Dylan? Bring your recorder thing. You have to get a picture of
this." She was staring at the board.

Dylan pulled his recorder out of his pocket and went to stand beside her.

"Bloody hell."

"Exactly."

The board was covered with pictures of abused children. Beaten
children. Neglected children. An infant left in the back seat of a car on a
hot day. Another squashed when dad sat down on the bus, forgetting it
was in the carrier he wore on his back. Another putting a Christmas
tree light in his mouth while mom watched, smiling. Another strapped
to dad's chest as he windsurfs. A trio eating Fritos and drinking beer
for supper in front of the tv. Another dropped as dad catches a ball at a
baseball game. Another in stripper costume being held up to a pole,
mom trying to wrap her fishnet-stockinged pudgy babyfat legs around
it. Another being taught how to hold a gun, dad trying to sort out the
uncooperative fingers to get the right one into the space with the trigger. A baby in a diaper that was duct taped to its body. Five electrocut-
ed toddlers. Four drowned babies.

"Dylan O'Toole?" a middle-aged woman approached them.

"Yes," he stood and offered his hand, "and Chris Reveille. She's—"

"Curious," Rev also stood and offered her hand. "And revolted."
She glanced behind her.

"Deb Rinette," the woman said, nodding, presumably at both her
curiosity and revulsion. "And none of those are photoshopped." They
paused a moment, as one does in mourning.

"If you'll follow me, I'll give you the tour. How are your articles coming?" she asked as she led them up a staircase, then down a hall that had classrooms on either side.

"Very well," Dylan lied. He'd stopped trying to organize everything weeks ago. It was just too much. The topic was too big. He yearned for his tambourine days with A Bunch of Drunken Indians. He still couldn't believe they finished the book about their blasphemy tour. Ah. They.

"So, as I think you know," Deb started her tour guide spiel, "there are two components to the course that people applying for a licence to parent must pass. Theory and Practicum. We start a new section of the first part every month, and the second part is sort of a proceed-as-you-go thing.

"In the first part," she nodded to a class in session, "we cover all the basics of raising a children. What children need to develop physically, emotionally, cognitively, and socially."

"Won't all that required premium care privilege the rich?" Rev asked.

"Please. A bag of TVP and a bunch of bananas costs less than a bag of chips. Milk is cheaper than beer. Broccoli and spinach cheaper than cigarettes. And the course will make sure people know exactly why milk is preferable to beer. We provide lots of pictures," she added sardonically.

"Do people just have to complete the course or must they achieve a certain grade?" Dylan asked.

"They must complete and pass. Different units have different standards as to what constitutes a pass."

"And are there any equivalency measures?"

"Yes," she replied. "Someone who has already taken courses in child development would get a pass at some of the units."

She stopped then and nodded into a classroom full of people watching a video. "They're starting on the socialization unit. We have videos showing many of the common, but thoughtless, and damaging, words, gestures, and behaviors—parents have no idea how much power they have. No idea."

"For instance?" Dylan prompted.

"Gender polarization. It's one of the critical foundations of patriarchy, one of the big things that defines who we are and messes us up so thoroughly. Individually, as a society, as a species. And parents are very much responsible for it." She led them into an empty classroom, and walked to the console at the front of the room.

"Watch," she said a few seconds later, directing their attention to the flatscreen at the front of the room. The video showed a little girl falling off her bicycle. The parent rushed up and asked if she was okay.

"Good parenting, right? Attentive, concern for injury."

Then a little boy fell off his bicycle. The parents smiled and encouraged him to get back on and try again.

"That sort of thing must happen a hundred times a day. There are so many studies showing that parents hold girl infants more than boy infants, they speak to them in a different tone, they react differently," she nodded to the screen, "to what they do and do not do. We cover at least a dozen of these differences in the course."

Dylan made a mental note to ask for copies of the videos.

"We have another series of videos using time-lapse to make the point."

"Could you describe one of those?" He assumed they were too long to watch right then.

"My favourite is the one in which we show a parent repeatedly insulting the child or otherwise undermining confidence and self-esteem. Then we pretend a fast-forward that shows the kid as a teenager and later as an adult, doing the kind of shit someone with no self-esteem does. Like, if it's a girl, staying in an abusive relationship. Not asking for a raise in pay."

"And if it's a boy?"

"Engaging in excessive posturing, persistently seeking out ways to prove himself. Constantly picking fights, breaking the law ... Another one shows parents not paying enough attention to their child, who then grows up to become the kind of adult who is constantly seeking attention, often in inappropriate ways."

She led them out of the classroom.

"We have similar videos showing the kind of parental behaviour that inadvertently encourages, or at least maintains, behaviors such as tantrums, disobedience, dependency, and so on."

A woman came out of the classroom at the end of the hall and turned toward them.

"Marie," Deb called out, stopping her as she approached. "This is Dylan O'Toole. He's writing the articles about the licensing parent legislation. This is Marie, one of our resident psychologists. Not only is Marie available, for anything, to people making their way through the courses, she was one of the people who prepared the videos."

"Pleased to meet you," she reached out and shook their hands. "A lot of damage, irreversible damage, occurs in the child's first few years," she said, clearly for Dylan's benefit, who obliged by holding his mini-recorder toward her. "And that's when only the parents are to blame. The kids don't go to school yet, they have no interaction with society—toys, advertising, what have you—except for what their parents permit. They have to know that."

Dylan nodded, glad he'd still had his recorder turned on. "Anything else you'd like to say?" His directed questions were to die for.

Marie thought a moment. "Being a parent is an awesome, overwhelming responsibility. Right up there with existential dread. After all, it involves existence. At its fundamental. And it's about time people understand that."

They parted then, Marie continuing on to wherever she was going, Deb leading Rev and Dylan to the end of the hall.

"But don't parents already know a lot of this stuff?" Rev asked. "I would guess, for example, that if you asked, many would say yes, beating a baby isn't the best way to make it stop crying."

"Of course," Deb replied. "Which is why the theoretical stuff is just part of the course. We're also testing for, and letting the applicants test themselves for, aptitude. We need to see whether they have the self-control, the personality, to apply all this theory. To *not* beat a baby when it won't stop crying.

"Furthermore, to answer a common objection," she turned to Dylan, "no, we don't have a lot of evidence to show that parents who have more knowledge of child development, as measured by a paper-and-pencil test, are better parents," she added. "So, again, the practicum."

She led into a stairwell and up another flight.

"Once they pass the practicum elements we have here, all prospective parents must spend one month as a teacher's aide in a nursery school classroom. A lot of the men balk at that. Apparently it's emasculating to play with little kids," she said, dryly. Rev grinned at her. "And the four hour stretch is a challenge for many."

Hearing raised voices, they paused in the next doorway.

"This is what I think of your fucking bag of flour!" a man said as he dropkicked it neatly out the window. It exploded impressively when it hit the sidewalk two floors below.

"Tell me he fails," Rev said in the ensuing silence.

Deb led them toward the next room.

"What about the objection that the practicum is unfair, because surely parents are better with their own kids?" Dylan asked. "Children with whom they have an emotional bond?"

"That can backfire. Often parents are worse with their own kids. Because, of course, they take it all personally. They figure their kids' failures reflect badly on them. And they're right. Up to a point. But usually the kid who strikes out at a little league baseball game doesn't do that just to embarrass dad."

"Right," Rev said. "I've seen those dads. The world revolves around them."

"Doesn't it just," she said in Rev's direction.

In the next classroom, a lesson on diaper changing was being given.

Rev opened her mouth, but Deb beat her to it. "We discourage the use of gas masks. It frightens the babies."

She led them onwards.

"The final exam is spending eighteen hours with a screaming infant," she said, nodding to the soundproofed room. In which there was indeed a screaming infant and an adult.

"How do you make sure the infants keeps it up that long. What do you do to them?" Rev was interested.

Deb gave her a look. "It's a robotic infant."

"Oh."

"Maybe this should be the entrance exam," Dylan suggested.

"Well, we're operating on the premise that understanding increases tolerance."

"Hm."

She consulted the clipboard on the door. "Bert here is in hour six."

The man was holding the infant, jiggling it, tears streaming down his cheeks. Bert's cheeks. They were Bert's tears. He stood up and started to walk around the room. He started singing a lullaby. He picked up a brightly-coloured toy and dangled it in front of the child. He picked up a bottle and offered it.

They passed on to the next room. Again, one screaming infant and one adult.

"Beth's in hour ten."

"I think Beth might be done," Rev said, as the woman collapsed onto the floor in the corner and started slowly banging her head against the wall, as the baby continued to wail from the crib into which she'd put her.

"Maybe not. We'll give her some time. The baby's safe in the crib."

In the next room, they saw a man pacing around the room, with the infant in his arms. He was very agitated. Which was clearly making things worse.

Suddenly the man shook the infant. Hard.

Its head fell off.

He stared, horrified.

Then he bent down, picked it up, and tried to put it back on.

Then he just—left. Walked right by them.

"He also fails, right?"

Deb led them to the end of the hall and back down the stairs.

"We also help the prospective parents with their plan of care," she said, half-turning to Dylan on the steps behind her.

"Plan of care?"

"Yes, one of the prerequisites for obtaining the license is having a plan of care—an account of how the child will be cared for 24/7 for 6 years, then almost 24/7 for another 12 years."

"I see."

"We discourage the traditional nuclear family arrangement—a man working full-time and a woman at home full-time."

"And why is that?" Rev asked. Mostly to get Deb to say it so Dylan would have it.

"It seems inevitably to reinforce the patriarchy, no matter how much the couple tries to fight it. The person making the money almost always ends up with the greater share of the power. And the person at home almost always ends up being the primary parent. And when those roles are gender-aligned ... "

"Bad things happen," Rev concluded.

"Indeed. What we're starting to see is the return of the extended family, whereby relatives of all sorts become part of the childraising process. We're also seeing arrangements of involving those who are not genetically related.

"And, this is just my own personal prediction, I think that as a result, we're going to start seeing an increase in job equity. With the demise of the male breadwinner and the rise of women, mothers or not, contracting to be financially responsible for raising a child, I think it's inevitable that women will start receiving equal pay for work of equal value, for work requiring equal skill, and for work requiring equal effort."

"Anything else you'd like to say?" Dylan asked her, frowning again at his stellar interview skills. But holding out his recorder. Which was on.

Deb thought for a moment. "Having to go through the process of obtaining a license will increase the likelihood that the kid is wanted. And surely it goes without saying that wanted kids are better off than unwanted kids. People who choose to do something typically do it better than those who are forced to do it."

"And yet, they're forced to take the course," Rev said. "They don't choose to be here."

"I disagree. Only those who want to become parents have to take the course. By choosing to be parents, therefore, they're choosing to be here."

Rev had to agree. It was, after all, the argument she had used every time one of her students had grumbled about courses that were mandatory in their program.

"But what about the backfire possibility?" Dylan asked. "The more someone wants a child, the more they may have very specific plans for it. So the more pressure there will be on the child to fulfil those plans, to meet those specific expectations. The less freedom it will have to turn into its own human being."

"Hopefully the course will make parents aware of the tendency and danger of doing that. 'Want' doesn't have to mean 'control'. You can want to go to Europe without wanting—without planning every specific detail."

"True, but people often do," Rev said. "Plan the details. Have specific desires about what they want their trip to Europe to be like."

"And they might not make the best parents. Hopefully what we do here will make that clear to them."

They were at the door.

"What I like best about the whole program," Deb added, "is that it makes parents more responsible for how their kids turn out. No longer can parents say they can't be blamed, they didn't know. Their license," she gestured to the building behind her, to everything they were doing, everything they were teaching, "proves they did."

T hose who teach the courses have a lot of power," Dylan commented next morning as he opened his laptop.

"Yeah, I just hope they get to use it" Rev said, sipping her coffee and staring out at the sparkling lake. "Remember what happened to me at the university? Fail too many students and you lose your job."

"But wasn't that because funding was attached to pass rates?"

"Is that the case in this case?"

Dylan made a note to ask.

"You didn't want to swing by the shelter yesterday," he noted, belatedly.

"No," Rev said. "I have no more questions to ask. I have no idea who did the deed. Or how to find out. And, in any case, charges against Susie have been dropped, remember?"

"Oh yeah."

They heard a car pull into the driveway then, and Loup ran out, tailing wagging.

"How does she know?" Rev wondered aloud. Flaker was coming for his first overnight. But Kit had never driven to their house before. "Can she actually smell Flaker? When he's inside a car? In our driveway?"

"Maybe," Dylan was surprised too. And seriously impressed if that was the case.

They went out to join Loup in welcoming Flaker.

"Hi," Kit said, her arms full.

"Hi," Rev and Dylan answered, taking various items from her.

Loup watched curiously, and with apparent approval, as Flaker, Kit, and Dylan put Flaker's blanket—grey with black and white sheep all over it—in her den. Flaker's dish was put by the back door of the cabin beside hers. Then it was moved around the corner from hers. Kit gave Flaker one of his toys, which she'd brought as well, hugged him, then drove off. Flaker watched until her car disappeared, then turned to Loup. The two of them chased each other around the cabin then ran off to the swampy end of the cove.

"GOING TO GET THE mail!" Dylan called out from the porch to Rev somewhere inside. Froot Loup stopped what she was doing and looked at Dylan. Flaker did the same. They'd both been bathed and were body surfing on the lawn.

"Wanna come?" They both said yes.

"Sure, give me a minute," Rev said.

Dylan heard her make a phone call.

"Hello, I have a— English. I'd like to schedule a pick-up, but it's— Arrange. Pick-up. Come get. Package. Yes. No. Well, that depends on whether— Jeezus, how can I speak to— YES! SPEAK TO A REPRE-SENTATIVE.   RE-PRE-SEN-TA-TIVE."

A few minutes later, he heard her hang up.

"I imagine a very near future in which the stupid people rule the world," she said to him on their way out the door, leaving her latest batch of LSAT questions in its FedEx envelope on the window ledge, "because they'll be the only ones able to communicate with all our automated systems, because their minds are unclouded by complexi-ty and subtlety."

"Hm."

Loup took her position twenty feet beside them in the bush and began to trot along. Flaker danced in front of them, happily. Dylan and Rev smiled. Until he kept it up. Kept dancing in front of them. Stepping in front of them. After five minutes of repeatedly bumping into him, stopping and walking around him, or tripping over him, Rev shot out an irritated "What the hell is he doing?"

"I think he's herding us," Dylan chuckled. "Around the stones."

"Oh for fuck's sake!" She'd tripped over him again. It was very frustrating.

"Flaker, no!" she said. But it was hopeless. He was born to herd.

"We need to take him to a sheep farm," she said several jerky steps later. "Once a week. Or something."

"I've got a better idea," Dylan said, smiling with anticipation.

WHEN THEY GOT BACK—just a few minutes later, since they'd abandoned the idea of going for a walk with Corn Flake, ever—Dylan rummaged around in one of boxes from their tour that he had yet to unpack, then went out into the yard.

"Corn Flake!"

Flaker went bounding toward him.

Dylan fired his bubble gun and a million bubbles shot into the air, dispersing in every direction.

And Flaker went wild trying to herd every last one of them.

"LET'S SIT DOWN AT THE water," Rev suggested later in the afternoon, when they had returned from kayaking on the lake and biking through the bush respectively. Apparently bikes were not in Flaker's must-be-herded category. Either that, or the bubbles had him all herded out.

"Good idea," Dylan said. It was late July, the worst of the bugs had passed.

So they got their coffee and headed down to the dock. Rev sat in the bear chair she'd bought and stained mahogany a few years ago. It needed to be redone, she thought. The sun's UV was clearly getting stronger. Dylan opened up the lawn chair he'd brought down and wondered about buying a second bear chair. Loup and Flaker went for a brief swim to cool off, quenched their thirst, then presumably found a patch of late sun to lie in.

They stared across the cove waiting for the magic time. When the sun got down to a certain point, there was something about the angle—there! It lit up the green and turned the whole cove a shimmering chartreuse. The shimmer bounced off the water and onto the trees, and they watched the light trembling in the trees, rippling the trees, as it moved from left to right across the cove—

And then a loud boat motor broke the silence.

"Fuck!" Rev said. Then with great resignation, stood up.

"What?" Dylan asked, clearly feeling like he was missing something.

"That's Numbnuts. He's going fishing. He goes around the edge of the whole lake at that speed, with a couple lines out the back of his boat. So he doesn't have to expend the effort of casting and reeling in."

"So ... "

"It takes about an hour. You want to listen to that engine for an hour?"

It was very loud. Likely an old engine. And outboard boat motors, such as those on small fishing boats, didn't have mufflers, of course. And since they were used on water, their sound travelled remarkably well.

"I don't, no," Dylan sighed, and stood up as well.

"And as soon as he passes us, you'll be breathing oil and gasoline fumes for a good fifteen minutes."

"Why don't they use those new electric motors?" he asked as they headed back up to the cabin. "They're so quiet you can't even hear them. He'd catch more fish that way. And no fumes. Which, of course, eventually settle into the lake. You'd think he'd like that part. He eats the fish he catches, doesn't he?"

"Actually, no, I think he throws them back."

"So— Then why—" Dylan was speechless.

"In any case, electric motors are for sissies," Rev explained.

"The jetskis are worse," she added. "They use about ten gallons per hour, and about twenty percent of that goes straight into the lake, uncombusted."

"But that's—that's just like pouring two gallons of gas into the lake! Per hour?!"

"Yup. As much, each year, all of them together, as the Exxon Valdez spill."

"And you've tried to get the lake proclaimed a no-jetski lake, I presume?"

"Nope. Didn't bother once I read that some coalition of cottage associations tried to get a bill passed that would allow local authorities to ban, or at least limit, jetskis on lakes in their jurisdictions. Anyway, Bombardier got involved and so of course they couldn't win. And a senator presented a private member's bill on the matter six times. Lost every time."

At the top of the hill, Rev paused. Flaker was herding a rabbit. And given the rabbit's random zigzagging, he was doing a virtuosic job, keeping the poor creature from escaping into the bush. Time and time again, Flaker anticipated with impressive reflexes and agility and blocked off its escape route, keeping it on the lawn.

"What the—" Dylan had stopped as well.

They watched as Corn Flake herded it to the side of the house. Curious, they followed—and saw Loup lying in wait, a short stack of rabbits, dead rabbits, beside her.

She pounced, barely, since Flaker had herded the hapless rabbit practically straight into her mouth, then shook it, threw it into the air, and rolled on it, then added it to the pile.

"What a team."

Next morning, they brought their coffee and pizza into the porch as usual. Dylan smiled when he saw that Flaker's blanket had been pulled halfway through the doggy door. Rev smiled when she saw that the mosquito netting was still intact.

"Maybe they're both—"

A howl suddenly split the air.

"Froot Loup!" Dylan cried out instantly, and ran back in, then out the back door.

"No, I think that *was* Froot Loup!" Rev said, right behind him.

Froot Loup was in the driveway, panting and pacing, clearly in distress. There was blood on her muzzle.

"Oh god," Dylan said, running up to her to check her for wounds.

"What is it, girl?" Rev said at the same time. "Did Timmy fall down the well? Again?"

Loup suddenly leapt away from Dylan's exploring hands and ran to the shed. If she crawled into her den, she might be really hurt, Dylan thought. But she ran back out seconds later with a bunch of the practice snares in her mouth.

"Flaker's caught in a snare!" Dylan got it instantly. He ran to his bike. Rev ran into the shed.

"Dylan!" she shouted as he pedalled after Loup. He turned, went back for the wire cutters she had in her hand, then sped away.

Rev got her car keys. Slow down, think. Dylan would have to deal with 'Beat' and 'Breathe'. The third First Aid 'B' was 'Bleed'. She ran for a freshly laundered tshirt and tore it into strips. And shock. Flaker would be in shock. She grabbed a blanket. Then she grabbed her cell phone and called Dr. Theresen to give her a heads up. She started her car, backed up, stopped, went back into the house for Froot Loup's harness and leash. And Flaker's leash. Then she drove to the trail entrance and waited for Dylan. And waited. She couldn't drive in. Just as she decided to get out and run in, she saw him in the distance, on foot, Corn Flake in his arms. Oh no. No, he was running, as best he could, Froot Loup trotting at his side. So Corn Flake must still be alive. She opened the back door.

"He caught his leg," Dylan panted. "Not his neck. So I think he might be okay. But it's cut deep." There was a short piece of wire still embedded. "I didn't think I should pull it out." He bent and awkwardly got into the back seat with Corn Flake still in his arms, head drooping. After just a moment's hesitation, Froot Loup leapt in beside him.

REV PULLED INTO THE into the vet's parking lot, quickly got out, opened Dylan's door, carefully closing it behind him so Froot Loup didn't jump out. He hurried to the front door of the vet's office, carrying Corn Flake, bundled in the blanket. They both heard Loup's howl and then a thump. They turned and saw her throw herself against the car window a second time.

"Jeezus!" Rev said.

"Here," Dylan carefully handed Flaker to Rev. "I'll see to her."

But once Rev was inside, he realized he didn't know quite what to do. Leash her and take her inside so she could see? No, that was out of the question. There might be other dogs there, and cats, possibly even rabbits, and besides, there's no way she'd know the vet was helping Flaker. It was quite possible, Dylan thought, that she'd go for Dr. Theresen's throat. He talked to her through the car window, soothing her, crooning to her, but it seemed to have no effect on her whatsoever. She howled and threw herself at the glass again. She was going to hurt herself, Dylan realized. Already, there was some blood from her muzzle smeared on the window. It was his job to protect her against herself, he thought, but should he actually get back inside the car with her? If he tried to restrain her— She was going berserk. Understandably so. First her mom died right there in front of her, and now her best buddy, possibly her mate, had died too—she had no way of knowing that he was still alive, that he would be okay, she didn't even know where they had taken him—ah. Dylan pulled out his cellphone and hoped Rev had hers with her.

"Yeah?"

"How's Corn Flake?"

"Fine. The wire cut pretty deep, there's some muscle damage, but the tendons and ligaments are okay. She put him under and is stitching him up now. He's going to be fine."

"Good. That's good. Loup's going berserk. Is there a window in the room she's doing surgery in?"

"I don't know. I'm in the waiting room."

"Ask. Please."

A few seconds later, Rev returned. "Yes. It's at the back. Why?"

"I think Loup needs to see him. Alive. I'm going to pull the car around. Hopefully she won't attack me when I get inside the car."

"It's that bad?"

"She's still throwing herself against the window. There's blood—" Dylan was near breaking point too.

"But Corn Flake's under anaesthesia. He's going to look dead."

"So wag his tail."

"What?"

"Go into the surgery room, open the curtains, and wag his tail so she can see he's alive."

"Okay. Yeah. Okay. Keys are in the ignition," she added.

Dylan turned back to Loup and started singing the lullaby he'd sung when she'd freaked about the fireworks. It had a very slight effect. He eased into the driver's seat. Started the car. And pulled around to the back. Carefully parked the car as close to the window as possible. Rev, gloved and masked, had already opened the curtains. Good. He got out and tried to direct Loup's attention through the car window and through the vet window. Not easy for someone who negotiates her way through life using scent and sound.

"Loup, look. There's Flaker. He's okay. It's okay, Loup. Look. See?"

Rev gently grabbed Flaker's eminently fluffy tail and wagged it.

That caught Loup's attention. She stilled.

"Again," Dylan called to Rev.

Rev wagged Flaker's tail again. Loup saw it. Whimpered. Sat down.

Rev wagged Flaker's tail yet again. Loup wagged her tail.

Dr. Theresen looked up from her work and out the window. She smiled. She'd always loved the elegant solution.

FIFTEEN MINUTES LATER, Dr. Theresen came out to see Loup.

"I'd really like to check her mouth," she said, "but there's no way— Back in a second." She returned with a syringe. "Do you think you can keep her calm and distracted at the front end, while I get this in the back end? It's just a sedative."

"Yes, I think so."

"The alternative is a tranquilizer gun, but I'd rather do it this way."

Dylan got into the back seat with Loup, who had calmed considerably once she saw Corn Flake—they kept the curtains open, and Rev continued to wag his tail every now and then—and started singing their lullaby. He carefully put his arm around her neck in case she suddenly tried to turn and snap at Dr. Theresen, who then reached in carefully through the window. No problem.

They waited until the sedative took effect, then carried her inside.

"Okay, all I'm seeing are cuts," she said, examining her mouth. "There are many, but they're all fine cuts. Nothing that needs stitches, and nothing that won't heal on its own. She must have tried to bite through the wire." She took a good look at her paws as well, thinking she may have tried to paw the snare away. Her paws were fine.

"How long of a drive do you have?" she asked. "I can make sure they don't fully come to until you're home. Normally, I like to keep the dogs here until they come out of anaesthesia. But Flaker's already coming around, and given Loup—"

"Actually," Dylan said, "it occurred to me—we've decided to have her spayed. Is that something you can do now—on such short notice? I mean, now that she's here, and—"

"Well, it is major surgery, and she'd have to be fully anaesthetized. But, yes, I could fit her in. Reschedule if necessary. Given her situation, it does make good sense to do it now, while she's here. Has she eaten in the last eight hours?"

"I don't think so. She hasn't had any kibble since last night, but the two of them were out and about this morning. It's quite possible they caught something. And ate it." He'd forgotten about their stack of rabbits.

"Or buried it for later," Dr. Theresen said. "My guess is that since she is so well fed at your place, any hunting she does is more for sport than anything. I think it's probably safe to proceed, but we'll take precautions."

SO DYLAN AND REV went home, worried, then returned at five o'clock for both Flaker and Loup.

"Both of them will be a bit out of it for a couple days until the anaesthesia wears off," Dr. Theresen started giving them the post-op instructions. "Loup more than Flaker. You can give them water. A light supper if they want. They may not, so not to worry. Start the antibiotics tonight though. They'll both probably just sleep until morning."

"Okay."

"It's important to know that not only will they feel drowsy, they'll be a little unsteady on their feet. So what you don't want is for them to try to get up and run around. They won't know their legs won't obey them until they fall and break something. Carry them both in and out of the car."

"Maybe we should take them to Kit's place then," Rev said to Dylan. "She's got that fenced in enclosure."

"Or we could just close the shed door. Or put a board across the doggy door in the porch. Loup's never been at the enclosure. Has she?" Dylan turned to the vet then. "We actually don't know. She spends several hours a day out and about on her own now."

"Given her distress at novelty," Dr. Theresen said, "I think her den or the porch might be the better option. If she wakes up in the enclosure, and it *is* new to her, she might freak like she did in the car."

"Okay, good, we'll do that."

"Keep the wounds clean and dry for seven to ten days. No out and about. No swimming. For either of them."

"Okay."

"If you have any questions, just call. But I think they'll both be fine. They make a good pair," she added, smiling.

"THAT WAS A GOOD idea," Rev said to Dylan once they were on their way home, "to get Loup spayed now. Both of them will be in recovery mode, with restricted activity, at the same time. It'll make it easier on both of them."

"It was, wasn't it. I hadn't thought about that part, but you're right."

"In fact, I'm thinking maybe we should ask Kit if we can keep Flaker for the week. In a couple days, when Loup's feeling better, she's going to want to go find him. If she hasn't already. In which case, she's going to howl outside his window or something. We're going to have to keep her at our place against her will or let her go and hope that she doesn't tear her stitches."

"Good point. And even if she does get to his place okay, he'll want to jump all silly with joy— If he stays at our place, they might be content to just lay around together all week."

"SO WE'RE GOING TO have to teach Corn Flake about snares," Rev said a little later.

"We are, yes. Loup will help," Dylan smiled, glancing into the back seat where the two of them lay, zonked out.

AROUND TEN O'CLOCK, Dylan was in the kitchen. Flaker and Loup were in the porch, in the double nest they'd made for them. Both were awake, but more than content to stay exactly where they were. He opened one of the cupboards and stared at it. Then he opened the fridge and stared at it.

"Coffee's in the coffee pot," Rev said helpfully, coming in for a slice of pizza. They'd replenished their supply. So it was fresh. Fresh pizza was better than fresh rabbit, Rev thought, taking a bite of the soft and gooey undercooked double cheese, green olives, and pineapple.

"No, yeah, I'm looking for something to make the antibiotic pills go down," he said.

"Oh, right." She thought for a moment. Peanut butter? No, they'd just lick around the pill. Stuff it into a chunk of cheese? It would probably fall out. She took another bite of her pizza.

"Bob liked his pills stuffed into a wiener," Dylan said distractedly.

"Well, maybe Loup and Flaker would like theirs the same way."

Dylan closed the other cupboard he'd opened and faced her. "You don't have any wieners."

"Do too."

"You're not supposed to have any wieners," he clarified.

She opened the freezer door and took out a package of veggie wieners.

"Ah! Brilliant!" Dylan microwaved the frozen block, then extricated one wiener from the package. He cut two one-inch pieces from it, stuffed a pill deep into each, and went back out to the porch.

KIT ARRIVED HALF AN hour later to pick up Flaker, her shift having ended at midnight. As soon as he heard her car, Flaker tried to get up. Dylan rushed to help him, then saw that Loup was also struggling to get up.

"I'll take Flaker," Rev said, picking him up and carrying him outside to the driveway. Dylan followed with Loup in his arms.

"What happened?" Kit cried as she saw Flaker's bandaged foot, and ran to take him from Rev before he squiggled out of her hold.

Then she saw Loup looking a little dopey, and she looked again at

Rev and Dylan for an explanation.

Settling on the yard, they quickly told her what had transpired over the last twenty-four hours.

"Poor liddle Corn Flake has a boo boo on his leg," she said, putting her arms around Flaker even more tightly. Rev rolled her eyes. Dylan grinned.

"Thank you so much for taking care of him," she said when she had finished lavishing Corn Flake with post-trauma affection and assurance.

Then she turned to Loup, "And thank *you* so much." She leaned toward Loup, hoping to hug her as well, giving Dylan a quick glance to see if it was all right. Loup said it was. She was Flaker's person.

"So we were wondering," Dylan said to Kit, "would you be agreeable to letting us keep Flaker for the week? We're thinking that—"

"Yes!"

"Yes?"

"I was coming here tail between my legs to ask if you guys could keep him for a few more days. Shit happened, and I have to go back at eight for another overnighter—"

"Eight as in, like, seven hours from now?" Rev asked.

Kit nodded. "And then I have to take a kid to frickin' Kenora for court. Which will be a two or three day trip, depending."

"All right, then," Dylan said, cheerily, ruffling Flaker's ears with his left hand and Loup's with his right.

Kit thanked them all again, profusely, then hugged Flaker goodbye, again, then left for some desperately needed sleep.

"Don't you just love it when everything falls into place?" Dylan said as they escorted Flaker and Loup back inside.

"Yeah. 'Cuz usually everything is fucked up and stays that way."

So today's the day of that televised debate," Dylan looked up from his work. With a sigh. He had way too much information already. And had made no headway in the week since Flaker had been injured and Loup spayed. He missed biking with her every day. And they still had three days to go. Three days during which she was at Flaker's place. Kit was back and they thought it would be good to keep the two of them together for the remaining days of their recovery. It was a perfect opportunity to familiarize Loup with the enclosure.

"Oh yeah," Rev said. "Can I come?"

"Can I stop you?" He grinned.

WHEN THEY ENTERED THE auditorium, they saw that it was quite full, and the panel on the stage consisted of representatives from various religions, the disability lobby, the civil liberties union, and a few others. Television cameras were placed around the stage. The debate, such as it was, seemed to be in full swing.

"The right to marry and have a family is a basic human right," the civil liberties rep pronounced, as Rev and Dylan edged their way into a couple empty seats. He was a grey-haired man in a business suit. It was hard to ignore his triple signatories of authority. And he knew it. "This legislation deprives us of that right. It should be abolished.

Immediately. It violates our right to privacy," he continued, "our right to physical integrity, our right to autonomy—I could go on and on!"

The moderator let him do just that.

Ten long minutes later, a woman representing the disability lobby got a word in edgewise. "The Parent Licensing Act is an insult to differently abled people everywhere." Cheers rose from one section of the audience. "Denying our right to reproduce is a slap in the face, an outright statement that our lives are less valuable. It's ablist. It's discrimination, pure and simple." More cheers.

After a few more minutes, Rev wondered when the members of the audience would have a chance to respond to the arguments. Scratch that. Respond to the claims. No one had actually made an argument yet. Well, except for the civil rights person. But he had presented no support whatsoever for the premise upon which his conclusion was based.

"God said 'Be fruitful and multiply'!" It was one of the religionists. "To do otherwise would be a sin!" Probably the Roman Catholic one. "A sin against nature! A sin against God!"

The moderator gave the floor back to the civil liberties guy. Because he'd indicated that he'd like to speak again. Gee, Rev marvelled. Is that all it took to get the floor when you were a gray-haired man in a business suit?

"The right to religious belief is integral to our freedom of thought. It is integral to ... "

They listened for another ten minutes. Ten minutes during which the moderator made no indication whatsoever that she understood the concept of relevance to mean anything other than 'more or less on the same topic'. And the participants made no indication whatsoever that they had actually heard, let alone understood, any of the other participants. What they thought they were participating in, Rev had no idea. This wasn't a discussion, let alone a debate. It was just serial sermonizing.

"I can't stand it," she muttered, finally, then stood up and strode toward the stage.

Oh god, Dylan thought, it's Texas all over again. He trotted behind her, stumbling as he made sure his minirecorder was on. At least here, they don't have guns. No, he groaned inwardly, they have hunting rifles instead.

"You're all flinging rights, and wrongs, at each other," she said loudly as she approached the stage, "not to mention a ton of red herrings and paper tigers and non sequiturs—" She marched up the short staircase to the stage. "Are any of you trained philosophers?"

They all looked at each other. Dumbly. Then shook their heads.

"Then good thing I happen to be here, huh?" She walked along the row shaking everyone's hand. "Chris Reveille, Philosophers, Inc. 'We help you figure out your shit.'"

Attempts by the moderator to beckon someone from offstage to get the crazy lady away from them failed.

"You, disability," she pointed to the woman from the disability lobby. "To say that the disabled have rights doesn't necessarily mean you have the right to create someone who will be disabled. Your right to do so is neither more nor less than anyone else's right to do so. If you think it's so okay to make someone blind, go ahead." Rev pulled out her Swiss army knife and handed it to her. "Make me blind.

"People are better off without disease, can that actually be contested?" Rev asked. "They're also better off without disability, generally speaking. Ask any adult who can't go to the bathroom by herself."

"If health and well-being *aren't* valuable," Dylan shouted from the side, struggling a bit to remember Purdy's exact words, "Why do you want to eliminate the obstacles society puts in your way? Obstacles *to* well-being."

Rev air-high-fived him. "Laura Purdy," she provided the credit for anyone who wanted to know. "Philosopher."

"But I'm *glad* I'm disabled!" the woman stood up to protest. Or would have, if her legs had worked. "Adversity makes you strong."

"Then why isn't everyone rushing out to throw themselves in front of a truck?"

The moderator was frantically making driving-a-truck gestures to someone offstage. It was an ambiguous message, at best.

"Preferring the absence of disability doesn't mean the lives of the disabled are of less value. It just means that given the choice between pain and reduced opportunities, and the absence of, we'd choose the latter.

"I mean, why in god's name *wouldn't* you want to get rid of the gene for Sickle Cell Anemia or Down's Syndrome or what have you? That's why we have the cultural taboo about incest and marrying your cousin."

"The policy is cruel—" the woman persisted.

"Not to let parents with genetic abnormalities have kids? Cruel? What do you call intentionally *making* a genetically abnormal kid?

"Why is genetic heritage is so important that you want to intentionally bring into the world a child who won't be able to walk?" She stared at the woman. Who had no answer.

"Muscular dystrophy today, anyone who can't run a marathon tomorrow?" someone from the audience spoke up. "It's a slippery slope!"

"Of course it's a slippery slope," Rev looked out at the audience, trying to find the speaker. "So what? Why are we so afraid to go from genetic correction to genetic enhancement? Maybe what we call normal isn't. What's the standard? And why is that the standard?"

"You know, it's interesting. I've always found that those who scream the loudest that we're not allowed to discriminate are those who are most unable to discriminate. To tell the difference between shades of good and bad, right and wrong, fair and unfair."

The moderator had left the stage. Perhaps also the building.

"And you. The Pro-Family wingnut. Familyism is just tribalism at its smallest."

The woman was outraged. At being called a wingnut. She didn't get the tribalism point.

"You all get married, have kids, spend twenty years raising them, and your goal, your best hope, is that they get married and have kids. And all *they* want for *their* kids is that *they* get married and have kids. And on and on. Such folly."

"I am not a wingnut!"

"Bible Boy? 'God said unto *them*, Be fruitful and multiply.' He was talking to Adam and Eve. Not you."

Dylan wondered if he'd mentioned to Rev that this was for *national* tv. Not just the local station. And it was live.

"And Little Miss Righteous? You've equivocated. Nature and God are not one in the same. And nature seems to prohibit procreation in many cases. Miscarriage. Infertility. Menopause.

"Also, I find your religion-inspired pronatalism a little hypocritical, because once the child is born, most religions go out of their way to incapacitate its development. 'Obey these rules without question.' There goes autonomous decision-making. Not to mention the development of the mind. Especially if that mind is inside a female body.

"Is there anything in the Bible about *when* to go forth and multiply? *With whom* to go forth and multiply? Or *how often?* Reproduction without ethics isn't pretty. It's evolution. Which," she added cryptically, as far as they were concerned, "should bother you just a little bit.

"No," the civil rights man corrected her, "I believe you're mistaken. Evolution is survival of the fittest.

"Right, and a species that has no constraints on reproduction ends up not fitting."

"What happens is the stupid and the brutish replicate ad nauseum, whereas the intelligent and considerate exercise a little self restraint. Guess what the species starts to look like? And the planet."

Dylan was nodding his head, cheering her on.

"We see it again and again, especially on islands. A species without any predators will replicate itself out of existence. Because unlimited reproduction plus limited resources equals ... ? People start killing each other for evermore scarce resources and eventually, one way or another, they all end up dead."

"So what do you propose?" he asked. Mocked, actually. "Eugenics?" Oh, the horror.

"Well, we don't have predators, so the writing's on the wall. So wouldn't it be better to plan things than let evolution run its blind course? Why can't we have a planned society? A postevolutionary society. A supra-evolutionary society.

"Except that we're not ready for that either," Rev trailed off. "Look at Nazi Germany. And China's a success only if you ignore the consequence that far more female babies are killed than male ... "

"China," he paused for effect, "is one of the biggest violators of human rights—"

"Oh yeah. Rights." He'd brought her back on track. "Where do I begin?" She paused, then said, to the gray-haired man in the business suit, "You do know you have the right to shut the fuck up, yeah?"

He was speechless. No one had ever told him to shut the fuck up before. Wonder what that's like, Rev thought in passing.

"First, it seems to me you're confusing 'I have a right to this' with 'I want this'. Unless you have a basis, a reason for *why* you have a right, the whole concept of rights is useless. So let me ask you, *on what basis* do you claim all the rights you say you have?"

"You tell us," the grey-haired man in the suit said, dripping with—hm, resentment.

"Well, there are several possibilities," Rev replied, equanimously. After all, this was standard fare for Phil101. "You could use a contractarian basis. We have whatever rights arise from the consensual agreement we make when we live in a society. In this case, usually rights are acquired, and there are reciprocal responsibilities or obligations or duties. Which no one seems to be talking about.

"Or you could use a utilitarian basis. Utilitarianism is usually about right, not rights, but we can still use it. We can say that that which results in the greatest good for the greatest number of people is a right.

"Some of you are saying the right to reproduce is a natural right, something we just have. Others, a human right, something we have just because we're human. In both cases, there seems to be this indefensible assumption that whatever we *can* do, we *should* do. Or at least *have a right* to do. Nuh-uh."

Dylan grinned at her philosophical eloquence.

"Shouldn't being a parent be, instead, an acquired right? Something we become entitled to do because we have met certain conditions?"

"But the desire to have a child is a basic human need," the disability woman spoke up, probably hoping to score woman-to-woman. "Surely you can't deny that," she smiled warmly at Rev.

"I do deny that." Rev did not smile back. Dylan, however, was smiling uncontrollably. "I feel no need whatsoever to have a child.

Besides which, why do you think you're entitled to have all your needs fulfilled?"

"Second, even if I concede *any* of the rights you've mentioned, *no right is absolute*. Our rights collide. All the time. So we have to figure out a way to determine whose rights trump. Or which rights trump.

"And that's not easy. So dismissing the legislation on the basis that it violates rights is—well, that's far too simple. Far too naïve."

The grey-haired man in a business suit almost had a coronary.

"She's good, eh?" Dylan grinned at the camera guy beside him.

"Besides all of which, shouldn't consequences trump rights. At least in this case? We're not talking being able to go to a movie. We're talking about making humans. The phrase 'have children' makes it sound so passive, so inconsequential. But it's not. At all."

"But state policing such as this fails to recognize people's autonomy." There was intelligent life in the audience. Who knew?

"On the contrary," Rev replied. "It's because people have autonomy, the capacity to make independent decisions, that such policing is required. To prevent the dumbfuck decisions they make."

"In fact," Rev paused. She had a thought. A brand new thought. "I think we need to question this whole notion of human rights."

Everyone gasped.

"Seriously. Do we—should we—have *any* rights just by virtue of being born? We are not accidental. We are not inevitable. We are, each of us, *made*. We are the products of intentional behaviour. We all exist because of someone's choice. And usually," she added, "given the mechanics, and given the power structures of our society, that someone is a man.

"Why should someone's individual choice automatically confer a whole barrage of rights onto the product? Rights that potentially impose on other people's freedoms? I may choose to write a novel. Should that choice entail any rights for the novel? Can I say my novel has the right to be purchased? That you must buy it? And read it? Of course not.

"Which is why," she followed her reasoning to its conclusion, "I'm not sure there should be *any* human rights. I'm not sure we should be entitled to anything, just because we exist. Just because someone decided to make us."

"Food, clothing, healthcare, education—" he *hadn't* had a coronary. "You're saying these shouldn't be basic human rights?"

"Well … ," she was saying that. And yet … "Okay, up to say, age eighteen, I'll grant those rights. Plus a bunch of others—the right to be free from harm, for sure. But after that? I say you have to earn the right—"

She had another new thought. "You know, we're lucky we consider the right to life to be a basic human right. Because if people had to *earn* that right, most of us would've been toast long ago."

I really wish Canada and the States would get on the bandwagon and start teaching critical thinking in school," she said the next morning. Not as she was working on some LSAT questions, but as she was thinking about the day before. "Remember *Sophie's World*?"

"That novel by the Norwegian writer?" Dylan had just returned from his twice daily bike ride to Kit's place to check on Loup. Both she and Flaker were almost completely healed.

"Yeah. Did you read it?"

"I did, yes."

"I found it such a weird novel," Rev said. "The philosophy was graduate level, but the plot and characters were so childish."

"And then you found out that in Europe, children were able to handle philosophizing at that level."

"Yes! Because it's taught starting in *grade* school!"

"For a while there," Dylan said, "we had Values Education, remember?"

"Yeah, back in the late 70s. What happened to that?"

"I don't know."

"Did you know that in France," Rev said, "students have to take a philosophy exam at the end of high school. It's a four hour exam posing a single question such as 'Can scientific truth be dangerous?' or 'Is it one's own responsibility to find happiness?'"

"Really? Most of our graduating university students would have trouble with that."

Rev burst out laughing. "Can you imagine our business students writing such an exam? *Having* to write such an exam?"

A WHILE LATER, "IT'S also a pity that business rules the world. Because that means that business students rule the world."

Dylan waited.

"Not only are they our 'C' students—our 'A' and 'B' students go into the sciences and the humanities. Not necessarily respectively," she added.

"But also, they have no capacity for joy or beauty. Partly I suspect that's a self-selection thing, but partly, it's because we don't require business students to take any arts courses. No music, no poetry, no painting. So no wonder they see the world, life, as a competition for more, and no wonder they measure GNP instead of GNH."

"Gross National Happiness," Dylan said. "I've heard of that. Bhutan's been using it since the 70s."

Rev nodded. "Business students wouldn't know where to begin to measure happiness. Most of them are men, so they're further crippled by an inability to reflect on their own happiness."

Dylan nodded. "Ask any man if he's happy, and he'll give you the cow look."

Rev waited.

"The look cows have on their faces when—ever?"

"Ah." She resumed then. "And do you know *why* business rules the world?"

Dylan waited.

"Because we don't require our humanities and sciences students to take any business courses. We don't know shit about strategy. We live by principle. Not by consequence. So we don't need a plan, and a back-up plan, we don't need to anticipate various outcomes and have responses, contingency plans, ready for each one. We just do what's right. So they outmanoeuvre us. All the time."

"Undistracted by what's right," Dylan added.

I'M HAPPY, DYLAN THOUGHT to himself a few days later. Loup was back, and Flaker was off with Kit somewhere for a couple days. Rev was sunk on her couch beside him. Very happy. And that was before he decided to roll a joint.

Half an hour later, Rev shouted, "That's who did it!"

"Did what?"

"The egg bank thing! The illegal fertilization! It had to have been someone from the tv panel!"

"Had it to have been?" Dylan asked, then grinned, then said it again. "Had it to have been." He giggled. Loup wagged her tail.

"Either the civil rights lobby or the disability lobby or the religious lobby— Wait, didn't we think of this before?" Rev asked.

"Did we? What did we do about it before?"

"Nothing?"

"Ah," he said. "That's where we went wrong then."

"So what are we going to do about it now?"

"I don't know."

"Maybe that's why we didn't do anything about it before," Rev concluded.

After a long while, Dylan asked, "Why exactly did we think of it before? And again now?"

"Because they've got means. Any one of those lobbies could have hired someone to just—eew. And they've got motive. The publicity would shine a spotlight on— On—" Rev deflated. "I confused the license thing with the egg bank thing again, didn't I. I keep thinking they're related."

"They both have to do with reproduction," Dylan said, in her defence.

"Yes! And— And— Nope, I lost it."

Five minutes later, she found it again.

"And both the new legislation and egg banks restrict men's access to women's eggs."

Dylan thought about that.

"But that's nothing new. Surely their location inside of women do that?"

"You'd think. But given the near universal acceptance of rape—"

"I wouldn't call it—"

"Name one country in which there is *not* a significant contingent of men who feel entitled to sexual access to women. Any woman. Any time. Who get angry if you say, in any way, 'No, I'm not sexually available. To you.'"

Dylan thought about that. Briefly. "So you're looking for a *real* man? An entitled fratboy of an asshole?"

She sighed. "Like looking for a needle in a haystack."

"No, it's like looking for a piece of hay in a haystack."

"No, that'd be easy."

"A *particular* piece of hay in a haystack."

"Aren't pieces of hay called straw? Straws?"

"Like looking for a straw in a haystack?"

A COUPLE HOURS LATER, the roar of a chain saw suddenly split the air.

"Holy— Have you hired someone to take down one of your trees?" Dylan stood up and went to the door. Loup got up as well.

"No, that's the guy across the lake. Next to the boat guy."

"Can't be," Dylan looked out in disbelief. "This loud?"

"Yup. The sound just skids across the lake and smashes into the other side. This side."

"But—"

"And because the land rises behind us, there's nowhere for it to go."

"It's like an echo chamber—"

"It's particularly bad here, I think, because of the cove."

"Ah—it's like being in a cave. Does he know? I mean, why can't he chainsaw *behind* his house?"

"Good question. The second one. As to the first, yes, he knows. At least, I've told him."

"Probably didn't believe you."

Rev nodded. "I'm a woman, so I must be exaggerating. Being dramatic. Hysterical over nothing. Plus he called me a complaining bitch," she added, "said he'd heard about me, that I was always complaining about something."

"To which you replied … "

"That if he had my keen observational skills, along with my perspicuity, he'd be a complaining bitch too. Not that it takes any keen observational skill to notice the sound of a chainsaw."

"How often does he do that?" Dylan sat back down. Loup followed. "Chain saw. Not call you a complaining bitch."

"As often as he wants. He has his firewood delivered as logs that he cuts himself, to save a few bucks."

"Can't he get them dumped behind his house?"

"He could."

The chain saw continued to whine ever so annoyingly. There was no way either of them could get any work done. Or even continue to sit outside. Or, probably, even inside. Even with all the windows closed. On such a beautiful summer day.

"But— So— You're just going to let him get away with that?" Dylan said with surprise.

"How exactly do I *not* let him 'get away with that'?" Rev asked with exasperation.

HALF AN HOUR LATER, Dylan returned. Limping. Loup, having accompanied him part way, then turned back because of the noise, ran to greet him.

"What happened?" Rev said, also running out to him, "Are you okay?"

"I think so, yes. In the middle of our 'discussion', the guy shoved me, and since a log was behind me, I landed flat on my ass. Hard."

"Your tailbone's probably—do we need to get an x-ray?" He wasn't getting any younger either.

"I don't think so. Let's see if it's better or worse tomorrow," he made it into the porch then gingerly sat down in his chair.

"You could press charges."

Dylan agreed. "It's his word against mine, but if he ever finds out Loup's with me, I'm concerned she might get 'accidentally' shot."

Rev noticed the 'but' where she'd've said 'and' and realized that Dylan hadn't automatically assumed that her word would be discounted. Wonder what that's like, she thought to herself.

"I'd like to say you're over-reacting, but that could definitely happen."

Dylan was silent for a long time.

"The thing is, it's not just here," Rev said, from the kitchen. "And it's not just about something as relatively inconsequential as chainsaw noise. Here," she said, handing Dylan an ice pack.

"In any conflict of interest, it's the more immature and unintelligent one who 'wins'," she continued, clearly having thought about the matter a great deal. "Because, on the one hand, they're unable to understand and evaluate reasoning, so they 'engage' emotionally and physically. And because, on the other hand, given their ethics, or lack of, they're more willing to go further. So if the conflict escalates, they'll stop at nothing. People don't just lose quiet and beauty," she nodded to the trees across the cove, "they lose their fingers, their children, their lives. When they stand up to bullies."

She paused for a moment, then asked with anger and frustration, "How do we solve the bully problem? That's the question. For civilization.

"Give them a job, opportunities, it's poverty at the root? Nonsense. Chainsaw guy has a job in town. You weren't threatening his livelihood, you weren't taking something he had or needed.

"Education? Teach bullies how to use their words? We tried that, you and I. As did all the teachers we saw dancing in the street. That doesn't work either. By the time they're six, it's too late, they're already using their fists."

"So we have to get at the parents. The parenting," Dylan concluded.

She nodded. "Much as it upsets the libertarian part of me and the anarchist part of me, both of which, or whom, recognize, now, that libertarianism and anarchy work only when people are capable of self-governance, and much as it could pave the way for *The Handmaid's Tale*, I'm in favour of this new legislation."

But then she added, "That's not to say that educated people won't also produce bullies. But surely there will be fewer of them, when people understand—everything. The importance of expressing love and affection, of teaching children how to get along, how to consider others, how to empathize. How not to be an immature stupid asshole."

"AND YET," REV SAID an hour later, "remember when we were interviewing Ms. Jackson? Our choices are a democracy of idiots or the risk of malevolent dictatorship?"

"Yeah."

"What if fail at keeping the dictatorship benevolent? I mean, if all it takes is one asshole with a gun and no morality— The democracy of idiots at least allows those of us who are conscious to have a life."

A couple days later, in the evening, when Rev and Dylan were in the kitchen getting something to eat and Loup was out and about, presumably doing the same thing, they suddenly heard the roar of an ATV followed by a banging on the back door. Rev opened the door, mainly to stop the banging. A severely beer-bellied man in a dirty jacket stood there, wavering slightly in a cloud of alcohol and gasoline fumes, with a hunting rifle. Pointed at her.

"You! Bitch! Mind your own fucking business!"

"Okay," Rev replied, agreeably enough. She thought. Dylan had moved to the door as well, but when he saw the rifle, he realized he'd made a mistake. He should've—would the guy notice if he turned around and headed to the porch, to circle around and—

"Don't move!" the guy said. Okay, the answer to that was 'yes'.

"At the egg place!"

Rev was still confused. And wondering, since the man's pants were threatening to fall down around his ankles, whether such men shouldn't buy their pants in maternity clothing departments.

"Asking questions!"

"Yes ... "

"About me!"

Ah. "You're the one who did it?"

"Damn right I'm the one who did it! Someone had to!"

"Why?" She had to know. Even at gunpoint, Rev had to know. That was just the kind of person she was. Well, that and the kind of person who was trying to stall so they could figure out how to—

"Bitches won't need us anymore, will they?" he asked Dylan belligerently.

Dylan doubted that anyone, bitch or no, had ever needed this particular specimen of the human race even *before* the widespread use of in vitro fertilization, but he wisely decided not to make that point. At that particular moment. Because the rifle had been getting progressively lower—

The man raised his rifle again.

And then got hit in the head with a dead beaver.

He went down. Knocked out cold. It was a big beaver.

Loup pounced on her beaver and a significant portion of the beaver's insides came to merge with the man's outsides as she repeatedly grabbed and shook her beaver, occasionally throwing it into the air. In her excitement, she wasn't too fussy about which of the many bits she grabbed, and although the man would later regret losing one of the bits she grabbed, one of *his* bits, the authorities wouldn't have to worry about future egg bank violations of the kind they'd been investigating of late. When the man came to, he'd have a story to tell his nonexistent grandkids.

They bound and gagged him, the latter Rev's idea, while they waited for the summoned police and an ambulance, the latter Dylan's idea.

THEY FOUND OUT A couple days later that the guy had no relationship whatsoever with any of the eggs in the bank. He was just someone whose 'MUST REPLICATE' gene took over his brain because he was too stupid to resist.

ince they were out of pizza, and low on Froot Loops and kibble, a trip into town was in order. Dylan had no more appointments—thank God—so they decided to make it a purely pleasure trip and check out the new exhibit at the art gallery. It was something to do with light and glass and prisms. They had to park some distance away, which puzzled Rev. Going to the art gallery wasn't high, she thought, on most people's list.

As soon as they rounded the corner, they saw a long line of people on the sidewalk, so long it disappeared around the next corner. Past the art gallery.

"What would so many people line up for?" Dylan asked. "Here?"

"A free pick-up truck?"

"No, look," he said as they got closer. "Most of them, a lot of them, are women."

Rev scanned the line as they passed it. Dylan was right.

"A free pick-up truck?"

It was about half and half for those under thirty, she'd say, and for those over, it was more women than men. Odd.

"Shania Twain's coming home?" he suggested.

"Actually, she was born in Windsor. And raised in Timmins. But maybe. Given people's desperate and irrational claims of association with fame and fortune, and … ," she trailed off, because sometimes she just didn't want to be bothered finishing her thoughts. But mostly she couldn't help it. " ... and the unlikelihood of Sudbury lining up for Celine Dion."

They followed the line around the corner and saw that it extended another two blocks, disappearing yet again around a corner.

"What the—" she was truly perplexed.

"Hey, dude, end of the line's that way," a young man said, as if they were American.

"He's not here for the vaccination," his buddy elbowed him, "he's too old."

Dylan stopped. "Ah, the— Am not."

"Are too."

"Am not."

"Are too."

"Is not," Rev said. That shut them up. "I'm the one who's too old," she added. "Don't you boys know anything about human physiology as it applies to male and female bodies?"

"That shut them up," Dylan said. "'Male and female bodies.'"

"So," she said half a block later, once they'd wrapped their heads around the idea that so many were lining up for the contraception vaccination, "do you want to interview some of these people?"

"No," he said.

Rev looked at him.

"I'm tired of the whole thing," he explained. "I think I've maxed out for the year on thinking about things of substance. I've met my quota."

Rev wondered what it would be like to have a quota one could meet. "Okay, I'll do it."

"Are you sure?"

"Who, what, when, where, and why. Piece of cake."

He handed over his mini recorder. Which he'd put into his pocket out of habit. Rev turned it on and approached the next pair of young men they came to.

"Who are you?" she said to the first one, who turned to her, a little taken aback.

"Michael Epps."

"What are you doing here?" She grinned at Dylan. She'd nailed the who and the what.

"Getting the vaccination."

"When was the last time you cleaned your bathroom?"

"Um, never." His buddy jostled him.

"Supplemental: When was the last time you *used* your bathroom?"

"This morning."

She let that percolate just a bit. While she thought of a where question.

"Where did you leave your spaghetti?"

"What?"

"Why are you getting the vaccination?"

"Um, so I don't get the call."

"Supplemental: What call?"

"The call that goes 'I'm pregnant, it's yours, pay up.'"

"My turn," his buddy said eagerly.

"Who are you?"

"Luke Smith." They started the exchange, Rev moving the recorder back and forth as if they were engaged in a tennis match. Dylan grinned.

"What are you doing here?"

"Getting the vaccination."

"When was the last time you cleaned your bathroom?"

"This morning!" he crowed.

"Where did you leave your spaghetti?"

"What?"

"Why are you getting the vaccination?"

"So when I get the call, I've got proof to the contrary. I'm gonna make a copy of my certificate, keep it safe, you know, in case I need it. I'm not ready to become a father yet," he added.

"Supplemental: What would it take?"

"I don't know."

"Then you're right. You're not ready yet."

Two young women further up the line looked eagerly at Rev. What she was doing looked like fun, and they wanted in on it. Rev obliged.

"Who are you?"

"Tara Mason."

"What are you doing here?"

"Getting the vaccination."

"When was the last time you cleaned your bathroom?"

"Tuesday. I do that Tuesdays."

"Where did you leave your spaghetti?"

"In the treehouse!" she practically shouted. Rev grinned.

"Why are you getting the vaccination?"

"Because the side-effects of the pill are horrible!"

Her friend stepped up, ready.

"Who are you?"

"Megan Thomson."

"What are you doing here?"

"Getting the vaccination."

"When was the last time you cleaned your bathroom?"

"Can't remember."

"Where did you leave your spaghetti?"

"Can't remember."

"Why are you getting the vaccination?"

"Because I can't remember to take the pill!" She grinned.

"Supplemental: Are you concerned that the government might require you be licensed before they give you the antidote?"

"I suppose that might happen, but it doesn't bother me too much. I don't really want kids."

"You don't think you might want them later?"

"Maybe," she conceded. "Apparently for a while in your mid-twenties, the desire gets really strong, but that's just the drugs talking." Rev poked Dylan. "It passes," the young woman shrugged.

More young people crowded around, eager to be interviewed. Dylan was delighted. And wondered when last he'd charged the battery on his mini-recorder.

"Who are you?"

"Carley Preston."

"What are you doing here?"

"Getting the vaccination."

"When was the last time you cleaned your bathroom?"

"Do not know."

"Where did you leave your spaghetti?"

"In the pot."

"Why are you getting the vaccination?"

"Because the condom keeps breaking. Freaks me out."

Rev turned to her male companion.

"Who are you?"

"Adrian Neilson."

"What are you doing here?"

"Getting the vaccination."

"When was the last time you cleaned your bathroom?"

"What?"

"Supplemental: Are you aware bathrooms have to be cleaned?"

"Yeah, but—" His female companion stared at him.

"Where did you leave your spaghetti?"

"What?"

"Why are you getting the vaccination?"

"Because my dad said I should."

She turned back to the young woman. "Supplemental: You don't want kids?"

"Well, I know you're supposed to get married, settle down, have kids, but—I don't really like kids." Rev high-fived her, but her companion stared at her.

"You don't want to have kids? We're not going to have a family?"

She stared at him. As if he'd just morphed into someone she didn't know.

"You don't really like kids either!"

He morphed back. "You're right. She's right," he said to Rev, "I don't really like kids either."

The line moved ahead, and Rev and Dylan stepped back. "Do you want me to interview some of the older ones?" Rev asked.

"I think we know what they're going to say.

"'Been there, done that, we have enough'?"

He nodded. "I'm more interested in what all these young people have to say."

The line stopped, and she turned to the young person who'd

stopped beside them.

"Who are you?"

"Trey Taggert."

"What are you doing here?"

"Getting the vaccination."

"When was the last time you cleaned your bathroom?"

"My mom does it," he replied. And suddenly felt a little ashamed.

"Where did you leave your spaghetti?"

"I don't know, but I'm sure I cleaned it up."

"Why are you getting the vaccination?"

"Because I plan to have lots and lots of recreational sex."

Dylan stepped up. "Supplemental: So why don't you just get a vasectomy?"

"I don't know, man, that's forever, I'm not ready to make any forever decisions yet."

"Supplemental," Dylan said. "Are you concerned that down the line you won't get the antidote unless you get licensed?"

"That wouldn't be a bad thing, would it?"

"YOU KNOW," REV SAID to Dylan a few minutes later, when Delightfully Delicious Delectables came into view, and she handed the mini-recorder back to him, "the vaccination may make the whole licensing thing a bit moot."

"It may, yes," Dylan thought. And decided he'd better finish his articles sooner rather than later.